"What do you want?" Kate asked

"I want what's mine."

"And what," she asked haltingly, "do you consider yours?"

"Don't worry, *chèr*. Not you... I meant my daughter."

The world tilted crazily around her. He had to be Mitch. Her sister's husband.

She had to come up with a plan. She couldn't let this stranger carry her niece off to an unknown future. Yet what could she do? She had no idea where he'd sent the little girl...had no idea where he lived.

If he disappeared now, she might never find Arianne again.

Should she tell him her twin had died? Perhaps he'd soften and handle the matter with compassion and reason. Then again, he might simply leave, glad to be rid of his ex-wife once and for all.

"Pack a suitcase for Arianne," he ordered her, interrupting her thoughts, "and one for yourself. We have a date with a judge. You left before our divorce was final. And guess what? The attorney you hired hadn't even passed the bar yet. He had no authority to act on your behalf. Nothing he handled was valid."

Kate stared at him. That meant... Oh, God, this man was Camryn's husband. And now he believed *her* to be his *wife*!

Dear Reader,

I wrote this book with deep affection for the offshore shrimpers in the Gulf of Mexico—men who face incredible dangers in their work, and do so with pride, a strict code of honor and an uncanny communion with nature. During my eighteen months of living and working on a commercial trawler named the *Lady Leone*, I came to admire Gulf shrimpers as true masters of the sea.

The hero of this book, Mitch Devereaux, is one of this breed, and of another proud race—the Cajuns of Louisiana. They're known for their strong family ties; distinctive music, food and dance; making a living off the land, swamp and sea; and an abiding love of a good party. They value zest for life, or, as they call it, joie de vivre. Mitch, however, lost his joie de vivre when his estranged wife ran off with his daughter. Nothing will stop him from tracking them down, bringing them home and forcing his wife to honor their joint-custody agreement.

Little does Mitch know that the woman he finds with his daughter is not his wife, but her identical twin, intent on protecting the baby she loves. This is the story of how Mitch regains his joie de vivre, and how Kate Jones finds the precious spice that has been missing from her life.

As you curl up in a comfy chair to read their story, I hope you *laissez les bons temps rouler*. A Cajun motto, it means, "Let the good times roll!"

Sincerely,

Donna Sterling

Wife by Deception
Donna Sterling

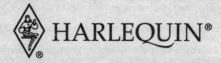

HARLEQUIN®

TORONTO • NEW YORK • LONDON
AMSTERDAM • PARIS • SYDNEY • HAMBURG
STOCKHOLM • ATHENS • TOKYO • MILAN • MADRID
PRAGUE • WARSAW • BUDAPEST • AUCKLAND

ISBN 0-373-71017-8

WIFE BY DECEPTION

I dedicate this to the Kozma clan, especially Eddie,
for "reading every word"; Kenny, for getting me to
the express mail office in time; and Michelle,
for venturing with me into the swampland…
and the Cajun dance hall. We passed a good time, *chèr*.

ACKNOWLEDGMENTS

Many thanks to Ron "Black" Guidry, for his swamp tour;
Jesse Lecompte Jr., for answering questions; Doug Lambert,
who has a great little shop in the French Quarter;
and Joe Cruse of *The Stormy Seas*, who will always
have a place in my heart. And special thanks to
Jacquie D'Alessandro, Susan Goggins, Carina Rock
and Ann White, for their insightful critiques.

PROLOGUE

Tallahassee, Florida
Early January

CAMRYN LISTENED for sounds in the early-morning still-ness of her sister's household. She heard only the patter of rain on the roof and the rustling of Florida wind through the palm tree near her window. No one seemed to be awake.

She climbed out of bed in stealthy silence.

Today was the day she'd hit the road for New York City. And Kate would discover she had a baby to watch for the next couple of weeks. Kate Jones, Ph.D., college professor, no less, should be able to figure out how to take care of a three-month-old.

Quietly Camryn dressed in the dark. The baby had bawled for hours after she'd brought her to Kate's house last night. Stunned to learn of her niece's existence, Kate had insisted they spend the night, then took charge of rocking, feeding and soothing the baby.

Camryn had expected she would. Despite the years they'd spent apart, she knew her sister. They were, after all, identical twins, and the only family each other had...other than the baby now. Kate would take good care of her until Camryn returned. She would have *asked* her to baby-sit if she hadn't been afraid Kate would put a kink in her plans. Much safer to force her cooperation.

After gathering her purse, her suitcase and Kate's car keys, Camryn tiptoed through the darkened house, tossed a letter onto the kitchen table, then hurried outside through the chill January rain to Kate's rather stodgy BMW. Camryn's Mustang convertible had given her problems. She didn't trust it on another long road trip. The BMW would have to do.

Moments later, she turned out of the elegant Tallahassee subdivision and onto the open highway, headed for New York City…and television stardom. *Prime-time soaps, here I come!* Everyone who knew anything about show business had assured her that the soap opera producers would take one look at the pictures of her with the baby and write them both into the script—mother and daughter. Her exceptionally gorgeous baby girl was just the gimmick she'd always needed to break into show business big-time.

And once she did, she'd have the means to solve her other problems, too. The one that had been driving her nuts lately was the need for a baby-sitter. The crying, the smelly diapers, the continual demand for attention were more than she could take. She'd originally intended to bring Arianne with her to New York right away, but after a hellish time on the road, she'd decided to leave Arianne with Kate, then come back for her after she made the all-important contacts and found a place to live near the studios.

Being free for a while felt good. Who knew mothering would be so difficult? She'd thought it would be an adventure…a new, exciting phase in her life. Movies and television had made motherhood seem so desirable.

So…*easy*. And while her ex and his family had been around to help, it hadn't seemed too difficult.

But the weeks since she'd struck out on her own had been torture. She supposed it wouldn't have been as bad if she hadn't lost all her money at poker. She'd had to take a singing gig in Atlanta, which hadn't paid enough for her to hire a baby-sitter *and* recoup her losses. She'd brought the baby to the club with her every evening until the manager put an end to it…and to Camryn's job.

She wasn't about to let Mitch know she needed help, though.

Give me full custody of her, Cam. Arianne would be better off.

Her hand clenched the steering wheel and she fumbled to light a cigarette. Flicking her gold lighter with a vengeance, she tossed her heavy blond hair over one shoulder and leaned toward the flame. Her professionally manicured nails shimmered crimson in the flickering light; her jeweled rings and bracelets flashed. She drew in a biting lungful of smoke.

She'd be damned if she'd give up her rights in their joint-custody arrangement. In fact, when she had more money, she'd take him to court for full custody. Arianne was her ticket to stardom. But she couldn't let Mitch know about her plans, of course, until contracts were signed with the television producers. Otherwise, he'd try to stop her.

Mitch was touchy when it came to Arianne. He'd made a big deal out of every mistake. Like when Camryn had taken the baby to New Orleans one night. If she'd known the crowd in the French Quarter would grow wild, she wouldn't have had all those margaritas. Even so, she'd been perfectly capable of handling the situation…except for the bail money, which, admittedly,

Mitch had to bring. The public drunkenness charge had been *so* unfair.

And then there was the time she'd left Arianne in the car while she placed a few quick bets at a casino. The security guard had called the phone number listed on the car's registration. Mitch had answered…then blew the whole incident *way* out of proportion. He told her that he would start proceedings to take her custody rights away from her.

She changed the phone number and address on the car's registration information the very next day. Mitch and she were divorced, damn it. What she did or where she went was none of his business. Later, after she'd left town in the dead of night with Arianne, she'd traded that car—her beloved 'Vette—for the Mustang in Birmingham. She hoped the switch would stop Mitch from tracking her down.

He might not appreciate her style of parenting, but she was still Arianne's mother. She had sacrificed her flawless figure and several months of her singing career to bring her into this world. For a few of those months, she'd even given up drinking and smoking. Or most of it, anyway. The baby was hers, and she'd take her wherever she wanted, *whenever* she wanted.

She wondered how Mitch had reacted to finding them gone. He was probably furious.

Served him right. He'd changed drastically from the first few weeks she'd known him. They'd had great times together at the start. But then she got pregnant, and he insisted she marry him. And all the fun stopped. He no longer tried to please her. All he cared about was the baby. Oh, and his precious shrimp boats.

Well, that was where he'd made his mistake. If he

didn't care about pleasing *her,* he wasn't going to have his daughter.

Besides, she had plans for Arianne. Big plans. She and Arianne were going to be television stars. Then she'd have money to hire a full-time nanny, as well as a powerful attorney to represent her in a custody hearing.

Feeling empowered, she took the next curve faster, leaning with the wheel to keep the car on the road. The effort won her a dark thrill. Things were definitely looking up.

She hoped Kate wouldn't be too angry that she'd left the baby with her. Kate had already been upset that Camryn hadn't contacted her about her marriage or the birth of her daughter. In a way, Kate herself was to blame for Camryn's failure to call her. She was always telling Camryn what to do. Even when they were growing up in the Tallahassee Methodist Children's Home, Kate had tried to run the show. She had such strong views on ''what's best.'' Few people had the strength to swim against that particular tide. She'd wear a person down before he knew the fight had even begun.

Like when she persuaded Camryn's first husband to turn himself in and serve out his sentence for insurance fraud. Or when she talked her second husband into admitting he was sleeping around. Could anyone blame her for hesitating to tell Kate about her third marriage?

She hadn't even mentioned to Mitch that she had a sister, let alone an identical twin, for fear that if they met, Kate would complicate matters. Camryn had been careful not to tell Kate much about Mitch, either... especially that he'd been granted joint custody. She might feel obligated to contact him.

Disturbed at the thought, Camryn pressed harder on the gas and took the curve in the slick, two-lane highway a little faster than she'd intended. The tires hydroplaned, and she fought to keep the BMW from fishtailing into the woods. Fear heated her insides. Her mouth filled with an acrid taste. Exhilaration gunned through her. Aah, what a rush!

She was feeling alive again! She wanted to celebrate. Maybe she'd stop at a convenience store for a wine cooler.

The next curve in the road came quicker than she expected, though, and she veered across the center line. She barely had time to focus on the oncoming headlights before her world spun…and screeched…and rolled…

And ended in thunderous conflagration.

CHAPTER ONE

Terrebonne Parish, Louisiana
July 4

THE CALL CAME during the Fourth of July crawfish boil in his parents' front yard on the bayou. The cell phone in his shirt pocket rang, and Mitch's heart paused.

No one but the detective would call him on this phone. The captains and crew members of his shrimp boats didn't know the number; they always contacted him by the radio he wore on his belt. So did his neighbors on the swamp. It had to be Chuck Arceneaux, the investigator he'd hired. And if the call wasn't urgent, Chuck would have left a message on his home answering machine.

The adults at the long picnic table fell silent, their gazes shifting to Mitch. They knew the significance of that ringing cell phone. His brawny, apron-clad father turned from the simmering crawfish kettle to watch him in sober expectation. His mother froze in the act of ladling jambalaya from a huge serving bowl, her eyes widening with hope and fear. The children seemed to sense the sudden tension, and all but the youngest of his nieces, nephews and cousins quieted. Even the hot Louisiana breeze seemed to halt its sighing through the willows and moss-draped cypress trees.

Mitch drew the phone from his pocket and answered it.

The investigator's flat, nasal voice greeted him. "All the dough you've been shelling out for those mailers finally paid off, Mitch. We got a possible lead."

A possible lead. Mitch shut his eyes and clenched his jaw, overcome with relief that the news hadn't been bad. Immediately following that relief came disappointment that the news hadn't been better. He'd been praying so damn long for the words *I've found your daughter. She's okay.* "What kind of lead, Chuck?"

"A man in Florida said he recognized a neighbor from the photos on a mailer. Said she goes by the name Kate Jones. He doesn't know much more than that about her. I've been staked out in front of the house, and a few minutes ago, a blonde stepped out onto the porch. She looks a lot like your wife."

Mitch grimaced at the term. He'd have preferred "ex-wife," although it wasn't technically correct. Camryn had taken off before they'd corrected major glitches in their divorce proceedings. Legally, they were still married—a situation he would remedy the moment he got his daughter back from her and knew that he'd be awarded custody. *Full* custody, this time. "Does she have a baby with her?"

"Haven't seen one yet, but I noticed a stroller in the garage."

Mitch's blood roared in his ears with a fierce surge of hope. *Please, God, let it be Camryn. And let Arianne be with her, safe and sound.* "Watch her. Don't let her out of your sight."

"This gal ain't going nowhere without me on her tail."

"Where are you in Florida?" Mitch demanded, rising

from the bench at the picnic table. He couldn't waste a moment. He had to get there before Camryn ran again.

"Tallahassee. But don't go off half-cocked. Think about how you want to handle this. You and I know she ran illegally with your kid, but you can't be sure how another state will deal with custody disputes. The law at home might be on your side, but you don't have any guarantees outside of Louisiana."

"That's why I'm bringing her back. And I'm not about to call the cops, if that's what you're worried about." Mitch knew better than to rely on anyone except himself. Camryn would flash her pretty smile and have the cops falling all over themselves to do her favors before he had a chance to show his joint custody papers. They'd probably arrest him and let her go free—to run with Arianne again.

If she still had Arianne. Mitch refused to put too much stock in the stroller the detective had noticed. Camryn could be staying with someone who had a baby. During her six months on the run, she might have left Arianne with a baby-sitter, or forgotten her outside a casino, or...

Mitch refused to think about the possibilities. The woman had a warped maternal instinct and absolutely no sense of responsibility. He believed she'd taken Arianne from him out of spite for what she considered his "interference" in her life. She'd resented the restraints imposed on her by marriage—as brief as their marriage had been—and even more, the demands of motherhood. She lived for fun and thrills. The risks she took in search of those thrills made Mitch's muscles clench. What a sap he was! As furious as she made him, he couldn't keep from worrying about Camryn as well as their daughter.

Their sweet baby daughter. *Arianne*. He hadn't seen

her in six months. She'd be nine months old by now. Did Camryn still have her? If so, was she taking decent care of her? He couldn't imagine her taking care of anyone for that long, let alone fulfilling the constant needs of a baby.

Then again, Camryn could do or be anything she set her mind to, at least for a while. She was a chameleon, changing colors to suit her mood or to get her wherever she wanted to go. He hoped her current whims included mothering Arianne.

If only he'd known Camryn before he'd gotten involved with her! But he'd been pretty damn irresponsible himself. He, too, had taken foolhardy risks in search of excitement. Like sleeping with a gorgeous stranger.

But he had to admit, it had been more for him than just thrill seeking. He'd been poleaxed by the sight of her. In that first blinding flash of reaction, he'd been sure she was the woman of his dreams. Her face, her eyes, her voice. Her body. Everything about her seemed so damn right…as if she'd stepped directly from his fantasies, custom-made for him alone. He'd honestly felt that fate had brought him to this one golden moment in time so that he could meet his soul mate. Never before had he been overcome by such a powerful certainty.

And never since.

Her beauty, vivaciousness and fun-loving spirit had kept him flying high through the first couple of weeks of their relationship. But gradually he realized that the deeper, more profound qualities he craved in a life partner simply weren't there.

She was like *flauteau*—the lush stretches of Louisiana grass and greenery that looked as solid as earth but were actually nothing more than vegetation floating on the surface of a swamp. A man foolish enough to step onto *flauteau* would sink beneath the dense foliage into stagnant, muddy water without leaving so much as a trace.

All flash was Camryn, without an inch of solid ground. And now he was drowning in his own foolishness over her.

When she told him she was going to have his baby, he insisted that she marry him. Old-fashioned of him, maybe, but he'd wanted at least the appearance of love for their child's sake, once she was old enough to understand things like parenthood and marriage.

It turned out that Camryn herself didn't know much about those things. She carried on a fairly convincing charade of wife and mother for as long as she could, but her true nature soon got the best of her. She craved fun and thrills and self-gratification, and when the conflict with him became too much for her, she filed for divorce. And then left town…before that divorce had been properly finalized…with Arianne. She'd barely been three months old.

And now, as he tried to track Camryn down, he was amazed at how little he knew about her. According to information gleaned from Arianne's birth certificate, Camryn had been born in Pennsylvania, but his search there proved fruitless. She'd said her parents were dead; he didn't know if she had any surviving family members. Her maiden name of "Jones" didn't help much in a computer search; every state in the country had thousands of them.

He hoped to God that he'd finally found her.

Mitch finished his conversation with the detective and returned his cell phone to his pocket, his mind whirling and his heart pounding. He had strategies to plan and preparations to make.

"*Mon Dieu!* Have they found our Arianne?" His

mother's breathless question and anxious expression jarred him from his thoughts. Every pair of eyes around the table reflected the same deep-seated concern.

"Maybe. I'm about to go find out." His throat nearly closed with emotion. "I might be bringing her home."

The prospect awed him. He'd missed her so damn much—holding her, feeding her, making her smile. Watching her bloom into the prettiest little thing he'd ever seen. *His daughter.* Had she needed him? Had she wondered where he was? Could she possibly even remember him?

His eldest sister whispered a prayer in French and made the sign of the cross. His younger sister hugged him. His father gripped his shoulder in silent support. His brother-in-law insisted on going with him, and everyone else chimed in with offers of help.

A small hand tugged on his shirt. Mitch glanced down at his four-year-old nephew, who stood on the picnic bench, his dark eyes wide with concern. In incredulous tones, he asked, "Are you *cwying,* Uncle Mitch?"

Mitch blinked back the sheen that had blurred his vision and swallowed against the swelling in his throat. "Nah. Too much hot sauce on my crawfish, that's all." He caught the boy to him in a playful hold and scrubbed his knuckles across his head, tousling the dark curls. "You didn't sprinkle more hot sauce in my jambalaya while I wasn't looking, did you, Claude?"

Claude giggled and swore that he hadn't.

Sensing a potential for roughhousing, the little boy's older cousins sprang from their seats. "*I* did it, Uncle Mitch! I put more hot sauce in your jambalaya!"

"No, *I* did!"

"*I* did."

Their impish grins and teasing claims eased some of

the tightness in Mitch's throat. Allowing himself the luxury of a moment, he captured as many kids as he could at one time, tickling each one he caught. They shrieked with laughter, scurried around him and mounted their own attack, some leaping onto his back from behind.

Mitch swore to himself that he'd bring his daughter home to join in the fun with her cousins. To dance to her uncle Mazoo's fiddle. Eat her *grand-mère*'s jambalaya. Wrap her papa around her little finger.

He'd bring Camryn back here, too—to resolve the legal glitches in their divorce proceedings, and to face the judge who had granted them joint custody. Despite the failed divorce, they *were* legally separated, and that custody agreement was legal and binding. She'd had no right to leave the state of Louisiana, or to keep his daughter away from him.

Yes, indeed, she would face the judge and pay whatever price he set for violating a court order. Maybe that would stop her from running away with Arianne again.

LATE FRIDAY AFTERNOON, KATE rolled the stroller up to the gate of the clubhouse area just in time to watch parents clamber out of the swimming pool with infants and toddlers in their arms, rivulets of water trickling from matted hair, slick swimsuits and sagging diapers. As everyone headed toward lounge chairs and beach towels, the instructor called out reminders of next week's class.

Drat. Kate had been hoping to watch at least some of this afternoon's swim class in session. The walk through the two adjacent subdivisions had taken longer than she'd expected, though. There'd been so many distractions along the way—flowers to sniff, kitties to pet, neighbors to enchant with Arianne's sunny, drool-shiny smile. And then there was Arianne's fondness for flinging her toys out of the stroller, just for the fun of having Kate retrieve them. The walk had taken *considerably* longer than expected.

Which was fine with Kate. It seemed to her that the journey itself was just as important as the destination— and they'd had a lovely journey. Maybe they would watch the swim class next week. At the neighborhood Fourth of July party yesterday, the lifeguard in her own subdivision had recommended this particular instructor for infant swimming lessons. Kate wanted to see for herself what methods the woman used.

She peered at the parents trudging past her toward the parking lot. A few moms and dads were talking and smiling. Others looked exhausted and harried. And... frustrated? Not a good sign.

Kate approached one young mother who had emerged from the pool area with a towel-wrapped infant huddled against her shoulder. Smiling at both the baby and his mother, Kate introduced herself as a resident from the neighboring subdivision. ''I'm thinking of enrolling my nine-month-old for swim lessons. Are you happy with the classes so far?''

''Oh, absolutely.'' The deeply tanned brunette, who smelled of chlorine and suntan lotion, lovingly towel-dried her son's reddish, downy-fine curls. ''Davey has learned so much in just two months. He can already hold his breath underwater. And he's only ten months old.'' She fairly beamed with pride.

''That's great. Does he enjoy the lessons?''

''Enjoy them?'' She sounded surprised at the question. ''Well, actually, he'd rather just play around in the pool with his toys than do what the teacher says. I suppose that's only to be expected.'' A flicker of frustration disrupted her smile. "And for some reason, he resists floating on his back."

Warning bells sounded in Kate's head. If any amount of coercion was involved in teaching a baby to swim, the instructor was probably teaching at *her* pace rather than the baby's. And, from the articles Kate had read on the subject, she'd learned that back floating was a skill to be explored later in a baby's progression.

No, she wouldn't subject Arianne to the stress of these particular lessons. She wanted her to enjoy learning, not shy away from it. She wanted the lessons to be a happy, peaceful time. An opportunity for physical and spiritual enrichment. A chance for her and Arianne to grow closer.

Maybe she should look into mother-baby yoga lessons, instead. "Thanks for the information," Kate said. "I think I'll wait another month or so before I sign Arianne up for swim lessons, though. You know, I've read some highly informative articles about infant swim lessons on the Internet."

"Really?"

Unable to resist the chance to save Davey from distressful lessons that might negatively affect his attitude toward learning, Kate told the woman how to find the articles she'd read.

Arianne, meanwhile, dropped the teething ring she'd been gnawing on, emitted a joyous squeal and pointed a stubby little finger at the pool. "Fwim!" Shifting her bright brown eyes to Kate, she repeated, "Fwim?"

Kate smiled at her with all the pride, warmth and tenderness brimming in her heart. Only nine months old, and she could already say *fwim*. She clearly had genius potential. "No, sweetie. We can't swim today. Tomorrow, maybe. In our own pool."

Arianne returned a still-hopeful gaze to the pool. Kate pulled a small foil-wrapped pack from her purse, knelt beside the stroller and distracted the little brown-eyed blonde with a teething biscuit.

Davey's mother shifted her towel-swathed son to her other hip and smiled at Arianne. To Kate, she said, "She's adorable. And she looks so much like you. You couldn't deny she's yours even if you wanted to."

Kate felt her smile falter. *Couldn't deny she's yours.* If only that were true. "Thanks. I…I guess I'd better head back home. It's quite a walk." After wishing the woman luck with Davey's lessons, Kate wheeled the stroller toward the sidewalk.

And tried not to let the innocent remark hurt too much. Hard to do, though, when the wound was still so raw. Because regardless of the fact that Arianne resembled her—same honey-blond hair, same brown eyes, even the same little cleft in her chin—she wasn't Kate's. Not biologically, or even legally, as of yet.

Her real mother had been killed.

Camryn.

A bittersweet pang went through Kate, as it always did when she thought of her sister. Then the grief set in. She was gone—her glamorous, high-flying rebel of a twin who had vexed her, angered her, worried her sick, but always brought tales of wild urban adventures that made Kate's own life seem boring in comparison. Camryn had been a dreamer, outrageously self-centered and as flighty as a kite in a high wind. She'd always gravitated toward the wrong crowd, set her sights on impractical goals and gone about reaching them in the hardest possible way. They'd argued more often than they'd laughed together, but her rare visits had added a certain zest to Kate's workaday life. There would be no more surprise-packed visits from out of the blue.

After six months, the grief had only begun to mellow.

At least she still had Arianne. A simple glance at her niece filled her with warm, comforting love...as well as concern. It had taken Kate more than five months—until last Friday, to be exact—to ask a lawyer about adoption proceedings. Because Arianne's father presented an unknown variable, she'd felt she had too much to risk by bringing Arianne to the attention of the courts.

Government bureaucracies always worried her. The Department of Family and Children Services had ruled her and Camryn's lives from the age of five—when they lost their parents in an automobile accident—until the day they turned eighteen. As humiliating and dehumanizing as that experience had been, they'd actually fared better than many of the children trapped within that frightening system. At least Cam and she had had each other.

Now Kate hesitated to contact the authorities for fear that some obscure regulation would result in their taking Arianne away from her. She shuddered to think of her dear little niece at the mercy of the heartless court system. Kate swore that Arianne would be raised by *her*— not shuffled around between foster homes or dumped into an orphanage, as Camryn and she had been.

But Kate knew she couldn't simply keep Arianne indefinitely. Too many questions would be asked—by doctors, school officials and the like. Kate believed in building a strong, unshakable foundation on which to base one's life. That foundation was a person's only real security. Arianne's foundation would require the paperwork that made her a legal citizen of the United States and Kate's legally-adopted daughter. Neither status was readily available without Arianne's birth certificate.

Her lawyer had warned her, too, that an adoption would be difficult without permission from Arianne's father. And Kate had no idea who he was or where he lived. She had no record of Arianne's birth, where she was born or even what her legal last name was.

"Isn't there a way around the red tape?" Kate had asked. "My sister told me Arianne's father doesn't want her. Even if we somehow learn his name, I doubt that we'll find him. Knowing the kind of men my sister was involved with, he's probably a drifter, or on the run from the law."

Although the attorney foresaw dozens of obstacles, he promised to delve into the matter as quickly and discreetly as possible.

For the umpteenth time, Kate fervently wished she'd gotten more details from Camryn about her ex-husband. Unfortunately, Camryn hadn't wanted to talk about him. All she'd told her was that his name was Mitch, he didn't want a wife or daughter and he'd been "mean."

"Abusive?" Kate had asked, horrified.

"Very," Camryn had confirmed in a choked whisper.

Kate had tried to pry more information from her, but to no avail. The very idea of a man abusing her sister and niece infuriated Kate. In order to get to sleep that night, she had to remind herself that in Camryn's mind, "abusive" could cover anything from physical battery to a refusal to fly her to Tahiti. She *had* seemed extremely upset at the very mention of this man's existence, though.

Then again, Camryn had closed the subject of her ex-husband with a sigh. "I don't know why I married him in the first place. I guess I'm just a sucker for a big,

strong male body and sexy golden-green eyes.'' An odd
wistfulness had crossed her face. ''And he does have the
sexiest eyes.''

Ah, Camryn! There'd been times when Kate had
wanted to shake her.

If only she'd shaken some information loose from her
that night. But Camryn had been too exhausted to chat
for long. She fell asleep within an hour. Kate, on the
other hand, spent half the night reeling from the news
that her twin had married again, given birth and divorced
since they'd last spoken. She mulled over those devel-
opments while walking the floor with Arianne, who'd
been wretchedly suffering from teething woes.

Kate hadn't handled a baby in years, but her vast experience from growing up in the Tallahassee Methodist
Children's Home came in handy that night...and ever
since.

It had been so typical of Camryn, dropping in unexpectedly after eighteen months without contact and
blindly assuming that Kate would baby-sit for weeks at
a time. She'd also stolen her car, leaving nothing but a
mechanically challenged convertible and a brief note that
thanked Kate in advance for keeping Arianne while
Camryn went to New York to get them roles in a soap
opera.

Oh, Cam.

The call had come less than an hour after Kate had
read the note. The highway patrol contacted her from
the number listed on the car's registration. Looking back,
Kate was glad that Camryn *had* taken her car, or Kate
might never have known what had become of her twin.
Whatever identification papers she'd carried had gone
up in flames. The head-on collision had rated only a brief

mention on the evening news, without names or pictures of the deceased.

Grief, regret and a terrible sense of loss haunted Kate, especially in the oppressive silence of night. During the day, she kept herself busy tending her motherless niece. Despite the financial strain and interruption to her career, Kate had taken the spring and summer semesters off from teaching to spend time with Arianne during these formative months of her life.

Kate had lost her twin after failing her in some fundamental way long ago. She couldn't remember a time she hadn't felt vaguely guilty over Camryn's emotional neediness. She should have tried harder to take her parents' place in Camryn's life; to supply more of the love she'd so clearly needed. Until the day she died in that fiery wreck, Camryn had been desperately searching for validation of her own worth…and always in the wrong places….

Kate swore she wouldn't allow Arianne to travel the same path. Bright, beautiful Arianne would remain her top priority from now on.

Kate felt only pleasure at the prospect. The baby filled a void in her heart that she hadn't known existed. She brought sweetness and warmth to her home and a deeper meaning to her life. Kate loved her more intensely with every passing day.

I'll take good care of her, Cam. I won't let you down again.

As she turned a corner into her own subdivision, clouds drifted across the late-afternoon sun, throwing the suburban Tallahassee street into momentary shade. She savored the respite from the July heat and pushed the stroller past neat lawns and brick homes toward her own modest ranch-style house.

By the time she reached the welcoming shadows inside her attached garage, Arianne was snoozing. Kate parked the stroller alongside the red Mustang convertible Camryn had left, ignoring the grief the sight of the car induced. Drawing the house key from a pocket of her khaki shorts, she turned to unlock the door.

A form loomed up from behind her. Before she could react, a hard hand came down over her mouth and jerked her backward against a large, solidly muscular body.

"Hello, Camryn," a gruff voice rasped in her ear. "Long time no see."

CHAPTER TWO

FEAR PARALYZED KATE into absolute stillness. Her assailant thought she was Camryn.

At the sound of footsteps behind her and a muffled murmur, she realized he wasn't alone. Though he'd greeted her in perfect English, he rattled off some brusque instructions to his accomplice in a language sounding like French. The only word she recognized meant "baby."

She tried to cry out, but the sound barely escaped the callused hand he'd clamped over her mouth. Dread slowed her heartbeats to a near standstill. Arianne was sleeping in the stroller behind her. *God, please don't let them take Arianne!*

With the key Kate had inserted in the lock, the man opened the door. His hand still covering her mouth, he nudged her inside.

Fear hammered through her. What did this stranger want with her—or rather, with her sister? Was he a jilted lover? Or maybe a psychotic fan from one of the bars where she'd performed. Or a bookie. A loan shark. Camryn may have owed him money. Stories of brutality flashed through Kate's mind, terrifying her.

With steellike strength, her assailant swept her down the short hallway and into the kitchen, where she looked for something to use as a weapon. Not a knife, fork, glass or bottle was anywhere in sight. The wall telephone hung a few feet away. If only she could get to it long enough to dial.

He dropped his hand from her mouth, gripped her shoulders, turned her around and pushed her down into a kitchen chair. Bracing his hands on its carved wooden arms, he leaned in close. "Don't even think about getting up. You're not going anywhere until I tell you to."

His lean, sun-browned face blazed with frightening anger. But it was his eyes that held her riveted—a vibrant, golden green, shocking in the ruggedness of his face. A memory stirred. Sexy green eyes... Her absolute terror pushed the memory beyond her reach.

He straightened to his full, imposing height, his fists on his hips, a threat in every tensed, muscled contour of his body. "Don't look so stunned to see me. You had to know I'd find you." His deep, rough voice held a hint of an accent she couldn't quite place. His thick hair shone in tawny waves, the color of a lion's mane, with his skin glowing slightly darker. From the sweep of his arrogant forehead to the long, clean line of his jaw, she saw no weakness in his face...only uncompromising strength and hardness. "I wouldn't have stopped looking, Camryn. Ever."

"You have the wrong person," Kate managed to whisper. "I'm not Camryn."

A harsh laugh tore from him. "And I suppose the baby isn't Arianne."

He knew Arianne. Fear engulfed Kate. "What do you want?"

"I want what's mine."

His deadly soft answer frightened her all the more. A terrible suspicion dawned. "And what," she asked haltingly, "do you consider yours?"

Grim humor glinted briefly in his gaze, surprising her.

"Don't worry, *chèr'*. Not you." The humor quickly vanished, leaving his expression granite cold. "I meant my daughter."

The world tilted crazily around Kate. He had to be Mitch. Arianne's father. The man whom Camryn had called "mean." And he'd come to take Arianne.

Kate rose from the chair in a horrified daze. "You can't take her. I won't let you."

Anger flushed beneath his tan. "The judge granted us joint custody. Joint! You had no right to run with her."

She shrank back from his fury, his thunderous words ringing in her head. *Joint custody. No right to run with her.* Could it be true?

"I've spent a fortune to track you down, Camryn. Nice try with the name change, *Kate—*" he uttered the name with scorn "—but the game is up. I'm taking Arianne."

"No, no, please," she whispered, her thoughts in a whirl. What he claimed might be true, or might not be. She knew nothing about him. Not even his last name. She couldn't let this stranger take the baby—especially not before she'd checked out his story. "Give me time...."

"You've had her long enough. It's my turn now."

Panic pressed in on her as she realized her own weak legal position. If he *was* the baby's father and had been granted custody, she'd have no legal claim on Arianne...or not much of one.

But he'd said that Camryn had the right to *joint* custody.

And he didn't know Camryn was dead.

"You can't just take her like this. She doesn't know you," Kate told him, reasoning with a frantic urgency. "She'll be frightened. She needs *me*."

"She's my daughter, and she doesn't know me. Whose fault is that?" His eyes blazed; his mouth pulled taut. "I'm taking her. And I'm suing for full custody."

Kate's lips parted, but no sound emerged. She shook her head in protest, her vision clouding with a sudden blur. Every maternal instinct in her cried out against handing her sweet baby girl over to this angry stranger. Where would he take her? Why did he want her? Again she remembered Camryn's claim that he'd been violent. He certainly seemed to be, the way he'd forced his way into her home and manhandled her. She had to think. Think!

She forced words through her clenched throat. "Let me bring her in now for supper. She'll be hungry."

"Don't worry. I've packed plenty of provisions for her."

Her panic escalated. "I'm bringing her in." She made a move to brush past him.

He caught her by the shoulders. "She's not there anymore."

Her eyes widened; her heart slowed. "What do you mean?"

"She's with…friends. Until I can join them."

When the news sank in, Kate cried out in pain and beat against his chest with fists to free herself from his grip. "Let me go! I've got to stop them. I can't let them take her like that."

He caught her fists, forced her arms behind her back and held her against his chest. When her struggles proved fruitless, she closed her eyes and swallowed a hysterical sob. In pained disbelief, she murmured, "You didn't even let me tell her goodbye."

"Did you let *me* tell her goodbye before you ran with her?"

Easing out of his loosened grasp, she refused to feel empathy for him. Camryn obviously had had good reason to run. Violence simmered beneath his surface like a pot about to boil over. She'd felt it in his grip, heard it in his voice, seen it in his gaze. "She isn't ready to leave home right now. She won't have any of her clothes or her toys." At a sudden remembrance, an ache went through her. "She won't even have her blanket."

"Her blanket? I have blankets. Plenty of blankets."

"But you don't have hers!" she shouted, glaring at him. "You don't care that she needs it to fall asleep at night, do you." Her lips trembled. She bit down on them, then added, "She holds it against her cheek and sucks her thumb." Though she tried to suppress the tears, they seeped from the outside corners of her eyes. She buried her face in her hands and succumbed to quiet sobs.

He shook her and issued a curt order. "That's enough. Stop the crying."

She sucked in her breath, sobs and all. Her chin came up, and her bottom lip tightened. The man was heartless. He was tearing a baby away from the only home she'd ever known, without any preparation at all.

"Go get her blanket," he said.

Stiffly she turned from him, and he followed her to the bedroom she had decorated as a nursery, with yellow walls, bright rainbows and teddy bears. The sight of the nursery now choked her with new tears, but she mastered them. The effort grew more difficult when she found the small patchwork blanket Arianne called her "bankie." Reverently Kate lifted it from the crib, savoring the softness and the subtle baby scent that clung to it. How could she live without Arianne?

"Here it is." Kate thrust it at him. "When she cries

for her *bankie,*" she finished on a whisper, "this is what she wants."

He took it and met her gaze. She saw only cold determination there. "Pack the rest of her things. Anything she might want."

She'd never met a man as cold and unfeeling. He looked so foreign and invasive in the cozy nursery— huge, hard and forbidding. She sensed a hair-trigger readiness about him, and knew that if she made one wrong move, he'd grab her.

She had to come up with a plan. She couldn't let this hateful stranger carry her niece off to an unknown future. Yet what could she do? She had no idea where he'd sent Arianne. She had no idea where he lived.

If he disappeared now, she might never find Arianne again.

Should she tell him she wasn't Camryn—that her twin had died? Perhaps his attitude would soften, and he'd handle the matter with compassion and reason. Then again, he might simply leave, glad to be rid of Camryn once and for all.

She couldn't let him go until she knew more.

"I'll have to get a suitcase to pack her things," Kate told him, stalling for time. She couldn't very well ask his name or where he lived without alerting him to the fact that she wasn't Camryn.

"Where do you keep your suitcases?" he asked.

"The hall closet."

"Lead the way." He trailed her to the closet and watched as she pulled out a sturdy gray suitcase. "Pack one with Arianne's things, and another for yourself."

She glanced at him in surprise as hope surged through her. Had she convinced him that Arianne needed her, at least temporarily? "You're letting me come?"

"Oh, yes, ma'am. In fact, I insist you do. You see, we have a date with a certain judge, you and I."

"A judge?" She frowned, perplexed. "In court? About...custody?"

He gave a dry, humorless laugh. "Custody will damn sure be on the agenda, along with other issues. Like divorce."

"Divorce?"

"You left before ours was final. And guess what? Turns out the attorney you hired hadn't even passed the bar yet. He had no authority to act on your behalf. Nothing he handled was valid."

Kate stared at him in sick dismay. Camryn hadn't been divorced. Which meant...oh, God...this man was her husband. And he now believed *her* to be *his wife!*

The nightmare just grew worse and worse.

Camryn must have been in a terrible panic to get away from him if she hadn't even waited for the divorce to be finalized. Foreboding coursed through Kate. Was she placing herself in danger by going with him?

Maybe she'd be wiser to tell him her true identity, and that Camryn was dead. But if she did, he might simply leave, and she'd have a hell of a time finding Arianne. He could easily disappear without ever telling her where he lived, or how to contact him. She might never see her niece again.

She couldn't allow that! Her sister had run away from this cold, heartless husband of hers. Kate would not willingly relinquish Arianne to him. If that meant impersonating her sister until she came up with a better plan, she'd do it. God help her!

She drew two suitcases from the hall closet.

He nodded curtly toward the nursery. "Go pack."

In seething silence, Kate carried the suitcases to the

nursery and packed one of them full of Arianne's clothes and toys. He watched her every move. When she'd finished, she moved on to her own bedroom, with her captor following closely. She set the empty suitcase on the bed and opened it, eyeing the telephone on the bedside table.

Even if she could get to the phone, who could she call? If she notified the police, Mitch would probably vanish rather than face possible complications. She had to stay with him at least until she discovered his last name, where he lived and where he'd sent Arianne. A telephone would do her no good now.

"Don't reach for that phone, Camryn," he warned, his perceptive gaze on her as he eased his tall form into an armchair near the door.

The threat was only implied, but she didn't doubt that he'd physically overpower her again. Remembering the awesome strength she'd felt coiled in his muscled body when he'd trapped her against his chest, she knew he'd have no problem brutalizing men much bigger than him—possibly several of them at a time—let alone one weaponless woman.

His stare alone frightened her. It seemed to have a disarming power of its own....

She looked away, pierced with a sudden, uncomfortable awareness of him as a man and the suggestive intimacy of the setting. Her bedroom. He believed her to be *his wife*—a woman he had once loved. At the very least, in the physical sense.

Flustered, she turned to the dresser drawer she had opened, anxious to finish her packing. Hurriedly she tossed jeans, shorts and tops into her suitcase. She then pulled open another drawer, and paused. Self-conscious warmth seeped beneath her skin. Calling herself a fool, she tried to ignore his infernal presence as she packed her panties and bras.

"Are those yours?"

The surprise in his question drew her glance back to him, then down to the cotton, pastel-hued underwear she'd just placed in the suitcase. The warmth in her face intensified. "Who else's would they be?"

He lifted one brow. "No black satin or red lace? Your taste in lingerie has, uh, changed."

"That's none of your business."

He almost smiled. "Amen."

Pursing her mouth, she shoved her underwear beneath the other clothing in her suitcase. She'd never bought the sexy kind of underwear Camryn had favored. Kate preferred the comfort of cotton to lace. Besides, who ever saw her in her underwear, anyway? Her work and her studies—and then Arianne—had dominated her time. She hadn't had a steady man in her life since her undergrad days.

Though she didn't care at all what this big rude lug thought of her, his comment had made her feel frumpy. In self-defense—and maybe to extinguish the mild amusement she seemed to have afforded him—she coolly remarked, "I try to please whatever man I'm *currently* involved with."

"Since when?"

She raised her brow at the chiding retort. He apparently didn't believe that Camryn had tried to please him. Kate was glad her sister hadn't wasted her time. She doubted there would have been much reward in the venture—other than, perhaps, in a strictly physical sense. That thought, however, brought to mind the possible physical rewards a man as blatantly virile as Mitch might confer upon a women...a subject she certainly didn't want to think about.

Abruptly she averted her gaze from him and continued packing.

"I hope whatever fool you're dating is the patient type, for his sake," Mitch said in a pleasant tone. "You're going to be gone for a while."

Kate halted in her work and frowned. "How long of a while?"

"A week or two...possibly longer, depending on what the judge decides."

Her stomach tightened with anxiety. Mitch clearly had every confidence that the court proceedings would go his way. "Where exactly are we going?"

"To the judge who married us, finalized our separation and granted us joint custody." He hadn't, of course, answered her question, although he probably thought he had.

"I have to tell certain people I'll be gone, or they'll worry."

"Too bad you didn't think of that when you ran away with my daughter. You just disappeared." He leaned forward, his arms resting across his knees. "I wouldn't trust you to call anyone, Camryn, so you're going to just disappear again. Shouldn't surprise anyone who knows you. You can spin whatever crazy tale you'd like when you get back."

Resentful at the control he had over her, Kate flung more clothes and a pair of shoes into the suitcase. In actuality, there wouldn't be many people who would miss her. Her parents had been dead since she was five years old, and she had no close relations left. She supposed that her neighbors might get curious about her extended absence, her friends might wonder where she was and her lawyer might leave messages on her answering machine, but no one would raise an alarm. She'd taken a leave from work, which meant co-workers wouldn't note her absence. She was entirely on her own. A sobering thought. She could disappear from the face of the earth and very few people would notice.

She stalked to her closet and rifled through her dresses and suits, looking for just the right one to wear into a courtroom.

"Don't tell me those are yours, too."

She jumped at the low, gravelly voice that came from right behind her. She hadn't heard him move from the chair, but now he stood peering over her shoulder at the neatly hanging garments in her closet. She understood his comment perfectly. She doubted that Camryn had ever worn a tailored suit or conservative dress in her life. Kate affected a nonchalant shrug. "So my tastes have changed."

He let out a laugh and wedged a broad shoulder against the wall beside her closet. "I get it now. The puzzle pieces are beginning to fit. You've got some rich fool believing you're a real prim and proper Miss Priss."

"Miss Priss!"

"With your practical underwear, your tailored suits, your hair all pinned and braided." He slipped his thumbs into his pockets and ambled across her room, nodding at the shelves that lined one side. "Leather-bound books in your bedroom, a piano in your living room." He looked genuinely amused. "So your new man's fallen for it, has he? Obviously so, since he must be paying the bills."

Jamming her balled-up knuckles onto her hips, Kate cast him a withering stare. How she hated his implication that Camryn had been living with a man for his money!

"How do you know I haven't worked for everything I have?"

"Come on, Cam. Even if you worked long enough to earn a little cash—which is doubtful, since you've only been gone for six months—money slips through your fingers like water."

He clearly thought very little of Camryn. The fact that he was basically right about her character did little to ease Kate's resentment. "Maybe I got financial help from my—" She stopped on the verge of saying *sister*. Did Mitch know that Camryn had a sister? If so, he clearly wasn't aware that they were identical twins. Perhaps it was better not to mention anything about sisters. Prudently, she finished with "My family."

"You told me you didn't have family."

A surprising pain accosted Kate. So Camryn hadn't acknowledged her existence at all. Pushing the pain aside out of pure necessity, she pursed her lips as if she'd been caught in a fib. "Okay, so maybe I don't have any *blood* relations. But I do have people who care about me enough to extend a loan."

"Maybe so. Maybe you borrowed the money to feather your elegant new nest. Won't your new boy-friend be surprised when your true colors shine through?"

"You know nothing about my life now. *Nothing.*"

His lips curved in mock appreciation. "You're good, Camryn. You're really good. I like your lady-of-the-manor act. I like your upscale clothes, and your sophisticated new look." He stopped beside her, leaned in too close and inhaled deeply. "And your expensive new perfume." His nearness sent a frisson of awareness through her bloodstream. "I even like your smooth new way of walking." His gaze roamed her face. "It's all very effective,'' he whispered. The odd intensity in his golden-green eyes suddenly cooled, leaving only contempt. ''But you can drop the act with me, *chèr'*. It won't do you any good. In case you've forgotten, I caught the last show.''

Thoroughly shaken, Kate drew back from him and gripped the edge of the dresser for support. Her hand itched to slap him. He'd invaded her personal space in a way no one ever had; in a way that disturbed her just as much as his earlier manhandling. She would resist the urge to slap him, though. He might kill her. Or, he might leave. Then what would the future hold for Arianne?

Only one thing Kate knew for sure—she needed more information.

She'd play the role he'd cast her in until she got it. And if, along the way, she discovered that this hot-tempered, hard-eyed man was indeed violent or emotionally cruel—''mean,'' as Camryn had described him—she wouldn't hesitate to take whatever steps were necessary to protect her niece.

Even if that meant running with her.

''I'm ready to go,'' she muttered between clenched teeth, her hands still gripping the edge of the dresser behind her, ''whenever you are.''

''Good.'' With a faint smile that didn't reach his eyes, he again leaned in too close. ''Then let me make it official. I'm placing you under citizen's arrest.'' From behind her came a *click-click* sound, and cold metal encircled her wrists. ''For the crime of kidnapping.''

She jerked her arms, found them bound together and stared at him in horrified surprise. He'd reached behind her and handcuffed her!

''Kidnapping,'' she repeated in panicked disbelief. ''You're charging me with *kidnapping?*''

"It was against custody orders for you to take Arianne out of state…which you well know. Not to mention the six months you kept her away from me."

Alarm buzzed in Kate's head. Could she, as the baby's aunt, be charged with kidnapping, or accessory to kidnapping? She didn't believe so, but she didn't know much about kidnapping laws. "If you really think I kidnapped her, why don't you just call the police, here and now?"

"You'd like that, wouldn't you? All you'd have to say is that it's your turn to keep the baby, and I'd be the one forced to prove otherwise. By the time they got the mess straightened out, you'd be long gone." He shook his head. "No, *chèr'*. The only place I know I'll get justice is in my neck of the woods."

His neck of the woods. Where, exactly, was that? From his use of the word *chèr'*, she guessed Louisiana…but she couldn't be sure. Cajun communities in Texas, Mississippi, even South Carolina and California, also used the term. She certainly couldn't ask him where he was from. If she was Camryn, she'd know.

Kate stiffened in fury as he gripped her arm and forced her into step beside him. He seemed pretty darn sure of himself. Maybe she'd tell the authorities her real name and charge *him* with kidnapping *her!* Perhaps then she'd be granted custody of Arianne.

"Don't worry about your suitcases," he said. "I'll send my driver in to get them once I have you situated in the van."

Situated? In a van? She didn't like the sound of that.

"Oh, and just in case you're planning on screaming when we step outside," he murmured, settling his palm against her nape, "all I have to do is apply the right amount of pressure *here*—" his thumb pressed into the sensitive indentation near her hairline "—to render you unconscious. You'd then have to make the entire trip bound and gagged." His hand remained cupped around her nape, making her all the more aware of his strength and heat and male toughness. "The choice is yours, *chèr'*."

She couldn't wait to have him thrown in jail for kidnapping her...and to get full, permanent custody of Arianne.

Assuming, of course, he really did intend to hand her over to the authorities. As he ushered her out the door, through the garage and into the back of a van with heavily tinted windows, her hands in cuffs and her neck encircled by that strong, ruthless hand, Kate began to have her doubts about that. If he hated Camryn enough, a man like him might simply murder her.

She wouldn't give in to the steadily mounting fear, though. She couldn't afford the luxury of cowardice.

Arianne needed her.

CHAPTER THREE

SHE'D NEVER BEEN a prisoner before. She was definitely one now.

Mitch had escorted her to the rear bench seat in a maroon passenger van parked just outside her garage. The van's tinted windows stopped outsiders from seeing in...which, of course, prevented the prisoner inside from signaling for help. The handcuffs binding her wrists behind her back also greatly curtailed her chances of attracting attention.

A dull sense of fear throbbed through her like a toothache.

He settled in beside her, blocking her access to the door. Dressed in a black T-shirt and jeans that emphasized the musculature of his chest, arms and thighs, he gave the impression of immense, ruthless power barely contained. He sat close enough for Kate to feel the heat from his sinewy arm, and she shifted as far away from him as possible in the suddenly tight confines of the back seat.

"Are these handcuffs really necessary?" she asked. "How on earth do you think I could possibly escape?"

"I wouldn't put anything past you, Cam," he murmured.

She bit back words of protest, afraid that if she didn't, he'd gag her.

The driver, a dark, burly man wearing a black sports

cap, a sleeveless green muscle shirt and tattoos on his impressive biceps, drove the van west from Tallahassee on I-10. Kate wondered how long the ride would be. And if she would survive it.

She truly was at the mercy of these men.

Mitch distracted her from her growing fear by reaching over the seat for her purse, which his cohort had carried to the van along with her luggage. As Mitch rifled through the contents of her suede handbag, she held her breath.

Her goal of reclaiming Arianne could very well depend on her impersonation of Camryn. The identification cards in her wallet would give her away. Although she could explain away the driver's license in the name of Kathryn Jones by saying she'd applied for it under her alias, its date of issue was nearly a year ago. If Mitch noticed the date, he'd realize that Camryn couldn't have been in Tallahassee at that time.

Another problem was the campus identification card naming her as Kathryn Jones, Ph.D., professor of history, Florida State University. Why would Camryn have gone to the trouble of manufacturing that?

Kate breathed freely again only when her captor nudged aside her wallet and pulled out, instead, a small container of pepper spray. She'd actually forgotten about that neat little defensive weapon. Since she had no intention of escaping before she discovered who he was, where he lived and where he'd sent Arianne, she hadn't concentrated on arming herself.

"Put this up for safekeeping, Darryl." He tossed the pepper spray to his driver, who caught it without taking his eyes from the road. "Wouldn't want my sweet bride bringing more tears to my eyes, would I?"

His sweet bride. The sarcasm was heavy in his otherwise light tone. Was he angry, not only because Camryn had taken the baby, but because she'd left him?

After latching the purse closed, he tossed it behind the seats, where they'd stored her luggage. Kate gave silent thanks that he hadn't examined her identification cards and unmasked her as an imposter. He probably would have dropped her off on the side of the road, leaving her no means of tracking Arianne. Unless, of course, she caught the license-plate number of the van—a feat she hadn't managed when he'd hurried her into the vehicle. But even a tag number didn't assure success of tracking down a determined person. For all she knew, the van could be stolen, or rented under a false name.

She made a mental note, though, to check the tag number at the first chance, as well as dispose of her identification cards, if those opportunities ever arose.

Her captor leaned forward and folded down the seat in front of them into a low bench. He then lounged back in his seat, extended his long legs across the bench and rested his arm along the back of her seat. The pose brought him even closer to her, while his vivid green gaze locked with hers. "So, tell me…why did you run with Arianne? And what have you been doing since you left? I'd like to know what kind of life my daughter has been leading."

Although he spoke softly, there was no mistaking his anger. Would something she'd say provoke him to violence? Her fear intensified. She was afraid to answer, yet afraid to remain silent.

Her drumming pulse and sweating palms brought back memories of childhood terror: late-night visits at the girls' dorm from a staff member in the children's home who talked gently, then lashed out with his belt…brutally, repeatedly, in a frenzied rage. He'd been fired when the girls had built up the collective nerve to report him—and he'd never applied that horrifying strap to Kate or Camryn—but the fear itself had scarred them both.

Kate would always be wary of quiet-talking, angry men.

"Well?" His tawny brows drew together in an impatient frown. "What have you been doing with Arianne?"

The very depth of her fear tripped some internal switch of Kate's. Imprisoned though she was, she wouldn't give in to the terror. She had to fight as she always had—by keeping in mind who she was and where she intended to go in life. She was no longer a helpless, parentless child in a world controlled by strangers, but a respected member of her community, a well-esteemed educator, whose word in court would carry considerable weight. She would fight her fear by keeping her wits about her, by using those wits against her captor until she knew enough about him to be sure of finding Arianne.

Straightening her spine, she gazed at him in her most quelling manner, the one that set wayward students to stuttering. "First *you* tell *me*...where have you sent Arianne?"

He stared at her in some surprise. Had he frightened Camryn so badly that she'd stopped talking back to him? Afraid that it might be so, Kate braced herself for a physical blow.

"You don't need to know where she is," he finally replied, his tone curt now rather than soft.

"Then you don't need to know where she's been."

A muscle flexed in his lean jaw, but he remained exactly as he'd been, in a deceptively casual pose with his arm resting on the back of her seat. The silence spun out into a long, tense standoff.

"If you really care about her, though," Kate added, "you do need to be aware of her dietary requirements."

"Dietary requirements?" he repeated in blank amazement, as if he'd never heard the term but found it fascinating.

"It means there are certain foods she can't—"

"I know what it means. I'm just surprised you do." His eyes had narrowed on her in a searching look that told her he hadn't meant the retort as an insult; he clearly *was* surprised that she'd used the term.

She saw then what she'd missed before—the keen intelligence in his eyes. Its magnitude startled her. She'd assumed that he, like the other men in Camryn's life, had more brawn than brains.

He was absolutely right. Camryn wouldn't have worded the concept quite that way. In fact, she probably wouldn't have given the subject itself more than a passing thought.

Kate compressed her lips in self-annoyance. To succeed in this impersonation, she'd have to stay in character. "I'm just telling you what the doctor said. Arianne has digestive prob—uh, stomachaches when she eats the wrong foods. It took a while, but we figured out the ones she can and can't eat."

"Like what?"

At least he'd bought the explanation, it seemed. Which had, after all, been true. Now she had to concentrate on finding clues to who was keeping the baby. Anxiety over Arianne's welfare clawed at her insides. "I'd rather talk to whoever is taking care of her."

"You'll speak to me. No one else."

She shrugged, glanced away and adopted Camryn's

most vacuous look. She hoped he couldn't detect the concern radiating from her heart like solar power.

"What can't she eat, Camryn?" Annoyance resounded in his deep, gruff voice.

She pursed her lips in the provocative way Camryn would to signify a secret she was keeping.

His jaw shifted; his gaze hardened. Perhaps he did care about Arianne, in his own twisted way. He probably viewed her as a prized possession—a trophy in his war with Camryn.

Kate wondered if he would resort to violence *now*. She'd sensed his temper rising.

After a long, disgruntled stare, though, he drew a cell phone from his pocket and punched in a number. His tone, when he spoke, was brusque. "How is she?"

Kate watched as he listened, her heart picking up speed. She desperately wanted to know the answer to that question. His rugged, angular face gave nothing away. She envisioned gangsterlike characters dealing with her sweet, frightened baby. She prayed that they'd be gentle. Caring. Competent…please, God…

"Have you fed her yet?" he asked into the phone.

Kate strained to hear the reply. She thought she heard peals of distress. Like a baby crying…Mama-Mama!

Her restraint broke, and she turned to Mitch imploringly. "*Please* bring her to me! She won't understand why I'm not there. Seeing only strangers will scare her."

"You're not getting your hands on her again."

"You don't really care about her at all, do you? If she's given milk-based formula, she'll get sick. She'll be in misery all night."

"Don't give her milk," he uttered into the phone.

"Soy-based formula," she stressed, and emphatically named a particular brand. "And no baby foods with spices, preservatives or added sugar. I feed her only fresh fruits and vegetables that I puree myself.'' Her throat cramped; her eyes misted. "She likes sweet potatoes, and…c-carrots.'' Turning her face away from him, she croaked in a half whisper, "And pears.''

Determinedly she fought against the tears. She would not cry in front of him.

"Sweet potatoes, carrots and pears,'' he repeated into the phone. "And fix 'em yourself. You know—with a blender.'' After a moment, he continued, "*Of course* you'll have to wait till you get home to do that. Until then, give her soy formula and, uh, crackers or something. Without salt or preservatives. I'm counting on you, Joey.''

Joey. Mitch's accomplice was named Joey. Whoever he was, she couldn't imagine him caring for the baby with the same nurturing tenderness that she herself would. She hated to imagine anything less. Anguished, she stared out the window at the blur of roadside forest whizzing by.

After he'd ended his conversation with the mysterious Joey, Mitch muttered, "Now you know how I felt for six whole months.''

She refused to believe him. He had no heart.

"But then, this is probably just another grand performance of yours to win my sympathy,'' he said. "Don't waste your time. I'm not about to let you go, or give you access to my daughter.''

Horrible man!

"If you really cared about her,'' he continued, "you wouldn't have deprived her of a father, grandparents, aunts, uncles and cousins.''

Kate tightened her lips in dismay. Grandparents, aunt, uncles, cousins? She'd never considered the possibility that Mitch had a family. It somehow made him seem more human. It also triggered an age-old response in her that she couldn't help—envy. A family with parents and siblings was, to her, an unattainable dream.

She had to remind herself that the simple fact of having a family didn't make this man a worthy father. He'd forced his way into her home. Kidnapped her. Kept her in chains. She had no trouble believing he'd abused Camryn and the baby.

If he had, he'd deserved every miserable minute of his six months' worth of anxiety. Assuming, of course, that he'd felt any. This kidnapping could just as easily stem from a sick desire to control his wife.

And as far as his family went, they were probably at the root of his antisocial behavior. She'd do everything she could to get Arianne away from him. As soon as she figured out how. She had to think, think, think!

The first logical step would be to learn his full name and where he lived. A peek at his driver's license would certainly help. Could she possibly lift his wallet? She'd never tried to pick a pocket before.

And she couldn't try now with her hands cuffed.

She shifted a tentative gaze to him. Her heart accelerated as their gazes locked. "I, um, don't mean to complain, but…uh…these handcuffs are getting uncomfortable."

He didn't look in the least sympathetic. But after a tense, silent moment, he shifted in his seat, drew a small key from his jeans pocket and reached around her. The heat of his nearness, the surprising appeal of his musky scent, the utterly masculine presence he radiated, clouded her mind with an uncomfortable awareness.

Yes, indeed, the man was dangerous. Although she loathed him, she understood why her sister had been

attracted to him. He was all man. And Kate herself had
relatively little experience with the breed. She literally
held her breath until the handcuffs swung free of her
wrists and he drew his well-muscled body away from
her.

She rubbed her wrists and averted her gaze.

Mitch settled back in his seat feeling nothing but resentment toward her. She was damn lucky he hadn't
wrung her pretty neck. She'd ripped out his heart by
taking Arianne and kept him in agony for six long
months…and didn't seem a damn bit sorry for it, either.

In fact, he sensed only an odd determination in her—
one that he didn't understand. What was she up to?
Something about the way she looked at him, the way
she held herself, the tone of her voice, even the words
she chose, seemed so…un-Camryn-like.

He had no doubt the change was deliberate. She was
obviously a better actress than he'd realized. Diabolical,
even. He had a fairly good guess as to *why* she'd
changed. She'd probably set her sights on a guy who
preferred a classier image for his woman than the one
she'd been projecting.

Her long, platinum-streaked blond hair, which she'd
usually worn flowing in sexy disarray, had been replaced
by a primly braided, dark blond upsweep. That alone
was enough to change her image completely. Also missing was the dramatic makeup that had added a wicked
allure to her natural beauty. If she was wearing makeup
at all, it was minimal. And she wasn't sporting her usual
jewelry—a profusion of bracelets, rings and necklaces,
as well as big, dangling earrings. Now she displayed
only a single sapphire ring, one demure gold chain and
tiny gold studs at her ears.

Her clothes were another remarkable difference. She'd

always favored tight short-shorts, halter tops and high-heeled strappy sandals. When she'd gone out for the evening—which she often had—she'd donned sensational low-cut dresses, usually in red or black. Always sexy, even after the pregnancy had compromised her chorus-girl figure. Now she wore relatively long khaki shorts, a simple sleeveless white blouse and low-heeled sandals.

Not that she wasn't still sexy. She was. Maybe more so. But he'd be damned if he'd think about *that*.

Disgruntled that he'd even noticed, he watched the passing scenery.

He couldn't stop thinking about the changes in her, though. Like the cotton underwear she'd packed in her suitcase instead of her usual see-through lace. Her current lover apparently wanted a woman drastically different from the real Camryn. Poor bastard.

The deception went much deeper than her clothes or appearance. Even her household had undergone a change. She'd never shown the slightest interest in making their house a home. It had never been more to her than a temporary resting place. The house she now lived in was as cozy and elegant a home as he'd ever seen.

But then, maybe the house wasn't hers. Because the investigator had spotted her yesterday—on the Fourth of July—he hadn't had the chance to discover anything at all about her current activities—whom she lived with, what she owned. Not that any of that information mattered much, now that he had her.

Mitch assumed the house belonged to the new man in her life. That would explain the house, the furniture, the leather-bound books, the piano. The guy was in for a rude awakening when Camryn's true colors began to shine through. Which, in time, they would.

It had taken Mitch himself quite a long while to understand her true character. When they were first married, she'd promised to be a good mother. She quit smoking and drinking for her unborn baby's sake, and actively tried to win his family's approval. Though their marriage wasn't based on love, he'd believed they stood a chance of making their parenthood work. By the fourth month of her pregnancy, though, the novelty of being his wife had worn off, and she'd begun sneaking off to bars and casinos every night in search of new thrills.

She had him served with divorce papers one month after the baby was born. She'd been ready to move on to greener pastures. Too bad she hadn't stayed to follow up on the legal details…like whether the divorce had gone through.

She'd put on quite a show for the court proceedings, especially at the custody hearing. She'd pulled her hair back with a bow, used very little makeup and wore a sweet yellow sundress to court. Fortunately for him, the judge knew her from various local bars and understood a good deal about her true character. Otherwise, he might not have believed Mitch when he'd testified to her negligence with Arianne.

Camryn was and always would be a self-centered party girl who wanted her kicks regardless of who suffered, including her infant daughter.

And that brought up more questions about this drastic change in her. If she was aiming to please a man, why had she chosen someone who clearly preferred a more sedate woman? Didn't sound like Camryn's idea of fun. Maybe the guy had money. Or…power.

That was a disturbing thought. Maybe this dramatic change in persona was part of a plan to arm herself with money and power. The poor sap she was involved with would probably meet them in the courtroom with a high-

powered attorney and deep pockets full of ready cash.
The prospect only strengthened his resolve to get her to
Louisiana to face a judge who knew the true story. No
amount of money or legal shenanigans would sway
Judge Breaux—not when it came to the welfare of a
child.

But what if she convinced the judge that motherhood
had changed her into a decent, caring, model parent?

That had to be the driving force behind the change in
her. Anxiety surged through Mitch. He knew Camryn
enough to be sure that the differences were only super-
ficial. When she had achieved her ends, she would revert
to her old fun-craving, irresponsible, negligent self.

Why, then, did she still want custody of the baby?

When she'd discovered she was pregnant, she'd considered it a new adventure. From things she'd told him,
he knew she'd envisioned motherhood as one big heart-
warming scene from a greeting-card commercial. But
reality slowly intruded into that idealized notion, and
boredom had set in. She'd been itching to leave Terrebonne Parish for a more exciting place.

He wasn't surprised that she'd skipped town, but he
hadn't expected her to take his daughter with her.

Nothing in her experience could have prepared her for
motherhood on her own. She'd had plenty of help with
the baby from his family, and after she'd left, he'd believed she would grow tired of the never-ending work
and responsibility of caring for Arianne by herself. He'd
expected her to send the baby back to him…or, God
forbid, abandon her to someone else's care.

Neither of those things had happened. This, more than
anything, puzzled him. Why did she continue to want
Arianne? A baby would only cramp her style and curtail
her freedom. She had to have some ulterior motive other

than motherly love. He honestly believed Camryn was incapable of such unselfish devotion.

What was on her mind? Or, more appropriately, up her sleeve?

It was then, as he sat staring out his passenger window and pondering the question, that he felt an odd little tug at the back pocket of his jeans. He froze in absolute incredulity.

She was lifting his wallet.

The idea was too ludicrous to believe. Did she think he wouldn't notice it missing? Did she intend to take his cash and credit cards?

Too curious to work up much of an anger, he allowed her to gradually pull the wallet free of his pocket, and through the reflection in the passenger window, watched her slip it into the pocket of her khaki shorts.

"Um, excuse me, but—" she was speaking to Darryl rather than him "—could you please stop at the next exit? I'd like to find a ladies' room."

Maybe she was hoping to escape him with the "ladies' room" ruse and skip out with his money. Nothing too new about that, he supposed. She'd maxed out his credit cards and spent all the cash she could before she divorced him. She'd then left town with his daughter. About the only thing he hadn't lost to her was his small house on the swamp, his fleet of shrimp boats and his heart. His heart remained strictly his own, thank God.

"Cap'n, you want me to stop?" Darryl asked him.

"Pull over here."

Camryn's lips parted in dismay as Darryl swerved the van onto the shoulder of the highway.

"We're stopping *here?*" she said. "You expect me to…to go in the woods?"

He lifted a shoulder. "It's up to you, *chèr'*. But we're

not stopping anywhere else, and we still have quite a ways to drive.''

Although clearly dismayed, she nodded and sat forward in the seat.

He clicked a handcuff around her wrist, and the other around his own. ''Ready?''

She gaped at the handcuffs binding her wrist to his, then stared at him in patent horror. ''You *don't* mean that you're…you're…coming *with* me!''

''You didn't think I'd let you loose in those woods, did you?''

He had to admire her acting ability. He could swear her objection was based on outraged modesty rather than a foiling of her escape plan. But he knew damn well she'd never been overly modest, even before they'd been married. At times she hadn't even bothered to close the bathroom door.

An oddly convincing blush crept into her face, and she pressed her lips into a thin, white line. ''You will *not* come with me,'' she decreed, her tone imperial and her bearing regal. ''I won't allow it.''

She really had that lady-of-the-manor act down pat. ''You think I should just let you out and, uh, trust you to return?''

''Absolutely.''

''So…you're trustworthy, are you, *chèr'?*''

Something flickered in her pretty brown eyes. Looked a little like guilt. Imagine that. She recovered quickly enough, though, and tilted her chin at a haughty angle. ''Yes, I am.''

''Then why do you have my wallet in your pocket?''

The color drained from her face, and she silently stared at him. Never had he seen her more at a loss. Not a lick of her former arrogance remained.

He held out his hand—the one that wasn't chained to hers.

Color rushed back into her cheeks as she dug into her back pocket and placed the wallet into his palm.

He flipped it open, glanced to see that his credit cards and cash remained in place, then slipped the wallet into his pocket. His shirt pocket, this time. "What were you planning—to skip the country, compliments of my American Express?"

"No. Of course not. I...I wasn't going to take anything from your wallet. I just...I just..."

He waited, curious as to what explanation she'd come up with.

She seemed fresh out of creativity, though. At least, for the moment. She bit her lip, looking utterly humiliated.

Something about her reaction bothered him. Crazy as it sounded, she seemed *too mortified*. The old Camryn would have been merely upset at being caught. A subtle difference, but one that he couldn't easily shake off.

Why did the change in her seem so deeply ingrained?

He didn't know, and he didn't like not knowing. He'd have to watch her every move. Good thing he intended to transport her by boat most of the way rather than car. Even if she succeeded in some trickery along the way, she couldn't do much damage in the Gulf. No one out there would interfere.

"You want to use the woods or not?" he demanded.

"No. I'll just wait."

He shrugged and sat back in his seat, forcing her to do likewise, since her wrist was cuffed to his.

"Could you please release my wrist?" she asked, her dignity back in place.

"Don't try to steal my wallet again," he warned as

he unlocked the cuff from his own wrist, then from hers. "Won't do you any good, anyway. Cash and credit cards won't mean much to you out there in the Gulf."

"The Gulf? Of...Mexico? Do you mean, we're going on a boat?"

Another odd response. "I damn sure wouldn't try crossing on a raft."

She digested that quip in silence, then asked, "What kind of boat?"

He turned and searched her face for signs of mockery or sarcasm. She *had* to know the answer to that question. Why had she asked it? "The *Lady Jeanette*," he told her.

And though he realized Camryn was a good actress and hesitated to believe anything she said or silently conveyed, he also knew that his reply hadn't told her a damn thing. The question was still as bright and bothersome in her eyes. How could she not know he'd meant one of his shrimp boats?

More perplexing still, he detected fear in her expression. *Fear.* Why would the thought of traveling on his boat frighten her? She'd enjoyed herself the last time she'd gone out to sea with him. She'd enjoyed herself a little too much, actually.

"Why are we going on a boat?" An almost undetectable tremor reverberated in her voice.

"Because I don't want you causing problems along the way. On the water, there's less chance of it."

Looking troubled, she searched his face, as if she suspected some hidden meaning.

Darryl called over his shoulder, "Is Joey gonna meet us at the dock, Cap'n?"

Before he had time to answer no, that he'd instructed Joey to head straight for home, Camryn cut in, "Joey?

The same Joey who has Arianne? Will he bring her, too?''

That question, more than anything, convinced Mitch that something was going very wrong here. Even Darryl glanced back through the rearview mirror to frown at the woman who'd asked the question.

"You know Joey, Cam," Mitch answered, watching her. "Why would you ask a question like that?"

From the blankness of her stare, he knew she hadn't caught his meaning. She clearly had no clue to what she'd said wrong.

"Do you mean—" she hesitated "—he *won't* be bringing Arianne to the dock?"

What in the *hell* was going on?

"I mean," said Mitch, "that Joey isn't a *he*. She's my sister."

His sister.

In the tense silence that followed, the facts of the situation rearranged themselves in Kate's mind. The person keeping Arianne was not the shady gangster character she had envisioned but a woman who held the same family relationship as she herself—Arianne's aunt. A measure of relief came with that knowledge, but only a slight measure. She had no solid reason to believe this Joey was any more competent or caring with babies than a strange man would be.

On the heel of those thoughts came the understanding that she'd made a huge mistake in referring to Joey as "he." Both Mitch and his driver were waiting for an explanation. *You know Joey, Cam. Why would you ask such a question?*

And this was just the beginning. If Mitch was taking her to "his neck of the woods," as he'd called it, she could be facing a community of people whom Camryn should know. How could she possibly bluff her way through this impersonation?

The answer occurred to her in a flash of unprecedented brilliance—an explanation that would cover her latest blunder and any she might make in the future, as well as offer Mitch an explanation that might help soften his attitude toward Camryn.

And though it would be a lie, it would be more of the truth than she'd told so far.

Meeting his frankly suspicious gaze, Kate said, "I wasn't going to mention this, since I doubt you'll believe me. But I suppose I do owe you an explanation." Taking in a stabilizing breath, she chose her words carefully. "In January, I was involved in an automobile accident. I sustained a head injury. Since then, there have been things I can't remember. Like, um—" she braced herself, half afraid to utter the rest of the explanation "—Arianne's last name. Or, where she was born... or—" she finished in a quieter tone "—who her father was."

She then waited for the bomb to hit target.

At first, his face didn't register a reaction. As the moment dragged out, his brows converged in a frown. "Are you trying to tell me...?"

He didn't finish the incredulous question, so Kate finished it for him. "That I don't know you. Or where you're from, or anything about you." When he continued to stare in stupefied silence, she added with fervent honesty, "That's why I took your wallet. I wanted to see your license...to find out your name."

CHAPTER FOUR

STUNNED INTO SPEECHLESSNESS, Mitch merely stared at her. Did she actually expect him to believe that she didn't remember him?

Thoroughly annoyed, he jerked his attention away from her to meet Darryl's eyes in the rearview mirror. His expression reflected Mitch's feelings perfectly. *Couldn't remember. Right!* Mitch squared his jaw and trained his gaze on the expressway ahead of them. He wouldn't waste his time responding to her nonsense.

What, he wondered, was the motive behind this ridiculous new claim of hers?

As they exited the expressway and sped down the two-lane rural highway toward Florida's Gulf Coast, her soft, hesitant voice broke the quiet. "When I first saw you today, the name 'Mitch' came to me." She paused and studied him with wide, beautiful, troubled brown eyes. "Is that your name?"

Mitch couldn't stop his lip from curling in derision. "No. It's André."

"André!" Her brows lifted, like golden wings poised for flight. Those brows soon converged above a frown of bewilderment. "Did anyone ever call you Mitch?"

"No."

"But...you *are* Arianne's father, right?"

That was about as much as Mitch could take. "You know damn well I am. I have no idea what you expect to gain by—'' He broke off as the reason for her amnesia ploy occurred to him. By claiming she couldn't remember him, she'd found an excuse for keeping the baby away for those six months. Despite the fact that she'd disobeyed the custody order by leaving Louisiana with Arianne, the judge might go easier on her.

He clenched his jaw and struggled not to curse. Clever of her. Very clever. But she wouldn't get away with it. He'd call his attorney and the investigator who'd found her. By the time she told her story to the court, he'd be prepared to expose her as a fraud.

''Your lies won't get you anywhere, *chèr*.''

''I believe you're the one who's lying,'' she charged with quiet conviction. ''I think your name *is* Mitch.''

Again, she'd managed to astound him. The intensity of her words and the suspicion in her gaze raised the hairs at the back of his neck. She *suspected* he was lying. But, of course, she had to *know*....

He searched the depths of her bewildered stare. ''What is it you want, Cam? Out of life, I mean. What would have to happen to make you 'happy ever after'?''

She looked surprised at the question. ''Well, I'd take Arianne home, and...and...''

''And what? Have some baby-sitter keep her while you sing in bars at night, sleep during the day and sneak off to drink and gamble in between?''

She gaped at him with an expression that only confused him more—as if the picture he'd painted horrified her; as if she resented his unflattering assumptions; as if he were doing her a grave injustice by reaching those conclusions.

But the Camryn he'd known wouldn't have found anything wrong with that scenario. She'd always tried to defend that very lifestyle.

"Is…is that what I *did?*" she asked.

Mitch knew then that he was in trouble. Deep trouble. Because even though he knew she was lying about the amnesia and couldn't possibly have changed her attitude and lifestyle *that much* in a span of only six months, he also found it hard to believe she was this good of an actress. She almost had him questioning his basic assumptions about her. *Almost.*

How the hell could he expect a judge to understand that she was, in fact, incorrigible? That motherhood ranked low on her priority list, far below personal gratification. That her desire for custody sprang from some self-serving ulterior motive. He absolutely *knew* all of this to be true about her, yet he could clearly see how a judge might be persuaded otherwise.

"By the time my attorney and witnesses get finished with you in court, you'll look like the worst kind of liar," he warned. "Take my advice and drop the act *now.*"

"Is that what you think? That I'm claiming not to remember you in order to sway the court?"

"If that's not the reason," he said softly, "then tell me what is."

Feeling trapped and uncomfortable in her role as Camryn, Kate grappled with the impulse to tell him the truth—that his wife had died, and that she, Kate, was horrified to think of anyone raising a child in the manner he'd described. She hadn't known that Camryn had gone back to drinking and gambling. She'd thought her sister had sworn off both addictions years ago.

But it seemed Camryn had reverted to her old ways. Had Mitch's abuse pushed her back into those destructive behaviors? Or…had she considered him "mean" for trying to stop her from them?

If only she could be sure!

All she knew for certain was how Mitch had treated *her*—forcing his way into her home, handcuffing her, kidnapping her. More than once she'd felt a fearsome anger simmering in him. Until she knew without a doubt that he wouldn't abuse Arianne, Kate couldn't confess the truth. Because if she learned that he'd deliberately hurt Camryn or the baby, she would use any edge she had—no matter how devious—to get Arianne away from him.

No, she wouldn't tell him her true identity. She'd save that for the judge. She'd then charge Mitch with false imprisonment, assault, kidnapping and any other offense her attorney could level against him. Unless, of course, she discovered that Mitch hadn't been abusive. What would she do then? *Give up Arianne?*

The thought hurt too much to contemplate. And so far, she found it impossible to believe that he could love Arianne more or give her a better life than she would. In fact, she had only his word that he *was* her father. She couldn't change her strategy now.

"Is Joey going to bring Arianne to the dock?" she asked, hoping against hope that she would.

"No. I don't trust you anywhere near Arianne. And I don't want her upset by anything you might do."

She glared at him, and they nursed their mutual animosity in silence.

Nearly an hour later, the van veered off the rural highway onto a crushed-shell driveway that ran alongside an abandoned, boarded-up seafood-processing plant. Behind it, the outriggers and mast pole of a shrimp boat came into view. The van then rounded the corner to the back parking lot, where a weathered wharf bordered the glimmering, dark green waters of a small cove.

At the wharf was docked a large commercial trawler. "Is that yours?" Kate asked in surprise. "A *shrimp boat?*"

Mitch answered only with a scornful quirk of his mouth. She supposed it *had* been a silly question. The trawler was, after all, the only boat at the dock. And as they drove closer, she saw the name painted on the stern. The *Lady Jeanette.*

The driver parked the van beneath scraggly palm trees near the end of the rickety wooden wharf, and Mitch reached for the door. "Stay here until I check out the boat, Darryl. Keep a close watch on our, uh, guest. Who knows how creative she might get? And don't let her loose, no matter what she says."

"Got 'er covered, Cap'n." The cold-eyed man with thinning black hair, a full mustache, well-trimmed goatee and anchor tattoos decorating his impressive biceps leaned his back against the driver's door and shifted a narrowed gaze to Kate. "She ain't going nowhere till you're ready."

With a brisk nod for Darryl and one last warning glare at Kate, Mitch left the van and headed toward the shrimp boat.

Fear stirred in her at the thought of being forced aboard a seagoing vessel by hostile men and taken far beyond the reaches of civilization. Not to mention the fact that she'd never been on anything larger than a ski boat, and that had been during her college years, in the relative safety of a bay.

"I don't understand why we're going by boat," she said, hoping to glean information from Darryl.

"Because Mitch is boss on da water. No one gets in his way." He spoke in a heavier, more distinct version of the dialect she'd noticed in Mitch's speech—a piquant blend of southern, French and possibly Canadian. It had to be Cajun.

"So his name *is* Mitch," she murmured, more to herself than to him.

Her captor snorted. "You got some nerve, lady. Saying you don't remember Mitch. If he'd let me, I'd take you way out yonder—" he jerked his head toward the sea "—and drag you in da try-net."

The fear Kate had been fighting spiked sharply in her breast. She had no idea what a try-net was, but she certainly didn't want to be dragged in one.

Undisguised animosity blazed from Darryl's coal-black eyes. "You know what you did to him. We all know. You stole his daughter, wasted all his money and broke his heart. He don't laugh. He don't joke. He don't dance at the *fais do do*. You took all da fun out of him. All his *joie de vivre*. He ain't da same Mitch no more...because of you."

Kate flinched at his hostility. Never before had she been the brunt of anyone's hatred. She didn't like the feeling. But surely a man who valued laughter, joking and dancing couldn't be all bad, could he?

She found it hard to visualize these tough, hard-edged men doing any of those things, though. And she wondered if what he'd said was true. Maybe Camryn had broken Mitch's heart. She doubted that. More than likely, he was merely furious because he'd lost control over her.

"Better hope when we get home," Darryl said, "his *maman* don't get her hands on you. She'd take you way back in da swamp and feed you to da gators."

Great. Just great. If she survived the boat trip, she'd have to contend with a family—or entire community—of hostile Cajuns. In the swamplands yet.

The thought of Arianne being held in the swamplands frightened her. She'd heard stories of people disappearing into the swamps of southern Louisiana, never to be seen again. Her panic served to revitalize her sense of purpose. No matter how afraid she was to board this boat, she had to do it. Even if she could find a way to escape from muscle-bound Mitch and his burly cohort, she might lose all contact with her niece. She couldn't risk that.

Come what may, she had to keep her link to Arianne intact.

As MITCH STRODE across the parking lot toward the dock, crushed oyster shells crunched beneath his boots, the late-afternoon sun glared in his eyes and a slight gulf breeze riffled through his hair, mercifully diluting the ovenlike July heat.

He breathed a grateful prayer at the sight of the *Lady Jeanette* awaiting him. At least something had gone as expected.

Although he'd hated to interrupt the shrimping trip of the crew he'd hired to run the *Lady Jeanette,* he'd called them in yesterday from Alabama waters. Remy had reported that they hadn't found much shrimp, anyway. "A waste of a good holiday," he'd grumbled. Less than a hundred pounds in two days, and mostly seventy-ninety count. Too small, too few, to even pay expenses. Which, of course, was the last thing Mitch needed on the heels of an expensive marriage, separation and hunt for his daughter.

For now, though, he was glad to have the *Lady Jeanette* at his service. She'd been his first and favorite boat, a seventy-five-foot, relatively shallow-drafting wood hull built in North Carolina. Although his three other boats were newer, faster steel hulls, none handled the sea with the same lilting grace as *Jeanette*. She also had the most comfortable quarters.

More to the point, she'd been the boat nearest to this isolated old dock between Panama City and Pensacola, a few hours' drive from Tallahassee down densely wooded highways and unpeopled back roads.

As he'd hoped, the dock was deserted. If Camryn screamed while he brought her aboard, no one would come to her rescue.

After drawing his cell phone from his pocket, Mitch keyed in the number for the private investigator. He had to disprove Camryn's ridiculous claim before they went to court. A few rings and he reached the investigator's recorded greeting. Irritated at the delay, he left a message for Chuck Arceneaux, relating the bare facts of his newest problem. He then dialed his attorney, who was also unavailable. Not too surprising, he supposed, considering it was suppertime on a Friday. July 5, no less. A holiday weekend. He suspected that neither his attorney nor the investigator would be available before Monday.

At least Chuck would have a definite starting point this time. Now that he knew Camryn's address and alias, he could probably trace her activities fairly easily. If those activities didn't include an automobile accident and serious head injury, she'd be facing a perjury charge as well as breaking the custody order…assuming, of course, she intended to tell the same story to the judge. Mitch believed she did. Why else would she bother to concoct such a tale, if not to defend herself in court?

Tense with anxiety, Mitch climbed a set of sun-bleached wooden steps and crossed the weathered planking to the *Lady Jeanette*. He couldn't wait to get out to sea again. At least there, he could think straight. Breathe easy. Make sense of his thoughts.

As he stepped over the bulwark and onto the back deck, a short, grizzled-haired figure strutted out from the wheelhouse. "*Ca va,* Mitch. How you makin'?" Remy, his long-time employee who usually captained the *Lady Jeanette,* sauntered to the back deck with a wide grin.

A tiny inset diamond glittered between his front teeth. This newest affectation never failed to amuse Mitch. The ugly, swarthy, ponytailed son of a gun was determined to draw the ladies' eyes. It seemed he'd found a surefire way. "You have your wife wit' you?" Remy asked, gazing curiously toward the tinted windows of the van.

"Don't call her my wife. If you're talking about Camryn, yeah. I have her."

Remy muttered a Cajun epithet about her to show moral support for Mitch, as his family often did. Not that Mitch encouraged hostile feelings toward her. Everyone in his tight-knit community knew she'd stolen his daughter, though. Many thought she'd also broken his heart. No one would forgive her those sins any time soon.

Except, perhaps, Remy. The middle-aged seaman always took joy in beautiful women. If he hadn't proved his loyalty over the years, Mitch wouldn't have included him in this voyage. Although Remy would take endless delight in Camryn's company, Mitch knew he'd help deliver her to the Terrebonne Parish authorities. To Remy, duty and loyalty to his captain at sea always came before pleasure. He was one of Mitch's best men.

"And your *fille*…you found her, too, eh?"

Mitch nodded and glanced out over the glistening, pickle-green water of the cove, not wanting to talk about his daughter. Too many emotions clashed within him.

For six months he'd agonized, wondering where Arianne was, whom she was with, how she was being treated. His relief at finding her washed through him in overwhelming tides, but his anxiety still burned. Though she seemed to have come through the ordeal okay, he couldn't be sure she hadn't suffered.

And his need to see her, hold her, reestablish his connection with her, hadn't yet been filled. He'd caught only a glimpse of her in Camryn's garage before Joey had whisked her away—a precaution Mitch had insisted on. In case some well-meaning lawman interrupted his plans for taking Camryn to Louisiana, he wanted Arianne safe at home with his family. He also saw no sense in exposing her to the inevitable animosity between her mother and him. He would not intentionally add to his daughter's distress.

All he could do now was hope that Joey and a longtime family friend had a safe trip back to Terrebonne Parish. If anyone could calm a distressed baby, it was Joey. She'd have her smiling in no time.

Wishing he could be there to see it, Mitch swept his gaze distractedly over the neat back deck of the shrimp boat. "Are we ready to go, Remy?"

"*Mais, oui,* Cap'n." A frown etched deep grooves in his forehead. "Da boat's ready, yes, but…"

"And your deckhands found transportation home?"

"Dey went out wit' another boat last night. But—"

"Then fire up the engine while I get the rest of our, uh, crew." Mitch turned away, deliberately ignoring the protest he knew Remy would make about leaving the dock today. He was in no mood to argue. And since Mitch was acting as captain on this trip, Remy would concede to his wishes.

Mitch himself would breathe a lot easier when he had

his wily prisoner safely offshore…on *his* turf, so to speak. She couldn't cause much trouble out there.

As he disembarked from the boat and strode back toward the van, though, he suddenly wasn't too sure of that. She probably *could* cause trouble if she put her mind to it. She obviously had depths to her character that he hadn't seen before.

Maybe it was time to change his strategy in dealing with her. Maybe he should follow her lead and play the game her way. If she believed herself to be winning him over, she'd be less likely to try something rash at sea. After all, if hell hath no fury like a woman scorned, he didn't want to court that fury while captaining the *Lady Jeanette*.

He'd simply have to hide his scorn. He'd treat her with the respect he'd show any woman—under normal circumstances—and engage her in conversation. He'd even play along with her amnesia tale if she persisted in it. Maybe he could get her talking. The more he knew about her life since she'd left him, the better prepared he'd be in court. And, of course, the more she talked, the better chance he had of tripping her up in the lie.

Before they reached port in Terrebonne Parish, he'd give her plenty of rope to hang herself.

KATE NOTICED a subtle difference in him the moment he returned to the van. It had to do with the open, friendly way he met her gaze as he settled into the back seat beside her and the warmer tone of his voice when he addressed her. "The boat's ready. The weather's holding out. The sea is calm. We should have a pretty smooth start to our trip." He almost *smiled* at her. Though his mouth didn't actually curve, the very end tilted slightly upward. His new amiability was enough to make her gape at him. "Let's go."

Darryl muttered something agreeable in the front seat, gathered things together and climbed from the van.

Kate scooted across the seat toward the door, her mind reeling. She'd barely recognized Mitch without his usual hostility and coldness. He seemed years younger, and a thousand times more…civilized. What had caused the change in his demeanor? Maybe the fact that they'd soon be out to sea, and on their way to "his neck of the woods."

Regardless of what had caused the difference, she devoutly welcomed it. She hadn't realized until this moment how much she'd been longing for a break from the anger directed at her. She simply wasn't used to being treated with hostility. Even if his pleasantness went no deeper than common courtesy, she welcomed the comparative warmth like a flower starving for sunlight.

When she reached the doorway where Mitch stood, Kate peered at him to see if she'd imagined the softening in his attitude. This time, he smiled. A slow, lazy smile—one that bracketed his mouth with deep dimples and emphasized the vertical cleft in his square chin; one that lit golden highlights in his eyes, like sunshine glinting on a dark green sea.

Kate roused herself from a sudden stupor to realize her heart was pounding and her breathing had stopped. Good heavens, his smile *transformed* him. He had to be one of the most handsome, sexiest men she'd ever seen—all rough-hewn masculinity, sun-bronzed flesh, contoured muscle…with a breathtaking smile, yet. Even the laugh lines fanning from the corners of his green eyes added a rugged appeal.

"I've been a little…brusque, haven't I?" he said.

Still dazed from his smile, she blinked, unsure she'd heard him correctly.

The smile mellowed into one of thoughtful contrition. "Camryn, I'm sorry for how I treated you today. I shouldn't have been so...rough. I guess I overreacted."

Astonishment left her momentarily speechless. He was *apologizing*. When she found her voice, all she thought to utter was "Y-yes."

"We have a serious matter to settle, but there's no reason we can't act civilized while we settle it."

"Civilized," she repeated, nodding in wholehearted agreement and tenuous relief. Surely a man who looked you straight in the eye and apologized with such sincerity wouldn't take you out on the high seas and murder you. Or drag you in a try-net. Would he?

With a satisfied nod, he reached out and settled his hands on her upper arms.

The unexpected contact startled her. Was he going to seal their presumed truce with a hug, or a *kiss?* A dizzying heat rushed through her at the thought.

His callused hands swept down her arms, brought her wrists together...and held them fast in one large palm while he reached beside him for the handcuffs. "I know you don't like being cuffed," he said in the same warm, amiable tone in which he'd apologized, "but it'll only be until we leave port and clear the channel." The cuffs locked around her wrists with an annoying *click*.

That effectively dispelled her stupor. "I thought you said we were going to act civilized. Do you call *this* civilized?" she demanded, lifting her bound wrists for emphasis.

"Until I know you won't try to escape, I have to take precautions." He somehow managed to make that seem reasonable. "Once we're at sea, I'll release you."

Annoyance stirred in her, and she wondered if he'd keep that promise. "I won't try to escape. I want to see the judge as much as you do."

"Good." He flashed her another smile, and she noticed the whiteness of his teeth against the bronze of his skin, and the golden highlights in his hair. Before she knew what he was about, he hooked his hand around her waist and scooped her up into his arms.

"I can walk!" she protested.

"No need."

She glared at him, resentful of the handcuffs, distrustful of his new friendliness and flustered by his physical closeness. With iron-strong arms, he held her tightly against his chest as he carried her. He smelled of sea salt, the summer Gulf breeze, exotic places and clean male sweat—an intensely *masculine* scent, somehow. Enticing.

Shaken by her suddenly sensual awareness of him, she concentrated on her resentment. She should find nothing about him appealing. He'd handcuffed her, for God's sake, and was bodily carrying her aboard a boat. And he'd taken her baby.

That thought renewed her anxiety. "If you're serious about treating each other with civility," she said, studying his face from an intimately close distance, praying that she might sway him, "may we please call your sister before we board the boat?"

His lips compressed slightly, and she knew he would refuse.

Before he had the chance, she raised her handcuffed wrists and lightly touched his face with her fingertips. Surprise flickered in his expression. "Please, Mitch. I really want to ask Joey about Arianne. And maybe…talk to the baby. Let her hear my voice, and…tell her everything will be okay.'' To her dismay, her throat tightened on the last few words.

He didn't slow his stride, and his jaw hardened with some emotion, as if her words had reminded him of unpleasantness. But after a silent moment, he murmured, ''We'll call ship-to-shore. Tonight.''

She nodded and pressed her lips together to keep them from trembling. She couldn't think about Arianne if she didn't want to cry. ''Thank you.''

Averting his gaze from her, he carried her up a short flight of steps, strode across a weathered dock and climbed with remarkable ease over the railing of the boat, like some Viking warrior returning to his ship with spoils of war.

A feeling of unreality came over Kate. She was well and truly on her way out to sea. How could that be? Just hours ago, she'd been strolling in her subdivision with Arianne, chatting with neighbors, discussing swim lessons, enjoying the holiday weekend. And now she'd been kidnapped, held prisoner and forced aboard a seagoing vessel.

Things like this didn't happen in her ordinary, darn-near-boring life. She, who'd never missed a day of school or work until she'd taken family leave, who'd never acted without thorough planning of every detail, who'd never experienced anything close to adventure, suddenly found herself shanghaied…by a man who believed her to be *his wife*.

Oddly enough, when she thought of her upcoming journey, it was the memory of his smile that caused her the greatest foreboding.

CHAPTER FIVE

THE STEADY RUMBLE of a huge engine beneath the floor-boards vibrated through Kate as she sat propped against pillows on the bed where Mitch had left her, still bound by the handcuffs. The oak-paneled captain's quarters consisted only of the neatly made double bed and a large chart table, with a narrow central walkway between.

Fore of the captain's quarters was the wheelhouse. Directly aft, the galley. Mitch had left the doors to both rooms open, allowing the slight breeze to flow through the stifling cabin. The dense Florida humidity, the per-vasive scents of sea brine and diesel fuel, the ceaseless vibration of the motor and the keen anxiety building in the pit of her stomach conspired to make Kate feel queasy.

And the boat hadn't even left the dock yet. How would she fare when the motion of the sea added to the mix?

The activity in the wheelhouse helped to distract her. From where she reclined on the bed, she could see Mitch standing with his broad back to her. Stationed at the wheel, he adjusted gadgets on a panel of electronics and issued orders to his crew—the surly, burly tattooed Dar-ryl and a stout, gray-haired, ponytailed man whom Mitch had called Remy. Kate caught only glimpses of him in passing. Neither man had accorded her so much as a glance since Mitch had carried her aboard and situated her in the captain's quarters with a promise to release her from the cuffs as soon as they were "outside."

"Outside?" she'd asked him.

"Outside the channel and the Intracoastal Waterway," Mitch had explained. At her blank stare, he'd clarified further, "In the open Gulf."

The open Gulf. An intimidating prospect to a landlubber like her. Even if Mitch had no murderous intentions, she knew that nature often posed a formidable danger for any boat venturing offshore. She couldn't help but wonder if Mitch was experienced enough as a captain to bring them safely through any storms or complications they might face.

A fast-paced masculine voice with a saucy Cajun dialect drew her attention to Remy, who appeared beside Mitch in the wheelhouse. "You know better 'n dat, Cap'n. Last time we left da dock on a Friday, we had all kind of bad luck. Da rudder fell off and da transmission went out. Why you want to risk it again?"

"The rudder fell off because you ran us onto a reef, and the transmission would have blown no matter when we'd left the dock. It had nothing to do with bad luck. I'm not postponing this trip."

"*Enfin!* You'll be sorry. Why not wait till after midnight? It's already seven-thirty. Just a few more hours, and it won't be Friday no more."

"No one's forcing you to come with me, Remy. But I'm leaving now."

"How you like it if I whistle in your wheelhouse, eh?" he threatened. "You won't be so cocky then."

"You won't whistle in the wheelhouse. You'd be more worried about it than I would."

Remy muttered something in Cajun French. Mitch responded in kind. The deckhand shook his ponytailed

head, curtly jammed a shabby purple sports cap in place
and trudged out of the wheelhouse.

Curiosity flared in Kate, reviving her usual hunger for
knowledge—an addiction every bit as strong as Camryn's craving for fun, and only piqued by her eight years
of college. She longed to ask about Remy's fear of leaving the dock on a Friday, and about whistling in the
wheelhouse, which, it seemed, made Mitch nervous, too.
She wondered what else allegedly caused bad luck on a
boat…and if the superstition about leaving the dock on
a Friday could possibly be true.

No, of course not.

Mitch stepped away from the wheel, and Kate heard
him call, "Cast off." Darryl yelled from the back deck,
Remy from the bow, and Mitch returned to the helm.
The boat soon idled into forward motion.

Kate sat up straight and raised her cuffed hands to the
small window above the bed. Sweeping aside the short
blue curtains, she watched the watery expanse gradually
grow between the boat and the wharf. Though the boat
moved slowly, she soon lost sight of the dock altogether.
Her apprehension grew, and she looked longingly at the
forested shoreline, wondering if she'd ever step foot on
solid ground again.

Heavy footsteps thudded on the side deck along the
far side of the cabin, and soon the murmur of conversation sounded in the wheelhouse. "I hope you right,
Cap'n" came Remy's voice from somewhere to the right
of Mitch. "You don't want no bad luck on dis trip wit'
your missus."

Mitch uttered a sharp reply, which Kate couldn't quite
make out. She felt shaken, though, to be called his "missus." She'd almost managed to forget the relationship
between Mitch and her sister…and the fact that she now

played the role of his wife. A vague qualm rolled in her stomach.

"A woman on board is another strike against you," Remy warned Mitch.

Kate pursed her lips in annoyance. Of all the insulting, sexist beliefs!

"I notice you never let *that* sacred rule of the sea bother you too much," Mitch said, sounding amused.

Remy barked a short, jolly laugh. "Never. A man has to draw da line somewhere, no?"

"Maybe so. But to me, *that* superstition is the only sensible one. A woman on board usually does means trouble."

Kate huffed out an indignant breath. Of all the nerve. Breaking into her home, kidnapping her and carrying her off in chains was bad enough, but spouting blatantly sexist statements was going *too far*. After her initial rush of annoyance ebbed, though, an inkling of hope came to her. Perhaps she could use this newly gained information to her advantage.

Decisively she swung her feet to the floor, rose from the bed and started for the wheelhouse. To balance herself against the slight swaying of the boat, she wedged her elbow against the chart table. When she reached the open doorway, she piped up from behind the three men standing near the helm, "Did I hear you say that a woman on board is bad luck?"

All three turned surprised gazes to her. No one answered her question.

She leaned her shoulder against the doorjamb to steady herself. "If that's true, there's still time to turn around and travel by car. Might be a good idea. After all, I'm not familiar with these 'rules of the sea.' Who knows what mistakes I might make? Like, um, whistling in the wheelhouse.''

"Yie, yie!" exclaimed Remy, his eyes growing round. "Don't do dat, *chèr'*. With t'ree strikes against us, we won't even make it back to da dock.''

Kate bit her lip to stifle a smile at the thoroughly startled expression on his comically expressive face. Even in his startlement, though, his eyes sparkled with unmistakable friendliness, and despite her unease with the entire situation, Kate found herself liking Remy.

A humorless laugh drew her attention to Darryl, who stood to the other side of Mitch. "Better not make too many mistakes, *chèr'*. We'd hate for you to fall overboard. Might be hard to swim in handcuffs. 'Specially wit' all dem hungry sharks out dere.'' Though he'd spoken lightly, the menacing glint in his eyes left no doubt that he'd intended to scare her.

And he'd succeeded.

"Then again," Mitch drawled, his gaze aimed straight ahead as he easily guided the boat between green and red channel markers, "I'm sure Darryl wouldn't mind jumping in to save you." His tone matched Darryl's in lightness, but there was no mistaking the underlying message.

Darryl shot a quick look at Mitch, curled his lip, crossed his hefty, tattooed arms and stared sullenly out at the water. Kate realized then that Darryl could be a dangerous enemy. And that Mitch, in his own quiet-spoken way, had come to her defense.

She couldn't have been more relieved.

"*I* would be happy to leap to your rescue anytime." Remy pulled himself up to his less-than-impressive height, snatched the New Orleans Saints cap from his head and crossed his heart. A wide smile displayed a brilliant diamond embedded between his two rather crooked front teeth.

Kate stared at that diamond in awe. Its prism-cut facets caught the late-afternoon sun and transformed the golden beams into wildly glittering rainbows. "Ooh." She clasped her cuffed hands to her breast in appreciation of the sheer *unexpectedness* of it. "How pretty!"

Surreptitiously watching through his sideview mirror, Mitch poked his tongue against his cheek and resisted the urge to grin. He swore Remy actually grew in stature. His chest definitely swelled by a good two inches, and though his white rubber shrimper boots technically never left the floor, his toes probably hovered somewhere above the grounded soles.

"Talk about *pretty*," Remy enthused, as he worshipfully regarded her—a reaction not completely unexpected by Mitch, mind you. "You done something new wit' your hair. *Très beaux!*"

"*Merci.*"

Mitch blinked in disbelief at her French reply. She'd never spoken a word of French when she'd been with him, or expressed any interest in doing so. She'd actually grown impatient when his family and friends occasionally spoke it.

He peered at her through the navigational mirror and sustained an even greater shock. She was not, as he'd expected, casting a provocative look at her admirer from beneath her lush lashes, or fanning Remy's fantasies with a flirtatious smile. She was simply gazing at him in amused camaraderie. A man would have a hard time reading anything sexual into that look.

Yet, for the first time in their relationship, a stab of envy pierced Mitch. She'd never gifted *him* with that particular brand of droll, sunny warmth. And although her hair trailed from her prim, braided upsweep in limp strands, her cotton blouse and khaki shorts were wrinkled from hours of travel and the dense humidity shone on her skin like a fine sheen of perspiration, he'd never seen her looking as beautiful. Not even in the first fateful moment he'd set eyes on her. And he'd been spellbound by her then.

The strike of a match and an acrid cloud of smoke in his face jarred him to his senses, and he jerked his attention to the waterway. Darryl muttered, "Want me to take over da wheel, Cap'n? Would be nice if we made it t'rough da channel without running aground."

Mitch clenched his teeth in self-annoyance. They hadn't been in danger of running aground, but Darryl had a good point. He'd been ridiculously distracted. What the hell had gotten into him?

"If you think my smile is nice, *chèr'*, wait till you try my *étouffée*," Remy boasted. "Or maybe I'll make dat gumbo you liked so much last time."

"She don't remember your gumbo, Remy," Darryl said with subtle sarcasm. "And she don't remember *you*. Or Mitch, either."

Another disturbing pang went through Mitch, although he wasn't sure why. Couldn't be injured pride, considering he didn't believe for a moment that she'd forgotten him. He chalked it up to anxiety over her motives for the ruse, and maybe anger at her for the deception.

"What you talkin' about, Darryl?" Remy asked in bewilderment. He then frowned questioningly at Camryn. "Of course you remember Mitch. And old Remy, too...no?"

Mitch couldn't help glancing her way again.

The expression of gentle apology on her face was so

damn convincing. "I'm sorry, Remy," she murmured in her summer-soft voice, "but I don't remember you, or your gumbo. You see, I…I was in an automobile accident and suffered a head injury. Since then, my memory has been…unreliable." She glanced at Mitch, and he resolutely returned his gaze to the waterway. "I don't remember Mitch, either, or any of the time I…spent with him."

Remy stared at her in astonishment.

"So much for your unforgettable gumbo, eh, Remy?" quipped Darryl, flicking the ash off his cigarette into an ashtray.

The gesture, along with the smoke, suddenly brought to Mitch's mind the fact that *Camryn wasn't smoking*. She hadn't asked for a single cigarette. Amazing, considering she'd always had a nicotine fit after ten minutes without one. When he thought back to his casual search of her purse, he realized that he'd found no cigarettes or lighter.

Odd. Very odd.

"Why don't you offer our guest a smoke?" Mitch suggested to Darryl. "Just to show you didn't mean anything by your threat to feed her to the sharks."

Darryl frowned, shrugged and reached for the cigarettes in his shirt pocket.

Camryn stopped him with, "No, thanks. I don't smoke."

Mitch pivoted from the wheel to stare at her. "Are you telling me you quit?"

"Y-yes." She seemed to shrink back in the doorway from his probing gaze. "After the accident."

Some sixth sense told him she was lying. But when Mitch remembered holding her during their various tussles of the day, he recalled only a light, sweet scent emanating from her. Like vanilla wafers, maybe. Not cigarette smoke. And though he hadn't been in her house for very long, he didn't recall seeing any ashtrays there.

Highly suspicious and somewhat confused, he sullenly turned back to his navigation.

"Good for you, *chèr'*." Remy beamed his approval at her. "Me, I quit four months ago. Don't like smudging up my diamond. Mitch, you lucky you never started. It's your turn now, Darryl. You should—"

"Sit down, Camryn," Mitch broke in. "Or better yet, go lie down on the bed." He suddenly wanted time alone with his crew to discuss some much-needed strategy. "We're almost out of the channel, and the swells will grow bigger. With your hands bound, you might lose your balance. You'll be safer on the bed." In a gentler tone, he added, "I'll take those cuffs off you as soon as I can."

He met her eyes in the mirror, expecting an objection or, at the very least, a pout. Oddly enough, though, she looked grateful. Grateful! And he knew it was because he'd spoken pleasantly to her; had shown concern for her well-being; had promised to release her from the cuffs. She was simply that easy to read.

Guilt pulsed through him, and he tried to squelch it. She'd stolen his daughter and kept her away for six months. She'd put his family through hell. And who knew what harm she'd done Arianne? He had every right to take her to the authorities for breaking their custody agreement. He'd done nothing that hadn't been necessary.

But he supposed he could have been nicer about it. Open hostility only made matters worse. Besides, as the old saying went, more flies were caught with honey. And he had some important "flies" he intended to catch…before she reached the courtroom.

Mitch watched through his navigational mirror as she turned toward the bedroom. Remy stepped forward and took her arm. With a gracious smile for him, she hobbled into the captain's quarters.

The moment she was out of easy earshot, Mitch explained his plans regarding Camryn in a discreet undertone to Darryl. After he'd finished and answered a couple of questions, Mitch said, "Take Remy to the back deck and fill him in. She's more apt to respond to him than to you or me."

Darryl nodded, looking considerably cheered by the traps they would set for her.

Mitch hoped they would trip her up in her lies, and soon. He wasn't sure he could take much more of her role playing. He was beginning to feel as if a stranger had taken over her body. Or that he'd never really known her at all.

"DROP THE OUTRIGGERS."

No sooner had Mitch's command boomed over the intercom than a loud *cr-r-reak* and *clang!* jarred the boat. Within moments, the speed of the boat increased to a humming pace; the vessel surged and rolled over waves; and a cool, clean-smelling wind whistled through the doorways and windows, riffling the curtains, the linen on the bed and the loose, sweat-dampened strands of her hair.

Clearly, the boat had left the channel. They were "outside."

An unexpected reaction stirred in Kate—one that defied all common sense and told her things about her character that she'd never suspected. *Anticipation.* Good

Lord, here she was a prisoner, bound in handcuffs, headed for a place that frightened her...yet she still wanted to see everything along the way; to learn everything she could about this alien new world in which she found herself. The lure of the unknown, she supposed. For the first time in her life, she somewhat understood Camryn's yearning for adventure. Kate nearly pressed her face to the small window above the bed to get a wider view of the scenery. All she could see was smooth, gray-green swells and the vague, smoky outline of the wooded shoreline growing more distant.

Sudden doubt tempered the odd anticipation. Would she ever return to that distant shore, or to the world she'd left behind? Was this journey taking her closer to Arianne, or farther away?

The heightened speed and movement of the boat soon increased her queasiness, and she worried about getting seasick. An uneasy heat pulsed through her, and she lay back against the pillows. Up and down, side to side...the motion seemed to get more pronounced.

Breathing deeply, she stared at the white stippled ceiling of the captain's quarters and tried to concentrate on *anything* rather than the sickening toss of the sea. Up and down...side to side...again and again... The ceiling itself began to spin, and all interest about the seascape dwindled. She now wanted only to curl up in a ball, close her eyes and...die, maybe. Or just lose her lunch. But that thought only made her feel worse.

Mitch soon materialized beside the bed, looking strong, vital. He seemed to emanate a palpable energy, an aura of unlimited authority and stamina. Life at sea clearly agreed with him. "Ready to get out of those cuffs?"

A sarcastic reply rose to her tongue, but she couldn't

summon the physical energy to utter it. A listless nod would have to suffice.

"Before I turn you loose," Mitch began in a pleasant yet uncompromising tone, "there are a few things I want to make clear. As always, I don't allow alcoholic beverages onboard the boat. But if you find a way to get your hands on any—and with Remy around, that's not impossible—I forbid you to drink. Break that rule, or any rule, and you'll end up back here, in this room, in handcuffs. Next, there will be no—"

"How long is this trip going to take?" Kate cut in, managing not to gasp or groan while she forced the words out.

He frowned and narrowed his gaze on her face, as if suddenly realizing that something wasn't exactly right with her, physically speaking. Perhaps her skin had turned green. "Two or three days, depending on the weather."

"Two or three days!" She gaped at him in abject dismay. She'd been expecting *hours,* not days. Good Lord. *Days!* "I'll never make it."

"Are you sick?"

She nodded, her misery growing.

"Let's get you out of these cuffs."

Wise choice, she thought, although she was no longer certain she could make it to the bathroom in time if the need arose, anyway.

Sitting beside her on the bed, he took her wrists between his large, work-hardened palms and unlocked the cuffs. Feeling listless and ill, she closed her eyes again and allowed her head to loll back on a pillow. "You're probably hungry," he said. "It's eight o'clock. Way past suppertime. I'll tell Remy to make you something light. I doubt you're in the mood for his *étouffée.*"

"No food," she croaked, fighting a wave of nausea.

"Soup. Or toast."

"Not hungry."

"Then try to sleep. A nap helped you get your sea legs last time."

"It did?" She squinted up at him with sudden hope.

He didn't answer, and through her blurry-eyed squint, she saw his mouth flatten at her question. It seemed that her alleged amnesia still annoyed him. She couldn't think about that now, though. The pitching of the sea was too bothersome, too ceaseless, too draining.

With a fervent prayer that she would "get her sea legs" as her twin apparently had, Kate shut her eyes and curled around a pillow to battle the nausea. Her attention was quickly claimed, though, by a crackle from the wheelhouse, a blurb of static, then the tinny blare of a man's unintelligible conversation from what had to be the radio.

The radio. She'd forgotten about the ship-to-shore radio. Fighting dizziness, she pushed up on her elbows. "Mitch, you said we'd call Joey to check on Arianne."

"She won't be home yet. I'd rather wait until—"

"Now," she insisted, calling upon all her strength to raise herself into a sitting position. "Please, Mitch. Let's call her now."

Amazingly enough, he didn't argue but braced her with a strong, steady arm as she rose from the bed and made her way to the wheelhouse, fighting nausea and dizziness with every step.

Though darkness had begun to encroach upon the mellow gold of evening, the breeze blowing through the wheelhouse felt hotter and heavier with the taste of salt. The electronics on and above the control panel glowed a soft, steady green, punctuated here and there with blinking red. Through the open starboard doorway, Kate saw the distant lights of the coastline, looking much like a constellation in a cloudy evening sky. The sky itself, though, as well as the sea, had disappeared into grayish shadows.

"Are you sure you're up to this?" Mitch asked as he helped her into one of the high-legged chairs near the helm.

"I'm fine," she lied, grasping the edge of the control panel with one hand and pressing the other to her churning stomach. A wave of sickly heat rushed to her head, and she sucked in deep breaths. "Just…hurry. Call her."

Reaching overhead for the radio, he fiddled with knobs, spoke into the handset and enunciated a telephone number, presumably to the marine operator. Kate tried to memorize the number, but the throbbing in her head and stomach distracted her too much. At least she knew the area code. If she had to search for Arianne, it would be a start. Then again, he *was* calling a cell phone. How much good would a cell phone number do her if Joey ran with the baby? But Mitch had said she was headed home….

"Don't talk until I give you the handset," he told Kate while they waited for the connection to be made. "I don't want you to upset Joey any more than necessary."

Kate frowned. She hadn't intended on upsetting his sister. Unless, of course, she heard anything that indicated she wasn't caring for Arianne properly. But then, how could she be sure of anything from a mere phone conversation? Tense with renewed worry, Kate nodded her cooperation, trying to ignore her stomachache and dizziness, which worsened with every treacherous dip and toss of the boat.

"Hello?" A hushed feminine voice wafted from the radio. As Mitch exchanged brief greetings with his sister, Kate heard the now-familiar Cajun dialect spoken with the genteel cadence of a young southern woman. "Fine, she's fine. Fast asleep. *Finally,*" she said in response to Mitch's question. "Can't talk any louder or I might wake her up. She fussed for hours, I swear. Our li'l Arianne sure can yell. But, hooo, Mitch, you should see her. An angel straight from heaven! All blond ringlets and big brown eyes. And your dimples. You really can see 'em now dat her cheeks have filled out. Rosy li'l cheeks. I told you I saw dimples."

Tenderness, awe and the huskiness of tears held in check sounded so clearly in Joey's voice that a lump rose to Kate's throat. This woman wouldn't hurt Arianne. At least, not intentionally. Whether she was a competent baby-sitter wasn't clear yet.

"Have you fed her?" Mitch's voice had taken on an odd huskiness, too, and Kate peered at him in curiosity. His dark, stoic face gave nothing away of his feelings, though.

Joey assured him she had fed her with the formula he had specified earlier, and Kate bit her tongue to keep from asking her own questions. If she wanted Mitch to call Joey for her on a regular basis throughout the trip, she'd have to respect his request to keep quiet.

"Does she look—" he glanced awkwardly at Kate, then away from her "—well cared for?"

Kate stiffened in affront.

"From what I can see." The surprise and skepticism in Joey's reply added insult to injury. What had these people expected—to find Arianne neglected and abused? How dared they! She'd been with her own mother, as far as they knew.

Kate's heart then gave a disquieting thump. *Would* Camryn have taken good care of the baby? If she'd fallen back into her drinking and gambling addictions, Kate really couldn't be sure of that. She couldn't deny that she herself would have had the same qualms, had she known.

She then thought of the numerous times Arianne had startled awake from a sound sleep with an agonized wail, then cried and trembled as if her little heart were breaking. Maybe Camryn had left her alone for long periods, or in the care of negligent strangers. Kate couldn't bear to believe that, though. It seemed more likely that the episodes were caused by feelings of loss after Camryn's death. Although Arianne called Kate ''Mama,'' she might have recognized on some level that she wasn't Camryn. Her sweet little Arianne was probably mourning her mother's death—*not* reacting to the trauma of neglect.

But the acute worry over both those possibilities exacerbated Kate's nausea…and strengthened her resolve that Arianne would not lose her own steadfast, loving care, no matter what she had to do to reclaim her.

''Camryn, do you want to talk to Joey?'' Mitch asked, clearly hesitant to allow the conversation at all.

Kate ignored his reluctance and determinedly reached for the handset, but Joey cut in with startling sharpness, ''I have nothing to say to *her*…except that I hope she gets what she deserves. A good long prison term.''

Mitch pulled the handset back from Kate. ''Let's not get into that right now, Joey. No sense in—''

''And if you start feeling bad, Camryn, it's because of Tante Louise's voodoo.''

Kate shot an alarmed glance at Mitch. She *was* feeling pretty bad.

Mitch slanted his mouth in mild scorn, and his gaze held a hint of droll humor. "Come on, now, Joey. You know Tante's spells never work."

"She used powerful gris-gris dis time, Mitch."

Kate couldn't help reflecting that Camryn *had* died.

Realizing the crazy turn of her thoughts, Kate shook her head to clear it. Voodoo, of all things! As a professor of history, she knew all about the practice of voodoo and black magic in Louisiana...and the power of simple suggestion. She wouldn't allow it to affect her.

A peal of distress suddenly shrilled from the ship-to-shore radio, followed by an infant's sobs and a pitiful wail of "Mama-Mama!"

Mitch winced. Kate's heart dropped.

Joey groaned. "She's up. Gotta go. Don't call again till I'm home, Mitch."

Choked with the need to comfort Arianne and a sharp, futile longing to hold her again, to take her back to their safe, sane, normal world, Kate gasped and lurched from the chair. Her nausea had risen to a desperate peak. Grabbing onto the nearby doorjamb, she propelled herself out into the bracing wind and salty sea mist.

And to the side rail.

Voodoo or not, she'd never been as sick in her life.

WHEN KATE AWOKE the next day, bright sunlight streamed through the curtains of the captain's quarters. Although the doors had been closed at both ends of the central walkway, the breeze swirling in from the open window blew refreshingly cooler than it had yesterday. Her head was no longer spinning. Her stomach wasn't churning. She still felt the rocking motion of the sea in the pit of her stomach, but her nausea had abated. At least, for now. And she was hungry. Ravenous, really. Maybe she was on her way to developing "sea legs."

To her surprise, she also found that she'd been covered with a light blanket. Had Mitch drawn it over her? She then remembered with almost dreamlike vagueness that he'd looped a steadying arm around her as she'd bent over the bulwark. When the worst of her seasickness had passed, he'd practically carried her to the bed, then wiped her forehead, face and throat with a blessedly cool washcloth.

He'd been unexpectedly kind.

Gratitude bloomed in her at the memory, and she had to remind herself not to read too much into his chivalry. Many factors could turn a basically decent man into an abusive beast—anger, drunkenness or mood swings. She couldn't assume that he hadn't abused Camryn just because he'd been nice this one time.

But she could no longer assume that Camryn's accusations against him were true, either. She had to set aside her anger, her fear, her personal bias and honestly get to know him. To do anything less would be terribly unfair to both Mitch and Arianne.

Lost in thought, she sat up in bed, cast off the blanket and paused at the sight of the pillow beside her. There was a dent in it. A head-size dent. And the bedcovers were rumpled…as if someone had slept on them. She supposed she could assume that she herself had rolled onto that side of the bed, but she wasn't a restless sleeper. At home, she never disrupted the other side of her queen-size bed. Perhaps the rocking of the boat had caused her to thrash about more than usual.

But she didn't think so. Leaning close to the pillow, she swore she detected a familiar masculine scent lingering on the linen. The scent conjured images of a bare, muscled body…and virile warmth and strength…within easy reaching distance, there in the alien darkness….

Flustered by her thoughts, she pushed abruptly away from the pillow and its subtle scent.

Dear God! Had Mitch slept with her? This was, after all, the captain's quarters. He probably felt it was his right to sleep here. And he did believe her to be his wife.

Those reflections shook her. She hadn't given a thought to the sleeping arrangements, mostly because she hadn't realized the journey would take several days. By the time she'd learned that disturbing fact, she'd been too sick to think straight. She was thinking quite clearly now, though. She had to know if he'd spent the night beside her. It hadn't been right of him, even though she'd been fully dressed and sound asleep the entire time.

She'd have to speak to him and set the situation straight. They had another night, possibly two, remaining of this wretched journey. She couldn't spend them in bed with Mitch!

CHAPTER SIX

KNOWING THAT SHE *had* to speak with Mitch about the unsettling question of last night's sleeping arrangements, yet concerned that she may have only imagined his scent on the pillow, Kate reluctantly opened the fore door of the captain's quarters and ventured into the sunny wheelhouse, trying to think of a way to pose her question without humiliating herself if her suspicions were wrong.

Mitch, however, wasn't at the wheel. Darryl sat there alone, his beefy, tattooed shoulders resting low in the captain's chair, his hefty legs propped up on the ledge beside the polished oak wheel, his mittlike hand wrapped around a steaming mug of chicory-scented coffee.

"Good morning," she greeted him.

Darryl responded with the briefest, surliest of nods, then returned his gaze to the sea.

Somewhat surprised that he'd acknowledged her greeting at all, Kate retraced her steps through the captain's quarters and followed a delectable aroma to the galley. She found Remy at the narrow gas stove, turning strips of sizzling meat in an iron skillet and singing a ditty about rabbit hunting in the swamp. Metal guardrails secured the skillet, a simmering kettle and a coffeepot on the burners. The redolence of the food wafted on the cross breezes from the open doorways of the galley. Beyond those doorways, the silent swells sparkled royal blue beneath a bright sky. Kate didn't believe she'd ever seen a more beautiful morning.

Breaking off his song, Remy nodded his ponytailed head, grinned and wished her a good morning. Kate wished him the same, then asked, "Where's Mitch?"

"Down in da engine room. He'll be working dere for a spell."

She relaxed slightly at the news, and realized she was actually glad for the reprieve. She'd much prefer brushing her teeth, combing her hair and showering before she met up with him again. Not because she cringed at the thought of Mitch seeing her looking her usual morning mess, she hastily assured herself, but simply to appease her own need to be freshly groomed. Nothing out of the ordinary about that.

Before she had the chance to duck into the bathroom—or the "head," as seamen called it—a loud, rhythmic banging forced her to glance back through the captain's quarters. The doors to the wheelhouse and galley, both of which she'd opened just moments ago, now swung on their hinges with the rocking of the boat, slamming against the walls in unison.

"You forgot to secure da doors," Remy noted from his post near the stove.

"Secure them?" she repeated.

"Hey!" Darryl bellowed from the wheelhouse. "Hook da damn doors, will ya?"

Hook. Good clue. Bristling at the rude command, though, Kate aimed a disapproving frown in his direction as she caught hold of the nearest swinging door. "Is he always such a ray of sunshine?"

"Oh, don't mind him. He and Mitch, dey grew up like brothers. Lived on da same bayou. Worked on da same shrimp boats from da time dey were kids. Darryl don't like no one who does Mitch wrong."

She flushed at the implied criticism but had to admit she understood Darryl's sentiment. She certainly found it difficult to like anyone whom she believed had hurt her friends or loved ones. What concerned her more than Darryl's dislike of her was the idea of kids working on shrimp boats. Stooping to latch the hook at the bottom of the door to the eye on the baseboard, she asked, "How old were they when they started working?"

"Seven, eight…some'm like dat. All us boys from home started around dat age. Dat's what makes us da best shrimpers in da Gulf."

Despite the pride in his voice, Kate was appalled that parents would allow young children to labor on commercial vessels. She frowned up at him from her stooped position beside the door. "Didn't they go to school?"

Remy grinned. "When dey had to. But truant officers never liked coming down to da swamps much. Or to da shrimp boats, when dey could even find 'em."

Biting her lip in consternation, Kate awkwardly rose, paced through the captain's quarters and stooped again to latch the wheelhouse door, resolutely ignoring Darryl's nearby presence at the helm. The roll of the boat pitched her sideways, and she grabbed for the doorjamb, missed it and landed solidly on her posterior. Wincing, she fervently hoped Darryl had missed her clumsy fall. Not bothering to check to see if he was watching, she pulled herself to her feet.

Life at sea was proving to be a complicated affair.

And the more she learned about Mitch's upbringing, the less she liked it. Swamps, voodoo and now child labor. And a clear disregard for education. Did he plan to raise Arianne in that environment?

Horrified at the very idea, she frowned as she made her way back to the galley. The hearty redolence of chicory coffee, baking bread and other appetizing aromas distracted her from the troubling thoughts and piqued her hunger. Despite her many concerns, she couldn't help feeling pleased that the seasickness had left her. "What are you making, Remy?"

"My famous *grillades* and grits." He glanced at her then, as if expecting some reaction.

"Grillades?" She pronounced the unfamiliar word as he had: *gree-odds*. "What are they?"

His brows converged. "You really don't remember my *grillades?*" He sounded incredulous. Apparently, he, like Mitch, was having a hard time accepting her amnesia tale. She supposed she didn't blame them. It was, after all, a lie...but the only way she could think to explain her ignorance. If they never really believed her, so be it. She was sticking to her story. Until she spoke to the judge, of course.

"I told you my memory isn't very reliable."

"Ca c'est dommage," Remy murmured as he turned toward the stove to stir a simmering kettle of grits. "Den da *grillades* will be a nice surprise for you, eh?"

"Is that what's baking?"

"Non. I'm baking da best croissants you ever put in your mouth. We have mayhaw jelly, too, made by my own sweet *nainaine.*"

Knowing only a smattering of rudimentary French from her undergrad years—which had sounded very little like the French he spoke—she asked, "Is Nainaine your wife?"

"Wife!" He barked a brief laugh. "Me? Nah. An old salty dog like me don't have time for no wife. I was talking 'bout my *nainaine*. My godmother. She gathers da mayhaw herself from da swamp."

Ah. The swamp again. Kate really preferred not to think about the swamp. But his comment about salty dogs having no time for wives made her wonder how often Mitch went to sea. If he earned his living by shrimping, he wouldn't have much time at all to spend with Arianne, even if he did win custody. Who, Kate wondered, would keep her?

Too upset by the idea that anyone other than herself might end up with the baby—her baby, the one she'd sworn to love and protect for the rest of their lives—she forced her thoughts away from the painful subject.

"Can't wait to try the *grillades* and the jelly," she said, managing a small smile for Remy. That much, at least, was true. She loved sampling unfamiliar regional foods and learning the history behind them. For now, though, she sorely wanted a shower. "While the croissants are baking, I think I'll take a shower." At a sharp glance from Remy, she added, "Would that be all right?" She'd almost forgotten that boats carry only a certain amount of fresh water in their tanks. She assumed, though, that this boat would have plenty, considering its size and the length of its journeys.

An odd look of uneasiness crossed Remy's face. "A shower? Sure, you can take a shower." He then raised his voice to a yell. "Hey, Darryl…is da shower set up yet?"

"Yeah, it's ready" came the reply.

"You in luck, *chèr'.*" Remy stood stirring the grits. "Da deck hose is hooked up to da ladder on da stern, all ready for your shower."

"Deck hose?" Kate repeated, uncomprehending. "On the stern?"

"Yeah, you know…on da back deck."

"But I…I thought I saw a shower stall in the bathroom."

"Oh, da shower stall in da head, you mean?" His swarthy face turned slightly red. "We don't carry enough fresh water to use it. But don't worry—a saltwater shower on da back deck feels just as good. A li'l colder, is all." His gaze flickered over the rumpled khaki shorts and sleeveless white blouse that she'd slept in. "Might wanna wear a bathing suit. Dat white blouse would turn yellow."

Kate gaped at him. "B-but I didn't bring a bathing suit. I…I don't have anything I can wear to take a shower in."

He lifted his shoulder and slanted her an amiable grin. "If dat's okay wit' you, *chèr'*, it's damn sure okay wit' me."

MITCH PAUSED, wrench in hand, over the auxiliary bilge pump he was repairing as the intercom in the engine room transmitted Remy's conversation with Camryn. He'd asked both Remy and Darryl to tune him in whenever they put their schemes into action.

Last night, after she'd gone to sleep, the three of them had plotted out a few ingenious tests to try today. He had no doubt that before the sun set, his crafty wife would trip herself up in her lies.

Amnesia. Hah. They'd see just how much she remembered.

Any moment now, she'd be demanding a freshwater shower. She knew damn well that the only time they took saltwater ones was when the freshwater ran low— usually near the end of a week-long trip, and only if someone got careless with the supply. She'd learned that lesson during their very first outing, after taking leisurely hot showers every day. When the water ran out, she'd had to settle for cold saltwater showers beneath the deck hose. She'd been none too happy about it.

Never had they run out of fresh water on the very first day of the trip, though. She would know that.

Her voice, soft and tentative, sounded again over the intercom. "Would it be okay if I fill the bathroom sink with fresh water for a sponge bath?"

Mitch stared at the intercom in disbelief. A sponge bath? Was she buying Remy's story that they were already low on fresh water? And was she really ready to settle for anything less than a full shower?

"I'm not sure Mitch'll like dat" came Remy's hesitant reply. "We try to save da fresh water for cooking, and…uh…you know, coffee."

Mitch waited, certain that she'd scoff at the idea that one little sinkful of water might deprive them of coffee. *Sacre Dieu!* She knew the water tanks held three thousand gallons.

"Is there a way, then," she asked, "that we can rig some kind of privacy booth where I could take a saltwater shower?"

Mitch almost dropped the wrench from his hand in astonishment. Not only did she seem willing to take a saltwater shower without putting up a fight, but she wanted privacy. The Camryn he'd known wouldn't have given that matter a thought. In fact, he'd been the one to insist she wear a bathing suit, at the very least, while she showered on the open back deck…and while she sunbathed on the roof of the cabin.

Which brought up another point: she'd left a bikini along with other clothes in the bottom drawer beneath the chart table. He hadn't gotten around to removing them yet. Would she somehow "find" that bikini, since she hadn't brought another, and she so dearly loved to sunbathe?

"Hey, Darryl," Remy shouted, "can you hang canvas around da stern ladder so Mrs. Devereaux can shower in private?"

"Devereaux," she repeated. "Is that Mitch's name?"

Mitch set his teeth on edge. Oh, she was good. Too good. She almost had him believing that she hadn't known.

"Mais, oui!" Remy exclaimed. "You don't even remember *dat?* You in bad shape."

From a distance came Darryl's almost inaudible reply. "Sure, I'll hang da canvas."

"Dere you go, *chèr',"* Remy said. "He'll have it up in no time."

Mitch waited in avid curiosity for her next move. How would she get out of taking a saltwater shower without admitting that she knew they had plenty of fresh water at the start of a trip? Despite her zest for adventure, her unpredictability and her never-ending love of novel situations, one thing about Camryn had always remained implacable: she required a hot freshwater shower every morning. During those last few days of her first trip with him, she had ranted and raged, demanding water for her showers, even though they had only a small amount left for cooking and emergency purposes.

No way would she give in peacefully now.

SHE HADN'T EXPECTED much from the saltwater shower, but by the time Darryl had constructed a crude canvas stall suspended by ropes from various parts of the rigging that creaked and groaned overhead, the morning had grown incredibly hot and humid. The cold, hard rush of water against her skin and through her hair felt amazingly exhilarating.

And how nice to know they wouldn't run out of saltwater!

Reveling beneath the forceful current of the deck hose, she tried first her own shampoo, then set it aside and reached for the bottle of golden dishwashing liquid Remy had given her. "Da only soap dat ladders real good in seawater." Most shampoo, he said, wouldn't "ladder." His prediction proved correct. She hadn't been able to work her shampoo into even the smallest lather, whereas the dishwashing liquid oozed the suds through her hair. It also left a pleasant, lemony scent. *For superior sudsing power in seawater, try new lemon Joy…for those times you must settle for the deck hose…*

Smiling at her own nonsense, she squeezed the water from her thick, tangled tresses and wrapped the beach towel securely around herself. Once she'd gathered her discarded clothing, she pushed through the flap of the canvas stall and padded across the gently bobbing deck, her eyes burning and her skin tingling. She felt revitalized, as if she'd just come from a brisk swim in the ocean. A little crusty, maybe. Not precisely *clean*. But, nevertheless, revitalized.

As she gazed at her surroundings, she also realized another pleasant fact. Despite the austerity of the boat itself—a functional work vessel with no ornamentation whatsoever—the vivid brilliance of the summer day provided all the beauty needed to satisfy the most aesthetic soul. The azure sky; the periwinkle water. The joyous shrieks of seagulls soaring in circles above the boat. The dense, salty taste of the wind, and its mysteriously tropical scent. The forceful heat of the summer sun, like laser rays from God's fingertips, igniting the undulating waves with the blaze of diamonds.

Oh, how she wished she could capture the extraordinary beauty and save it forever. Savor it. *Share* it.

Wistful, somehow, yet spiritually energized, she turned from the natural splendor and nearly walked headlong into Mitch. His hands shot out and gripped her shoulders to stop her from reeling backward.

Ah. Talk about natural splendor. Backlit with the bright, fearless blue of the sky and water, his tanned face and wind-tossed hair glowed with the sun's own radiance. Gloriously shirtless, his muscular arms and shoulders glinted with the sweat of recent physical exertion. His tight, faded jeans, streaked with engine grease, rode low across lean hips. And his chest, honed to a perfection achieved only by years of heavy manual labor, glistened with golden-brown curls.

He was, in a word, awesome. Breathtaking. A Greek or Roman sea god, surely. A god who smelled of sea brine, chicory coffee and engine grease.

"What are you doing out here alone?" The suspicion in his deep voice jarred her out of the spell she'd somehow fallen under. His green gaze inched from her dripping hair to the slopes of her neck, shoulders and arms. The slow perusal and the tightness of his hold propelled a slew of hot tingles through her. Disbelievingly, then, he asked, "You...showered?"

Despite her awareness of him—or maybe to deny that awareness—she slanted her mouth in a wry grin. "What gave me away?"

His gaze held steady, as if he hadn't expected a lighthearted response from her and wasn't sure how to answer. In the ensuing silence, the feel of his workhardened palms and fingers biting into her skin sent rivers of warmth through her, until that warmth dominated her mind and she could focus on little else.

Slowly, he released her shoulders. "How was it?"

With her mind hopelessly muddled in the aftermath of his touch and the virile beauty of his face and body, she stuttered, "H-how was…what?"

"Your shower."

"Shower. Oh! Yes. It was…invigorating."

For some reason, he looked mildly stunned at that.

Unable to think clearly enough to analyze his response, she drew back from him with an awkward laugh. She suddenly felt very naked beneath her towel. "And now I'm hungry enough to eat a whale." The sea breeze caught a few tendrils of her hair and trailed them across her face. Already beginning to dry, those few blond strands shimmered with tiny prisms in the blazing summer sun…and felt like cool silk against her oddly sensitized skin. She whisked her wayward hair behind one ear. "Is breakfast ready yet?"

He continued to watch her in an unsettling way. "Yeah," he answered absently. Gesturing toward the port-side walkway, he murmured, "After you."

Glad that their relationship had, at least, progressed to a civilized truce, Kate graced him with an approving nod, much as she would a student whose work was improving. She then gripped her towel with renewed strength and forced herself to walk, not run, toward the cabin.

She sensed him keeping pace behind her.

Somewhat breathless by the time she neared the port doorway, she forced her mind away from his overpoweringly male presence and thought, instead, of his kindness last night. She also remembered her suspicion that he'd slept with her. The thought was more shocking than ever. Her steps gradually slowed. She really did have to speak with him about both issues. Her stomach did a slow dip at the thought of broaching the latter subject. Deciding to start with the easier, she halted in the open doorway and turned to him.

"By the way, Mitch," she began, tightening one hand in the damp towel clasped to her chest and gripping the doorjamb with the other, more out of nervousness than any real need, "I want to thank you for last night."

He ambled to a halt beside her and leaned against the opposite side of the doorway. His tall, broad-shouldered form cast a cooling shadow over her. With a mystified lilt of his brows, he repeated, "Last night?"

Her cheeks heated. From the way he'd said "last night," a casual observer might think she'd been referring to sex. Flustered that Remy or Darryl might have overheard, she hurriedly specified, "You helped me while I was sick."

He nodded and waited, as if expecting more of an explanation to follow.

"I mean, it was nice of you to…to hold me steady at the rail."

His eyes narrowed. "You're thanking me for holding you at the rail? Did you think I'd just let you fall overboard?"

"I have to admit, it did cross my mind." She smiled to lighten the words, and hoped he hadn't taken offense.

He merely stared at her.

Clearing a sudden fluttering from her throat, she continued, "And you helped me get to bed, too."

"Easier than having you pass out on the wheelhouse floor, *chèr'*."

My, but he was intent on denying any finer, nobler

instincts! "I believe you also brought me a cool cloth. And wiped my face. And…covered me with a blanket."

A slight flush stole beneath the tan of his rugged, angular face, and he lifted a broad shoulder in an "it was nothing, forget it" shrug. He looked boyishly embarrassed.

Absurdly delighted to find that vulnerability in him, she couldn't help a small, almost secret smile. "Anyway, I just wanted to thank you."

His gaze probed hers with alarming intensity. The silence grew warm and heavy. "You're welcome."

All thoughts of discussing their sleeping arrangements fled from her mind. The tension between them was too strong at the moment. She couldn't possibly broach the subject of sharing a bed. Visions of his sleek, muscled body lying beside her sent ripples of heat through her stomach. Gripping her togalike towel with both hands, she turned and fled to the captain's quarters.

Mitch remained in the port doorway and watched her go. It took a while, but gradually he gathered himself together enough to think straight. He felt as if he'd suffered a series of physical shocks…and all because of the changes in her. What the hell was going on? He couldn't put his finger on the exact nature of those changes, but she was very different from what she used to be.

Why had that truth hit him so hard just then? She'd thanked him plenty of times in the past. For lots of things. Gifts he'd given her, favors he'd done for her. But would the Camryn he'd known have thanked him for those few acts of basic human decency last night?

No. She'd have expected them. Despite how bitterly he'd chastised her or how angry they'd made each other, she'd known she could count on him to bring her through any crisis, if necessary. She'd taken that fact for granted. Oh, she might have uttered a "thanks" while he helped her through a bout of seasickness, but she wouldn't have given the matter another thought. She damn sure wouldn't have approached him about it the next day. That was more in line with what a stranger would do. Or, someone who honestly appreciated every act of kindness shown to her. Camryn didn't fit into either category.

Perhaps *that* had been what had shaken him—the sincere warmth in her thanks. It hinted at a depth of feeling that Camryn simply didn't have. Or rather, that the "old" Camryn hadn't had.

The possibility that she'd somehow developed new depths shook the hell out of him. And so did the connection he'd felt with her. For in the midst of her gratitude, he'd also caught the glow of humor. She'd known that her thanks had made him uncomfortable; he'd always had a hard time handling thanks or praise. With nothing more than silent laughter in her gaze, she'd teased him about that difficulty...in a soft, warm, accepting way.

Never before had she touched him on such a subtle, nonverbal level.

"Hey, Cap'n," Remy called to him from his seat at the galley booth. "You hungry?"

"Hell, yeah." Mitch sauntered into the galley, snatched his gray T-shirt from where he'd draped it over the back of the booth seat and quickly shrugged into it. He then poured himself a cup of coffee and dropped onto the bench across the booth from Remy. The fragrance of sautéed beef, garlic and onions, freshly baked bread and chicory coffee made him realize how hungry he was.

He didn't intend to eat, though, until Camryn had

joined them. He wanted a good excuse to be there when she refused the *grillades* and mayhaw jelly.

Remy, he noticed, was just finishing up the last few bites of his own breakfast.

"Has Darryl eaten yet?" Mitch asked, grateful that he had two competent helpers to take turns at the wheel.

Remy nodded, his mouth too full to speak.

"You two haven't finished all the *grillades,* have you?" he teased, knowing full well that they both waited in avid curiosity to see if Camryn would pass or fail the test they'd devised for her.

"We value our lives more 'n dat, Cap'n."

Mitch smiled and settled back for a long wait. That was another defining quality about Camryn—she took a good long while blow-drying her hair, putting on her makeup and getting ready to face the world in the morning. She was, to say the least, "high maintenance."

He tried to put the time to good use by recalling all the things about her that had annoyed him the most. Unfortunately, thoughts of their conversation this morning kept interfering. He couldn't stop from seeing, *feeling,* the genuine warmth that had transformed her smile in a way that had driven the very breath from him.

It had been the second time this morning that she'd succeeded in shaking his composure. The first time had been different, though, and even harder to understand. When he'd climbed up from the engine room to find her standing at the rail, wearing a towel that covered her only to midthigh, enjoying the gorgeous summer morning as if she wanted to inhale it, he'd stopped dead in his tracks. And when she'd nearly walked into him, he'd caught her by her slender shoulders, looked into honey-brown eyes that brimmed with profound appreciation of the beauty around them...and he'd been zapped with a charge of longing that left him momentarily paralyzed.

He supposed he could chalk the reaction up to her physical beauty, and to the fact that he hadn't had a woman for a long time. But the bothersome need for absolute self-honesty refused to let him off that easily.

Sure, her face, body and long, shapely legs were enough to strike any man dumb, especially with beads of water glistening on her smooth, lightly tanned skin, dripping from her hair and sparkling in her curling lashes. But he himself had grown immune to her beauty. He'd come to see her as an empty promise. A taunt. A reminder of the mistake he'd made when he'd first set eyes on her, believing he'd found his life mate.

No, the strong, sudden yearning that had gripped him this morning had *not* been strictly sexual, or even for Camryn herself. It had been the old aching need for that unknown woman; the one who was destined for him. The one he would love with his whole heart and soul, if only he could find her. The one who would fill the terrible emptiness that had grown to frightening proportions within him.

Okay. So it seemed he associated his ideal woman with the physical beauty he found in Camryn. He couldn't deny there was something uniquely appealing about her face, her form, her hair. Even her soft, smoky voice. Ironic. And frustrating. He'd thought he'd moved far beyond the time when her attributes affected him at all...even if the longing she now provoked was for an unknown woman rather than her. The point was, she'd made him feel...*something*. And that wasn't good.

One thing for certain—he wouldn't let her take any more deck-hose showers. Not if she'd be traipsing around in damp towels with droplets sparkling on her lashes. Neither he nor his crew needed that kind of distraction.

The door to the captain's quarters opened, surprising him into alertness. Barely five minutes had passed since he'd sat down. No way could she be dressed and ready this soon.

"Mmm. Something smells wonderful," murmured the soft, smoky voice he'd been trying to put from his mind.

Again, she surprised him. With a sunny smile for Remy, she strolled out of the captain's quarters dressed in a soft, scooped-neck yellow T-shirt that hinted at her curves without actually clinging, and slim white shorts that weren't as long as her khaki ones of yesterday, but not cut nearly as high on her shapely thighs as the cut-offs she used to wear. Her hair was neatly combed, but still damp, and shorter than he'd expected. Flowing freely today instead of pinned up in a twist as it had been, her smooth, thick bob barely brushed her shoulders. She wore no earrings, bracelets or makeup, other than, possibly, clear lip gloss. She looked young, fresh and appealingly innocent.

And he felt another tug of longing. Not for her—damn it!—but for the woman he had *wanted* her to be. Illogical anger quickly followed, and he tightened his hold on his coffee cup. She would never be that woman.

Was she deliberately messing with his mind? Could she possibly know how these changes in her appealed to him? He couldn't allow himself to forget his earlier suspicions—that she'd taken on a new appearance to lure some unsuspecting, upper-crust guy into her life, and that she ultimately intended to win the court's favor to get full custody of Arianne. Was she also trying to play *him* for a fool?

She wouldn't succeed. At any of it. Her true colors would shine through soon enough.

"Come sit down, Mrs. Devereaux," Remy invited, surging to his feet, his gray ponytail swishing beneath his New Orleans Saints cap. "I'll fix you a plate."

Mrs. Devereaux. Mitch tried not to scowl. The name was another reminder of his mistake.

"Thanks, Remy." Camryn accepted a steaming cup of coffee from him. Strangely enough, she took it black, without her usual double dose of cream. "But would you mind calling me 'Cam'? I haven't been a 'Mrs.' for quite some time." With a glance at Mitch, she added, "At least, not that I know of. Being called by my married name makes me feel like a…fraud." She flushed at the last word and hurriedly lifted the cup to her mouth.

Mitch stared at her. He felt as if she'd psychically divined his discomfort with her use of his name. And though he was glad, *very* glad, that she'd asked to be called by a name other than "Mrs. Devereaux," he was also a little annoyed. He wasn't exactly sure why.

Remy mumbled something about being honored to call her "Cam," then turned to the stove to fill a plate for her.

She settled across from Mitch at the booth and cast him an oddly shy smile. As if his presence somehow flustered her.

He hadn't realized until now how beguiling a certain amount of shyness could be in a woman. It hinted at intriguing vulnerabilities. He wouldn't forget, though, that her shy manner was part of an act. Had to be. She'd never been shy with anyone, let alone him.

"I'll take a plate now, too, Remy," he said, refusing to return her smile. Her skin seemed especially luminous this morning, and the subtle fragrance wafting from her reminded him of lemons and freshly netted seashells.

"You know, Mitch," she said in a pleasant, conversational tone, sounding more like a polite stranger than his wife—"ex" or otherwise— "I'm not an expert on commercial vessels, but I'm sure there's a way to carry a considerable amount of freshwater. I mean, think of how much cruise ships must carry. I realize your tanks couldn't possibly contain as much as a cruise ship's, of course, but maybe you should look into finding a bigger tank."

Mitch sipped his coffee and studied her face. She seemed entirely earnest, as if she only wanted to help. As if she expected him to say, *Wow, what a great idea.* As if she honestly didn't know that they already carried three thousand friggin' gallons.

Remy saved him from having to reply by distracting them with steaming plates of grits with rich, saucy *grillades.* He also set out a platter of golden-brown croissants, a dish of butter and a jar of homemade mayhaw jelly.

The appetizing spread of food reminded Mitch of the significance of this breakfast. He'd almost forgotten. This would be Camryn's next test. He hoped the results would make things more clear than the shower test had. Her willingness to take the deck-hose shower—and her apparent delight with it—had only confused him more.

He'd bet his bottom dollar she'd find a way to avoid Remy's *grillades,* and the mayhaw jelly, too. That alone might not prove enough to convince a judge that she was lying about her memory loss...but if she ate only a plain croissant, he himself would know that she damn sure remembered what happened the last time she tried these good old down-home Cajun foods.

"Is this the *grillades?*" She regarded the heaping mound of beef, onions and tomatoes over grits with eager, wide-eyed interest.

"Da best *grillades,* east or west of da Mississip," Remy assured her, taking the place beside her where his own cup of chicory coffee awaited him.

"Mmm, grilled onions, I see. There's garlic in it, too, isn't there?"

"Some."

Inhaling the pungent fragrance of the unfamiliar dish, Kate closed her eyes and tried to identify the other spicy scent. Unable to recall where she'd last smelled it, she glanced at Remy, who was watching her with an expectant expression of a great chef awaiting approval of his newest creation.

Oddly enough, she noticed a watchful expression on Mitch's face, too. Why?

Was he simply doubting her inability to remember the *grillades…* or *was he growing suspicious that she wasn't Camryn?*

No, surely not! But a mild sense of panic hit her at the possibility. She wasn't ready for her impersonation to end yet. Although she knew his family name now, as well as the name of his boat, and had a fairly good idea that he came from the swamplands of Louisiana, she hadn't learned enough about the man himself, or his community. Until she did, she needed a way to discover the all-important, intimate details of his personality, his temperament. His home. Otherwise, how could she know if he was fit to raise Arianne?

She, who had worried only yesterday about the quality of Arianne's swim lessons, now had to decide whether this stranger was capable of giving her the love, guidance and support so vital to a child's future. No, Kate decided. She couldn't allow the impersonation to end yet.

She couldn't let him get suspicious that she wasn't, in fact, Camryn.

Had these *grillades* been a favorite dish of hers? Remy seemed to believe so. *"You really don't remember my* grillades?" he'd asked with an incredulous stare. If she didn't want to blow her impersonation, she needed to proceed with caution. A head injury might explain why she'd forgotten things that Camryn should have known, but it wouldn't have changed her taste in food.

Determined to swear she loved the *grillades* and finish every bite, she picked up her fork and optimistically dug into the creamy, sauce-covered grits, tomatoes, onions and beef. She noticed that Mitch had already begun eating his. He seemed to be enjoying it.

Kate's first taste was surprisingly delicious. No wonder her sister had loved the dish. She flashed a smile of approval at Remy.

But before she'd thoroughly chewed the first mouthful, the burning began. A hot, peppery burn in her mouth and throat. And her nose, her eyes. *Cayenne!* That was the fragrance she'd been trying to pinpoint. He'd used quite a lot of it, too. And maybe some hot sauce. And roasted jalapeños. Good heavens, maybe liquid *fire!*

She felt her face, her entire body, heat up to an alarming degree. With a tortured moan, she dropped her fork, grabbed her paper napkin and discreetly spit the burning mouthful into its folds. Her eyes watered and streamed, and the fire in her mouth continued to grow, as if she'd swilled pure acid.

"Don't give her water," Mitch said, his face nothing but a blur to her. She frowned at that heartless, infuriating blur, until he added, "Get her an icy cola. It'll stop the burning faster."

Remy, who had already left her side, fumbled around in the refrigerator and spoke in rapid French, his tone clearly remorseful, while Kate half rose from her seat, choking and coughing and fanning her mouth in growing desperation. A frosty glass was put into her hand, and she drank deeply of the contents. Slowly, much too slowly, the burning decreased, and she sank back down into her seat. But when she'd finished the cola, the fire promptly returned. Gasping, she reached for the ice-filled glass again.

"Dat's it, Cam," Remy murmured encouragingly from somewhere beside her. "Suck on da ice. Dat'll help more'n anything."

She followed his advice, and when the burning finally stopped—and the ice in her mouth had completely melted away—she drew in a breath, wiped her eyes with the back of her hand and leveled a bewildered gaze at Remy. "This was one of my favorite dishes?" she managed to ask. She couldn't imagine her sister enjoying anything that peppery. Then again, in the course of her worldly travels—and her marriage to a hot-blooded Cajun—maybe Camryn *had* developed a taste for hot and spicy.

That thought sent another wave of heat through her and provoked a spasm of coughing.

Remy patted her on the back, his contrition palpable. "Maybe I put too much Tiger sauce and cayenne pepper in it dis time."

"Maybe," she mouthed. Once her breathing capabilities had fully returned and the tears had cleared from her eyes, she noticed Mitch studying her again in that unsettling, unreadable way. "Or maybe I've just been away from Cajun cooking for too long," she croaked, happy to note that her voice had been only temporary impaired. "I've kept a pretty bland diet since the accident."

"Yeah, dat's probably it," Remy agreed, removing her plate of *grillades* from the table.

Incredulously, Kate watched Mitch help himself to another heaping forkful of his *grillades*. How on earth could the man eat anything so wickedly hot? Apparently noticing her fascination, he smiled slightly at her while he drew the fork from his mouth. Though he didn't say a word, she knew what he was telling her. *The hotter, the better,* chèr'.

There was something undeniably sexy about a man with an appetite for *hot*. The wayward direction of her thoughts shocked her, and she felt her face heat up again, almost as much as it had from the pepper.

"You still want a croissant, Cam?" Remy asked.

Thankful for the distraction, she awarded him with a warm smile. "Oh, yes, please. I wouldn't miss your *nainaine*'s homemade jelly for the world."

He handed her a smaller plate than the one he'd removed, and she helped herself to a golden-brown croissant. After slicing open the flaky, crescent-shaped roll, she topped it with a sparkling scoop of jelly.

"The jelly doesn't have pepper or Tiger sauce in it...does it?" she asked, only half joking.

"Non, non, non," Remy assured her emphatically. "I promise, it don't."

A hunger pang squeezed her stomach, reminding Kate that she hadn't eaten since lunchtime yesterday. Lifting the croissant from the plate, she opened her mouth to take a bite.

A hand shot out from across the table and caught her

wrist, stopping its forward progress. She stared for a brief, uncomprehending moment at the strong, large, sun-bronzed hand wrapped around her relatively delicate wrist, feeling the steely strength of his hold.

Bewildered, she met Mitch's gaze. *What the heck was he doing?*

"Is that mayhaw jelly?" he asked, maintaining his hold on her wrist.

She nodded.

"Don't eat it."

"Pardon me?"

"The mayhaw jelly. You're allergic to it."

"Allergic?"

"You tried it at my parents' house. Your mouth swelled up, and you broke out in hives."

Their eyes held for a long moment as Kate digested the import of his words. Allergic! The thought made her shudder. Both she and Camryn had suffered allergic re-actions to various foods, including strawberries and kiwi. She had no doubt that Mitch was telling the truth…and that she'd be just as allergic to mayhaw as her twin had been.

"Thank you." She felt ridiculously moved that he'd saved her from unpleasantness. *And* ridiculously aware of his hand still gripping her wrist, where her pulse pounded much too fast beneath his hard fingers.

Only when he'd released her and retracted his hand to his side of the table did Kate's good sense return. She dropped the croissant onto her plate and wiped her hands vigorously on the fresh napkin Remy had supplied. She owed Mitch another thank-you, she realized, for his timely intervention. Did that intervention mean he still believed she was Camryn? Was he starting to give cre-dence to her claim that she'd lost her memory?

"*Enfin!* I didn't know nothing about dat allergy," Remy swore, spreading his palms out in an expression of abject apology. "What a rotten breakfast I make for you, eh?"

Kate blinked as she recognized a certain sheepishness in Remy's expression. *Had* he known about Camryn's allergy? More important, had Mitch known that the jelly was mayhaw? He'd allowed her to spread it on her croissant and lift it to her mouth before he'd stopped her. Maybe he'd wanted to test her, to see if she would eat it. Maybe the *grillades* had been a test, too.

Kate suddenly felt as if she were stranded in the middle of a minefield. One false step, and she'd be blown to bits. A silly reaction, she supposed. As long as their tests always had to do with her memory loss, she'd be okay. She truly didn't know anything about Mitch or his life with Camryn, so he couldn't possibly trip her up into revealing more than her memory loss should allow.

But what if he started testing her in regard to the real problem—the one she hoped he knew nothing about? The question of her identity.

No. He had no reason to suspect that Camryn had an identical twin, let alone that she was now impersonating her. For the umpteenth time, she whispered a grateful prayer for the inspiration that had prompted her amnesia story. She never could have pulled off the impersonation without it.

"Why don't you bring out some of your *maman's* blackberry jam, Remy," Mitch suggested. "It's always been a favorite of Camryn's."

That much was true. "Blackberry would be wonderful." She made a move to slide out from her seat at the booth. "You don't have to wait on me, though, Remy. I'm perfectly capable of—"

"Non, non," Remy insisted, gesturing her back down into her seat. "Now I *know* you're not kidding about dat memory loss. When I work wit' Mitch, dis kitchen is mine."

"Oh! I'm sorry. I didn't mean to—"

"Da good thing about not rememberin', though," he cut in as he refilled her coffee cup with robust chicory brew, "is dat you get to taste my *maman*'s blackberry jam for da first time again. Hooo, you gonna pass a good time now, *chèr'.*"

She couldn't help returning his grin.

Rising from his seat and edging past the short, grizzled-haired deckhand, Mitch slanted him a glance. His gaze, warm with indulgent humor, then connected with Kate's...and for a moment, they actually agreed on something. *Remy's okay, eh?*

The moment ended far too quickly. Mitch turned to the sink, placed his empty plate and cup in the soapy water. "Think I'll go relieve Darryl at the wheel," he said to Remy. "Thanks for breakfast, *mon ami.*" He laid a hand briefly on the older man's back. *"Très bon."* Without a word or even a parting glance for Kate, he sauntered toward the doorway that led to the captain's quarters and wheelhouse.

"Um, Mitch," she called, stopping him near the doorway.

He tossed a questioning look over one broad shoulder.

"Can we call Joey to see how Arianne slept last night?"

"Later."

She smiled, relieved.

His eyes dipped to her smile, as if compelled there against his will. Her heart tripped into double-time. "By the way," he murmured, his eyes slowly rising to meet hers, "I fixed the problem with the shower stall. No need for any more deck-hose showers."

She blinked and frowned. "But I thought you didn't have enough freshwater for—"

"Now we do."

Mystified but pleased, she slowly nodded.

He turned for the door.

"Oh, and Mitch."

He stopped again, looking rather reluctant to face her.

"Thanks for saving me from a bad case of hives."

His full, wide lips twisted slightly, which deepened a particularly attractive dimple to the left of his mouth. "I'm turning out to be quite the hero, ain't I?" The words, though softly spoken in true southern form, rang of self-derision. "Keep her out of trouble, Remy. I'd rather not slay any more dragons."

CHAPTER SEVEN

HE'D THOUGHT he had her pegged. Thought he knew her, through and through. Yet Camryn had managed to surprise him three times that morning—first with the saltwater shower, then twice over breakfast. He still couldn't believe she'd tried the *grillades,* and he had no doubt she would have taken a big bite of mayhaw jelly if he hadn't stopped her.

As the sun climbed high into the vivid azure sky and the easterly wind kicked up a following sea, Mitch set the *Lady Jeanette* on autopilot and kept a casual watch on the radar, the depth recorder and the vast horizon as she sped across Alabama waters. He also listened to Remy and Camryn over the intercom.

"Hey, Cam…how 'bout some poker? Fifty-cent limit, eh?" Remy proposed. "I think da deck of cards you left after our last game is still round here somewhere."

Mitch expected her to jump at the chance to ream Remy in poker again. The cards he'd mentioned were marked, as Mitch had discovered during their marital separation while playing an idle game of solitaire. Remy hadn't been pleased to learn he'd been fleeced. On the other hand, he was a little too Cajun not to admire the smoothness of her scam. Mitch had settled the score by giving Remy the cards, with the understanding that he wouldn't get himself killed by using them in a serious game.

Certain that Camryn would remember which deck Remy was referring to—and use the marked cards to her advantage again—Mitch nearly choked on his coffee when she turned Remy down. "I'm not really in a card-playing mood."

Not in a card-playing mood. He never thought he'd hear those words pass her lips.

"She knows we're testing her," Darryl muttered from the starboard doorway.

"Maybe." Though he knew it was possible, Mitch didn't really buy that explanation.

Moments later, she surprised them again. "I'd rather take a tour of the boat," she told Remy, "if you're willing to be my guide." With his usual gallantry, he assured her he'd be delighted. "Great!" she said. "Let's start on the afterdeck."

The afterdeck. Why had she started calling the back deck by a term they'd never used? That detail was too subtle to be part of a plan. At least, any plan of Camryn's. But then, maybe the new man in her life owned a yacht or sailboat, and she'd picked up the lingo from him. The thought irked Mitch far more than it should have.

"Afterdeck?" Remy repeated blankly. "Oh, you mean, da back deck?"

Their voices faded as Remy escorted her out of the galley, then came in clear again from the intercom on the stern. "What are those arms called that hold the nets?" she asked with enthusiasm that sounded so damn genuine.

"Outriggers."

"They look like giant wings spread out over the water. I feel like we're riding on the back of some huge seabird that's soaring across a blue, blue sky."

Mitch shook his head in astonishment. The only thing she'd ever waxed poetic about before had been an outstanding poker hand, or the thrill she'd milked from trying something dangerous. But...*outriggers?* Nah. Had his aunt's voodoo spells summoned some dispossessed spirit to take over his wife's body?

"What are those big slabs of wood beneath the outriggers?" she asked Remy.

"We call 'em 'doors.' Dey drag da bottom and spread out da nets."

"Drag the bottom? Is that where the shrimp live—on the floor of the Gulf?"

"Mostly. When dey ain't migrating, dey burrow in da sand and mud."

As she asked questions about locating the shrimp and Remy explained the function of the try-net, Mitch marveled over her interest in such technicalities. Never before had she expressed the slightest curiosity about the rigging or the process of shrimping. Her enthusiasm had always been reserved for things like rooftop sunbathing, poker games with his crew, chatting with captains of other boats over the radio, dining on ultrafresh seafood and the occasional sports fishing they indulged in when shrimp was hard to find.

Another favorite pastime of hers had been guzzling from the flask Remy smuggled on board. That was the next test she would face—Remy's flask. Mitch awaited that all-important test with keen anticipation.

He waited a good long while. Remy's tour lasted a couple of hours. When he'd finished explaining all the equipment on the back deck and had shown her around the engine room, he finally made the offer. "If you get thirsty for something stronger 'n water, *chèr'*, my flask is in da same place it used to be. Just help yourself."

Powerful temptation for a woman like Camryn. If she asked Remy to get the flask for her, he would invent some task that had to be done immediately, which would force her to seek out the flask herself. The moment she made her way to the crew's quarters and dug into his hiding place, they'd have her dead-to-rights. How could she explain knowing where he'd kept his flask if she'd lost all memory of their previous trips?

Mitch held his breath while waiting for her reply.

"Flask?" she said, sounding surprised. "You mean, like, booze?"

"Yeah, you know. Da good homemade kind. Like I always say, *'Laissez les bons temps rouler.'* In case you forgot, dat means, 'Let da good times roll.'"

"Oh, Remy! Drinking on board a boat can't be safe. Mitch told me he forbids it. What if we have an emergency? Oh, my goodness…you don't take a turn *at the wheel* if you've been drinking, do you? I'm sorry, I don't mean to sound judgmental, and I probably seem hypocritical to you, if I used to drink with you, but—"

"I won't tell Mitch," Remy cut in. "It'll be our li'l secret, I promise."

"I'm sorry, Remy. Alcohol on board a vessel like this is simply too dangerous. I'm going to have to insist that you pour that liquor out."

Mitch exchanged an incredulous glance with Darryl, who looked as stunned as Mitch felt. She, a hardcore adventurer and suspected alcoholic, wanted him to pour the whiskey out? Had she given up drinking? Was that the miracle behind the profound changes in her?

"Aw, no, Cam," Remy said.

"Then at least tell Mitch you have it."

"But he'll t'row it overboard."

They argued for a while, and to Mitch's astonishment,

she and Remy soon appeared in the port-side doorway of the wheelhouse. "Uh, Cap'n, I need to talk to you," Remy mumbled.

Switching off the intercom, he asked a slack-jawed Darryl to step out of the wheelhouse. Under Camryn's watchful eye, Remy then "confessed" to having a flask on board—which Mitch didn't believe he even had. He'd agreed to make the offer to Camryn only to see if she'd know where to find the flask. Had she looked, she wouldn't have found one.

"Thank you, Remy," Mitch replied to his confession, trying to sound sufficiently stern despite his shock at Camryn's actions, "for, uh, coming forward."

"Wasn't *my* idea." He glanced tellingly at Camryn.

"Yeah, well, you and I will discuss this matter later." He then dismissed Remy and turned to search Camryn's face for signs of cunning. He saw only earnest concern.

"I...I'm sorry if I embarrassed him, but you *did* say you prohibited drinking, and I understand why. It doesn't take much alcohol to impair a person's judgment," she said, "or make him lose his balance. He might get hurt, or even killed. He might fall overboard!"

Stunned, Mitch acknowledged her words with only a nod. Safety had never been a concern of hers. She'd been a consummate risk taker. Not only had she shared a flask with Remy, she'd then climbed out onto the outrigger and balanced above shark-infested waters. Mitch swore he'd lost ten years of his life, trying to force her in to safety.

That had been the last trip he'd allowed her to take. It had also been the last time Remy had brought whiskey on board, as far as Mitch knew. If he hadn't sworn on his beloved mother's grave to never bring another drop, Mitch would have fired him.

He now found it almost impossible to believe that the woman who had climbed out on that outrigger was reporting Remy's offer of whiskey. Yet, she was.

"I'll take care of the matter," Mitch promised, feeling as if he himself had sustained a blow to the head. "While I do, why don't you just, uh, relax? Sunbathe on the roof, or...or something." As an afterthought, he added, "But don't try diving off, and keep your clothes on."

She gaped at him as if he'd gone crazy.

It was then that an awesome certainty gripped him. *She didn't remember.* She honestly didn't remember sunbathing naked on the roof or diving overboard, just as she hadn't remembered eating Remy's *grillades*...or that the *Lady Jeanette* carried enough freshwater for showers. Had she really been in an accident that robbed her of her memory? And if so, had that accident caused her to give up drinking and gambling...and all the other wild behavior that had driven him crazy? He found that hard to believe. But what else could account for the changes?

"Coffee," he mumbled, trying to bring some semblance of order to his chaotic thoughts. "I'd like some coffee. Would you mind making a fresh pot while I talk to Remy?"

She assured him that she wouldn't mind at all.

The moment she left the wheelhouse, Mitch closed the doors for privacy, reached for the radio and placed a ship-to-shore call to an old buddy who happened to be a cousin of the investigator he'd used. "I know Chuck is probably spending the holiday weekend with his family, but could you find him for me? I need to talk to him. It's important."

The investigator returned his call within the hour, and Mitch told him about the newest complications. "I have to know if she's been in a serious accident, Chuck, and if she sustained a head injury that could cause amnesia. It sounds unlikely as hell, I know, but I have reason to believe it.''

"I'll do what I can, Mitch, but I'm in the Bahamas with my wife. Plus, it's a holiday weekend in the States. Offices are closed, people are off from work. Don't expect much information any time soon.''

"I'd appreciate any information you can find, Chuck. Any at all.''

An hour later, while his crew kept Camryn occupied in some distant area of the boat, Chuck called back. "I had an associate do a computer search in the Florida county where we found her. He dug up some interesting info under the alias she's been using. You know, 'Kate Jones.' A car registered in that name *was* involved in an accident, and the driver *was* Camryn."

Mitch's hand tightened around the radio transmitter. "When?''

"January. Two weeks after she skipped town.''

"Was it a serious accident?''

"A head-on collision. Both vehicles were totaled, and there were fatalities.''

"Fatalities? My God.'' A feeling of unreality settled over him. "Who died?''

"Well...uh—'' Chuck let out a short, dry laugh "—that's where the information gets confusing.'' He sounded oddly hesitant. Almost embarrassed. "As a matter of fact, *all* of the information is confusing. Whoever keyed the data into the computer must have been celebrating some holiday or another. Made a lot of mistakes. The report left me asking things like, when did she register the car under her alias, and how did she do that when her driver's license still had her as Camryn.

And who exactly was killed? You just can't depend on computerized reports for a clear picture. I'll check out the details as soon as I get home. That won't be until Thursday. My wife will have my head if I cut our vacation short.''

Mitch forced a lightness to his voice. ''Relax and enjoy your vacation, Chuck. Sorry for interrupting it. I'll talk to you when you get back.'' He then thanked him for the information he'd related, disconnected from the call and stared off into space.

Camryn hadn't been lying about the accident. And if the collision had been serious enough to include fatalities, she could have easily sustained a severe head injury. The experience could have caused some life-altering realizations, too.

It seemed that things were very different from what he'd been assuming. He had to talk to her. Learn all the facts. Set aside his preconceived ideas about her. The accident had happened only two weeks after she'd left his hometown, which meant she might not have deliberately kept Arianne from him for those six months.

She might have honestly forgotten that he existed.

After many hours of listening to her, observing her, *testing* her, he no longer found that notion as preposterous as he once had.

KATE WAS GLAD that Remy wasn't holding a grudge against her for insisting he report his whiskey to Mitch. He smiled at her with his usual cheer while he served a supper of *boudin,* which he pronounced ''boo-dan,'' a delicious Cajun sausage made of pork, rice and onions that she found only slightly spicy, and croissants left over from breakfast.

After supper, Kate wandered out to the back rail,

stared at the churning wake and thought about the danger Camryn had put herself in. *Diving off the roof.* The very idea sent angst shooting through Kate's stomach. She was glad she hadn't known of her activities at sea, or she would have lived in a state of constant anxiety.

Actually, she *had* lived in state of constant anxiety…at least, whenever she'd contemplated her sister. Distancing herself from Camryn, physically and emotionally, had been her only means of staying sane. That realization only worsened her sense of guilt. If she'd tried harder to remain a part of Camryn's life, could she have changed her?

Too troubled by the question, she thought, instead, of the main source of joy in her life—Arianne. How was she faring with Joey? Was she being fed the right foods, and kept clean and dry? The need to hold her again throbbed like an ache. How she missed the lively weight in her arms; the softness of her rosy skin and silky blond hair; the fragrance of formula, baby powder and vanilla wafers….

"Hey, Cam," Remy greeted her, strolling up to stand beside her at the rail. "How you making?" The gray ponytail trailing from the back of his shabby purple sports cap riffled in the breeze, which had cooled slightly since midday.

"How am I…making?" she repeated, blinking herself out of a reverie to focus on the deckhand's craggy, weathered face.

He shrugged and grinned, which made the diamond between his crooked front teeth glitter in the slanted rays of late-afternoon sunshine. "It means, how you doing? What's up? How you making out?"

"I'm fine," she replied with a slight smile.

"You look like you lost your best friend."

In a way, she supposed she had. And she wasn't sure she'd get her back, either. "Guess I'm just thinking about my…my daughter." The term suddenly seemed fraudulent. Since Camryn's death, she'd intended to adopt Arianne, which would give her the right to call her "daughter." She doubted she'd ever have a legal claim to Arianne now. She couldn't envision Mitch Devereaux signing away his parental rights, especially to a woman who had deceived him. And she still knew so little about his character, his home, his way with children. "I miss her."

Remy looked uncomfortable with the confidence. "Yeah, Mitch missed her, too." The comment held no rancor or accusation. It was just a simple statement of fact. Maybe that was why it shook her more than Mitch's earlier ranting about Camryn kidnapping his daughter. Had he felt the same sense of loss, worry and pain that now had Kate on the verge of tears?

She had to change the subject if she didn't want those tears to break through her composure. "Remy, I hope you're not too upset that I told Mitch about your whiskey."

"Who, me…upset? Nah! He took my flask away, but dat's okay. 'Specially since we left da dock on a Friday. Maybe you saved me from a bad accident, eh?"

"Maybe you should worry more about da woman on board bringing you bad luck dan leaving da dock on a Friday" came a morose grumbling from behind them. They turned to find Darryl climbing out of the hold—the cavernous storage room belowdecks—with an armload of sand-encrusted netting. A strong smell of fish and sea brine emanated from the massive load of heavy twine. "She brought Mitch plenty bad luck, no?"

"Aw, don't start no problems." Remy clearly disliked conflict, while Darryl seemed itching for a confrontation.

"No, please, tell me." Kate paced toward Darryl as he set the load of netting down on the deck. Maybe by encouraging him to vent his anger, she'd relieve him of some of his hostility. "How did I bring Mitch bad luck?"

"You mean, besides costing him his life's savings, his *joie de vivre* and his best boat?"

Ah. New information. "I cost him his best boat?"

Darryl squinted at her with cold dark eyes, while the anchor tattoos on his meaty arms moved with the tensing of his muscles. "You gambled away all his money, den cost him a fortune to track down his daughter. He had to sell da *Miss Josette* to make ends meet."

"Was a nice vessel," Remy lamented. "A freezer boat. Wit' an air-conditioned cabin."

An illogical pang of guilt assailed her. Although she herself had had nothing to do with Mitch's loss, she believed her sister had. Had he been forced to sell a better boat and settle for this one to make his living? She wondered how much of his money Camryn had spent. If she'd returned to gambling, she could have blown incredible amounts.

And a man prone to violence might have been pushed beyond his limit. She hated to think that Mitch might have taken his anger out on her.

"But you know it ain't all Cam's fault dat he's in a jam," Remy protested. "Times are bad. Chemical spills mess up da water. Fuel and ice cost too much. Shrimp are hard to find."

"And some boat owners get messed up wit' women who bleed 'em dry." Darryl sat on the hatch cover, withdrew a small knife from the pocket of his jeans and grabbed a fistful of netting. "If you don't call dat bad luck, I don't know what is."

"You ain't seen bad luck till you leave da dock on a Friday," Remy retorted. "I'm hoping I'm wrong, but…we'll see."

After that ominous pronouncement, Remy took a seat across from Darryl on a low stool and reached for a handful of netting. Kate settled onto another stool and watched the men work with knives and sewing tools to repair tears in the net. To Remy, she said, "Yesterday you mentioned that whistling in the wheelhouse brings bad luck, too. Are there any other no-no's?"

"A few. If you're working in da galley, never open a can wit' da label upside down. Don't leave da hatch cover upside down, either. And never say da *A* word on board a shrimp boat."

"The *A* word?" She glanced at Remy with lively interest. "And what would that be?"

"Don't say it," Darryl cut in sharply.

Surprised, Kate studied his stern, dark face. "So you, too, believe in these 'rules of the sea'?"

He didn't answer but scowled and returned his attention to his net repairing.

"He only believes in dat one," Remy explained. "Da last time he said da *A* word on board a boat, we got a bad phone call. Da woman he loves married another man."

Darryl glowered at him. "Dat's no one's business but mine."

"Now she's a widow, and he has a second chance, but he ain't taking it."

"Shut up, Remy."

Alarmed at the menace on Darryl's face, Kate turned

the conversation to safer channels. "Can you *spell* the *A* word for me, Remy?"

"Don't even spell it," Darryl warned him, "'cause she'll say it."

"No, I won't," she vowed. "I want to know what it is so I *don't* say it. Is it a navigational term?" Remy shook his head, and she asked, "Something children would consider to be bad?"

"No, it's a common, everyday word. Something you might have around da house."

Overcome with curiosity, she resorted to guessing. "Is it…*a-p-p-l-e?*"

Remy repeated the letters. "Dat spells *apple,* right?"

She nodded, mildly surprised that he hadn't been sure.

"I thought so." He looked highly pleased with himself for having deciphered the word. She remembered then that he hadn't attended school very often. "But dat's not da *A* word." At a glare from Darryl, he added, "You better ask Darryl about it, not me. Don't want no trouble, eh?"

"Camryn." The deep, vibrantly masculine voice blared across the deck from the intercom. Kate's heart did an odd little flip. "Come to the wheelhouse, will you please?"

"Sure. I'll be right there." She'd managed to sound nonchalant, although her pulse had sped up and her knees felt weak as she rose from the low stool…and all because Mitch had called for her. Not a good sign. Definitely not a good sign.

Why had he called her? Was he ready to telephone Joey? Hoping so, she left Darryl and Remy toiling on the back deck and made her way to the wheelhouse.

As she stepped through the starboard doorway, Mitch leveled her a long, bracing glance that brought a disturbing warmth to her cheeks. Wearing tight jeans and a dark, cotton Henley that allowed a glimpse of chest hairs curling just below his strong throat, he sat low in the captain's chair, his legs extended comfortably before him, his muscular arms crossed over his chest. He looked perfectly at ease, but Kate sensed tension in him. The intensity of his gaze left no doubt that something important was on his mind.

Something to do with her.

"Come sit down, *chèr'*."

Chèr'. It meant "darling" or "dear." He hadn't called her that in quite a while. And when he had, he'd meant it sarcastically, of course. This time, it had sounded different. Warmer, softer. But she couldn't imagine why his attitude toward her might have softened.

To subdue her own growing tension, she took a seat beside him and forced a nonchalant smile. "So, how you making?"

He blinked at the Cajun greeting, but continued to search her face. "What injuries did you suffer?"

She frowned. "Pardon me?"

"In the accident. The one that caused your memory loss. In what ways were you hurt?"

His sudden interest in the accident gave her pause. Was he asking because he'd come to believe her story about the memory loss, or because he doubted it? Either way, she didn't want to talk about accidents. She'd been grasping at straws, like a person sinking in quicksand, when she'd mentioned an accident in the first place.

"I don't remember much about it. And my other injuries are irrelevant. I see no sense in discussing them when we could be calling Joey."

"What happened, Cam. I want—"

"But *I* want to call Joey, and find out how Arianne is doing. She's in a strange place, with people she doesn't know. I want to…to hear her voice, and let her hear mine." Her throat had tightened, and she pressed her lips together while she collected herself.

Slowly, Mitch nodded and rose from his chair. He towered above her, lean and broad shouldered, and smelling of chicory, sea breeze and soap. His purposeful, green-eyed gaze fairly pinned her to the chair. "Okay. We'll call. Then you and I will talk. Agreed?"

She didn't like the "talk" part but had no choice, really. "Okay."

He called Joey. Her soft, southern voice with its pretty Cajun cadence sounded more relaxed than the last time Kate had heard it over the ship-to-shore radio. She assured Mitch that Arianne had slept through the night, was eating the foods he'd specified and having a wonderful time playing with Claude, whom Kate assumed was another child.

Joey's voice lost its softness, though, when Mitch told her that Camryn wanted to speak to Arianne. "Absolutely not. Dat would only make her cry again. I don't want her upset."

Kate wanted to argue, but she had to admit that Joey's reasoning was sound. She had no choice but to take Joey's word for it that Arianne was fine…until she herself had the chance to see the kind of care she was receiving.

Joey went on to describe the baby's delight with a bubble bath, then said in rather awed tones, "She really surprised me just before bedtime. She found one o' dem fancy French cookbooks Mama likes to give for Christmas, brought it to me and climbed up onto my lap. I swear, Mitch…someone must have been *reading* to dis child!''

Kate wondered why Joey considered that surprising. She then remembered that Mitch's community didn't seem to value education much from what Remy had told her. Remy himself had barely been able to spell the word *apple*. And now Joey was stunned by the notion of a child enjoying a book.

Mitch shot Kate a glance, and she saw surprise there, too. ''Who reads to her?'' he asked.

''*I* do.''

Incredulity showed in his face.

''You, Camryn?'' boomed Joey's voice from the radio. ''You read to your daughter? When? Between hands of poker, or shots of whiskey? You barely had time to feed her while you lived here. Too much excitement in da bars and casinos to waste time wit' your new baby. Which makes me wonder why you even want her. Must have some scheme up your sleeve.''

Anger, defensiveness and the need to believe she was wrong about Camryn rose like leaping flames within Kate. ''How dare you? You know nothing about me. Nothing!'' Yet even as she said it, she remembered Camryn's note. She'd been on her way to New York City to get her and Arianne roles on a soap opera.

''Oh, I know plenty 'bout you,'' Joey retorted. ''You're sly and selfish, and you didn't care dat stealing Arianne would break Mitch's heart. You don't want him getting in da way of your fun and games, and you—''

''That's enough, Joey.'' Mitch's command rang with finality. ''I didn't call to hear you rant and rage. I'm glad Arianne's calmed down. You need to do that, too. Kiss her for me. Take good care of her. Tell Claude I'm bringing him a big old seashell from the bottom of the Gulf, just for being good to his little cousin.''

He then broke the connection, hung up the radio handset and turned questioning eyes to Kate. She sensed a soul-deep disturbance in him—as if he realized something was very wrong with the picture she presented, but he couldn't pinpoint what.

She wished she could clear up his confusion, but her need for the impersonation was as strong now as ever. She wanted to see not only the face Mitch Devereaux showed to the world but the one he revealed only to those who knew him best. His wife would be exposed to his secret side before a stranger would. Kate also wanted an inside glimpse of where he lived and how he lived…and who would be taking care of Arianne while he was out at sea.

No, she couldn't reveal the truth about her identity yet or the accident that had killed Camryn. She'd told Mitch at the very start that she wasn't Camryn, and he'd chosen not to believe her. He would learn his mistake when he turned her over to the authorities.

She suddenly dreaded the coming of that day.

''Let's go talk,'' he said.

Flicking on the intercom, he called Remy to relieve him at the wheel. He then took hold of Kate's hand and led her from the wheelhouse to the captain's quarters, where he grabbed a thick, colorful beach blanket. With her hand still firmly encased in his—a wonderfully gratifying feeling, she realized—he escorted her to the back deck and stopped near the steel-and-wood, door-high structure that sheltered the stairway to the engine room. The ''doghouse,'' Remy had called it.

''Climb up,'' Mitch said, releasing her hand.

"Up?" She frowned at him, puzzled. The stairway to the engine room went *down*.

He gestured toward the ladder rungs built onto the side of the doghouse. "To the roof."

Anxiety rippled through her. She wasn't sure about climbing onto a rocking roof in the middle of the sea. Not that she was particularly afraid of heights or water. But somehow the combination left her quaking in her sandals. She simply wasn't the adventurous twin. She found all the adventure she needed in books or videos. *Oh, Cam! How did I ever come to be living your life? I'm just not good at it!*

Hanging back from the ladder, she waved Mitch on ahead of her. "You first."

With a sidelong glance that spoke again of bewilderment, he reached for a handgrip, climbed the few steel rungs and stepped onto the roof of the cabin. He probably wondered what had caused her to lose her nerve; to turn into a yellow-bellied chicken, as Camryn had often called her when they were kids.

Had Camryn's bravery and adventurous spirit thrilled Mitch? He'd told her not to jump off the roof, but that only meant he took his responsibility as captain seriously. Maybe he'd found Camryn's wildness to be invigorating. Her previous husbands and boyfriends had.

"You're not afraid, are you?" he called down to her.

"No, no, of course not." Swallowing her fear, Kate gritted her teeth and climbed after him. When she reached the top and stood on the slightly inclined roof, dizziness overtook her. She felt so high…on a rough black surface that dipped and rolled with the motion of the boat…surrounded by nothing but miles and miles of purple-blue waves and golden sky. If she tumbled over the edge, she wasn't sure which way she'd fall—into the bottomless water or the endless sky.

Not the adventurous one. No way to pretend I am. Keep breathing, darn it. Just focus on the breathing.

A strong, steady arm came around her shoulders, and Mitch ushered her to the center of the roof. He laid out a blanket, then guided her down onto it. They sat with their backs to the wind, their faces to the stern. The wind whipped her hair wildly about her.

Gradually, her dizziness lessened. And she realized she was clinging to Mitch's tautly muscled forearm with both hands. Forcing her fingers to release him, she summoned her flagging courage and braved a glance around.

The view was breathtaking. Backlit with the heavy gold of late afternoon, the violet water stretched on into eternity. Gulls swooped, screeched and circled the boat, as if they knew fish would be hauled onto that deck eventually. The nets billowed in the breeze from the lowered outriggers. The wind hummed an exotic song in her ears, and the taste of brine flavored every breath.

And there, alongside the boat, were fins cutting silently through the water, keeping easy pace with the *Lady Jeanette.*

"Sharks! Oh my God, Mitch—" Kate threw a panicked glance at him "—if we fall off this roof..."

"We're not going to fall." Again he slid a protective arm around her shoulders and tugged her against the reassuring warmth of his large, solid body. "And those aren't sharks."

"They're not?" With breathless fascination, she watched the shiny gray-black creatures rise in a graceful arc above the waves, then dive again, their movements perfectly synchronized. "Porpoises," she breathed. They swam and rose and dived beside the boat until they vanished somewhere into the vast, blue deep.

And a sweet serenity stole over her. Heaven wouldn't share such beauty with her if she wasn't meant to enjoy it. The sun, wind and salt seeped deep into her pores, and she swore the combination could heal anything that ailed the soul.

"Talk to me, Cam."

Then again, maybe not. Tearing her attention away from the beauty of their surroundings, she met his troubled gaze with grave misgivings. "I'm not sure it's a good idea to stay up here long," she hedged. "It's after six, but the sun is still hot and dangerous."

"It's seven-thirty. And I thought I saw you putting on sunscreen a while ago."

"Oh. Yeah." She bit her lip, feeling cornered. She'd actually been slathering sunscreen on all day. "Guess I'd forgotten."

"You agreed we'd talk." His windblown hair danced around a face bronzed by many days such as this, and his green eyes looked deeper, more turbulent, than the sea. He needed answers. And she wanted to give them. "Now is the time, Cam. Tell me everything about the accident…and why you've changed so damn much."

She couldn't, of course. But knowing that she would eventually have to own up to her deception—in a matter of days—Kate suddenly felt the need to prepare him the best she could for the truth. She could tell him *some* of the facts about the accident, couldn't she?

"It happened early on a rainy morning in January. The police said I'd been speeding. I don't remember the crash itself, but it was a head-on collision. With a truck." The horror of the truth suddenly rose out of nowhere, like an evil apparition, and wrapped its hands tightly around her throat. Kate couldn't go on.

"Did anyone...die?"

She shot him a startled glance. Why had he asked that question? Had he somehow discovered the truth? No, she didn't believe so. Intense bewilderment emanated from him. "Yes," she whispered, too haunted by her loss to completely deny it.

"How many people?"

"Two." The pain burned like a freshly torn wound, and her heart thudded with heavy grief. "The truck driver," she said through an aching throat, "and...my sister."

CHAPTER EIGHT

"YOUR SISTER?" Mitch supposed he should have been immune to the surprises she sprang on him, but he wasn't. He felt as if he'd been blindsided into a tailspin. "You told me you had no family."

She stared straight ahead, over the water, and tears welled up in her eyes. "I lied."

"Why?"

"I'm not sure. It's one of those things that I…don't remember." A small tear inched down her face in a wildly crooked path, spurred on by the wind. "She and I hadn't been getting along very well." She swallowed hard, then swung her wide, honey-brown gaze to his. The pain he saw there made his chest tighten. "She disapproved of my drinking and gambling." A small, bittersweet smile twisted her mouth. "Almost every time we were together, she butted into my affairs." The tears trickled over her bottom lashes. "She was always telling me what to do."

Like me, he thought.

"Now she's gone," she said in a choked voice, "and I'd give anything to have her back, to get one more chance to make things r-right."

He gathered her to him and let her cry, which she did, long and hard. Sobs racked her slender body, and he held her close. After a while, he pulled her down with him to lie on the blanket, his cheek against her hair, his hand stroking her back. He'd comforted sobbing females more than a few times in his life, but something about her pain cut through his defenses and made his throat ache in sympathy.

"I should have done things so differently," she said between sobs.

He recognized then a major source of her pain. Guilt. Did she blame herself for her sister's death? *The police said I'd been speeding,* she'd said. He remembered the reckless way she'd always driven. He'd been afraid to allow Arianne in the car with her.

A sudden concern shot through his gut, and he whispered hoarsely into her hair, "Was Arianne in the car with you?"

"No, no." She shook her head against his chest. "Thank God, no."

The question served to curtail her weeping, and soon she lay still in his arms. After a moment, though, she stiffened and drew back far enough to peer at him. He detected embarrassment in her expression. "I'm sorry I...cried all over you. I didn't mean to break down like that. I—"

"It's okay, *chèr'.*" He ran a hand through her silky hair; brushed a wayward strand back from her face. "If I lost one of my sisters, I'd break down, too. I'd be devastated."

She relaxed somewhat, and rested her head on his arm to maintain their eye contact. Her embarrassment, so uncharacteristic, reminded him of how much she'd changed, and the fact that she didn't know him. For all intents and purposes, he was holding a stranger. Why did that idea appeal to him? He wasn't sure, but he suddenly wanted to know everything about her.

"How much of your life have you forgotten?"

"That's hard to say," she replied slowly. "I remember my childhood, and most of my adulthood. I guess I've lost whatever happened in the past couple of years. I don't remember anything about you, our marriage or our break-up. I remember very little about Arianne's birth, other than the fact she's mine."

"In other words, the only part of your life that you've blocked out is the time you spent with me." Ridiculous to feel hurt over that.

"No!" But after reconsidering, she allowed, "Well, maybe. But I didn't *purposely* block it out. At least, I don't think I did. Unless—" she searched his eyes with something like suspicion "—I had some *reason* to want to forget it."

He scowled. Was she trying to blame *him* for her memory loss? "If you had a reason, it was probably all the trouble you got yourself into." The statement brought to mind other topics they needed to address. "Have you stopped drinking and gambling altogether?"

"Yes."

Guilt over her sister's death would have been a strong motivating factor. "That couldn't have been easy."

Her expression intensified, but she didn't comment, and he couldn't read her emotions. She clearly wasn't ready to discuss her battle with the addictions. He thought about the struggle she must have gone through, and guilt nipped at him. He'd given up on her. Written her off as hopeless. But how could he have done otherwise? He'd tried to force her into a treatment center, but she'd refused to cooperate. Shortly after, she'd filed for divorce. He'd been able to do little else than watch her race down the road to ruin, taking Arianne along for the ride.

"Are you seeing a doctor about your memory loss?" he asked.

"Yes."

"A good one?"

"My doctor is one of the best."

"If you need help with medical bills, send them to me." A crazy offer. He had little cash to spare. But he wouldn't turn his back on her. She was, after all, the mother of his child. Which made her family. "I'll help you all I can."

Her brows lifted in clear surprise at the offer. "Thank you. That's very kind. But I'm doing fine."

Kind? She considered an offer of money from him "kind"…and turned it down? She'd always considered money from him her due—massive amounts of it—even after their separation. Obviously she'd come to some major realizations after her sister's death. Perhaps the change in her also had to do with her abstinence from alcohol. He'd known alcoholics whose twelve-step programs had brought about miraculous transformations.

Rather than dwell on her personality changes, though, he opted to focus on the money issue. His curiosity was strong. "How are you 'doing fine'? You never had money before."

She looked uncomfortable with his question. "My sister left me everything she had." Grief flashed in her eyes again, but she forced a slight smile and changed the subject. "You said you have sisters. I'm assuming that means more than one. How many?"

"Three. No brothers. Two brothers-in-law. Lots of cousins, nieces, nephews." Strange, to be telling her basic facts about his family, when she'd spent a good deal of time with them.

Wistfully, she murmured, "Having a big family must be wonderful."

Wonderful? She had come to despise his family. With good reason. They despised her. He rather liked the idea that she'd forgotten that. "Do you have any other relatives you neglected to mention?"

"No. All I have now is Arianne." A potent mix of anxiety and maternal love shone so clearly in her expression that his breath caught. A vision of her materialized in his head—her mouth curved in the gentle smile he'd noticed on her lately and his daughter cuddled on her lap, pointing a stubby baby finger at pictures in a book.

He forced the cozy picture from his mind. He couldn't go there. Couldn't think about her and Arianne. Too many confusing issues rushed at him at once. He needed time to reflect on the drastic way the situation had changed, and to determine the ways that it hadn't.

Intent on turning the conversation away from their daughter, he asked, "Was your sister older or younger than you?"

An odd little light that resembled humor leaped into her eyes. "A little younger."

Curious now, he probed, "What was she like?"

"Charming. Lively. Fun." She lapsed into an unfocused stare, as if fondly picturing her sibling. "People said we resembled each other, but—" she made a little moue and shook her head "—she was much prettier than me."

"Prettier. I can't imagine that." And he realized it was true. He'd always thought she was physically beautiful, but now, with her new vulnerability and classy softness—and an inner serenity and emotional depth she'd always been lacking—he simply *could not* imagine a woman more gorgeous.

It clearly had been the wrong thing to admit. She blushed with sudden self-consciousness and shifted her gaze away from him. Another change, it seemed. She'd always been hungry for compliments, as if her self-worth depended on them. "I...I guess I should go in now."

As she made a move to free herself from his arms, he tightened his embrace. She glanced at him in surprise.

"Not yet." He wasn't quite ready for the closeness to end. And he had more questions. Important questions. Maybe...too important? Ruthlessly ignoring his sudden qualms, he continued, "The house where you're living. Whose is it?"

She hesitated, and he suspected his first impression had been correct. She was living with a man. Mitch felt his muscles subtly clench as he waited to hear her say it.

"It's mine." When he continued to stare at her, silently demanding an explanation, she added, "It belonged to Kate."

"Kate?" He frowned. Hadn't that been the alias she'd used?

"My sister."

"Your sister! 'Kate Jones' was your sister's name?"

She nodded, and he almost laughed at Chuck's misinterpretation of the facts. She hadn't been living under an alias, after all. The neighbor who had reported seeing Camryn at the house had simply been confused between the two sisters when he'd told Chuck she went by the name of "Kate Jones." No wonder Chuck had seemed puzzled over the computer report. Apparently, Camryn had been driving Kate's car when the accident occurred.

Mystery solved. He was damn glad. He'd been bothered by her alias. It smacked of intricate, long-term plans to evade him. Now, though, it appeared she'd simply taken the baby to her sister's house. Maybe she would have returned in a few days if the accident hadn't erased her memory of him...and killed her sister.

"So, the piano and leather-bound books had been hers?"

"Yes."

Again, he felt relieved. "Then I'm sorry for my comments about...well, you taking money from some guy. I was out of line."

"Apology accepted."

He peered at her. "*Is* there...some guy?"

A flush tinted her cheeks. "No."

The degree of relief he felt at her answer set off an inner alarm. Why should he care whether she was romantically involved with someone? Their marriage was just a bothersome technicality now. She could date whomever she chose. Unless, of course, her choice of companions adversely affected Arianne.

That was the basis of his concern, he assured himself. He had every right to ask about the men in her life. But he had no business lying here with her. Holding her. Enjoying her softness, her womanly scent...and the incredible changes in her personality.

It damn sure wouldn't do. The last thing he needed was to be attracted to Camryn again. The first time had been a crazy, impulsive mistake. Though he'd met her less than two years ago, he'd been ages younger. A thousand times more foolish. The madness itself hadn't lasted long. Barely beyond their first few nights. He was still paying the price, though. He couldn't afford to forget that.

"We should go in." He propped himself up on an

elbow and faced windward. "The wind is shifting. A norther's blowing in." He withdrew his arm from around her. "I feel rain on the way."

"You *feel* it?" She cast him a doubtful glance.

He merely smiled. She'd see soon enough. As they sat up and she moved away from him, he immediately missed the warmth of holding her. Which wasn't good. It really, really wasn't.

"Maybe you should listen to weather forecasts," she suggested. "Might be helpful."

If anyone else had said it, he'd swear they were being sarcastic. She, however, seemed perfectly earnest. He managed not to laugh. "Of course I listen to weather forecasts. Couldn't survive out here very long without 'em. But you can't count on the weatherman to predict every little squall that kicks up over the Gulf."

"So, you count on your intuition?"

"Not intuition. More of a taste in the air when rain is headed our way. A smell, a feel." He shrugged. "Sometimes a crosswind will blow the rain clouds in another direction, though." He stood up, held out a hand and helped her to her feet. "No one always knows what Mother Nature will do. Just when you think you might, she'll spring one of her grand surprises."

"The sky *is* growing gray," she murmured, sounding disappointed by that fact. "Guess we won't see a spectacular sunset."

"Not tonight." After tossing the blanket over his arm, he took hold of her elbow and ushered her to the ladder that descended from the roof. He was glad the sun would be sinking behind a safe gray cover of clouds. Radiant sunsets had a way of igniting painful yearnings. Those yearnings always had to do with a woman he'd never met; the woman who was meant for him. The one with whom he'd share sunsets in an intensely personal way.

It was the same yearning he'd felt when he'd seen Camryn after her shower this morning.

In his present state of unrest, he didn't think he could handle the feeling of emptiness that always followed the yearning.

SHE SHOULDN'T HAVE doubted him. Twenty minutes later, while Kate indulged in a hot, freshwater shower— a luxury she still wasn't sure how Mitch had managed to provide—she noticed she was having difficulty standing upright beneath the spray. The rocking of the boat pitched her to one side of the narrow stall, then to the other, like a pinball in an arcade game.

Thunder pealed in the nearby distance, and a knock shook the bathroom door. "Hey, Cam. Mitch said to get outta da water," yelled Remy. "You ain't supposed to shower in a storm."

Storm. She didn't like the sound of that. She preferred the way Mitch had put it: "rain." Anxiety rooted in her gut.

"Dere might be lightning," Remy added.

Quickly she rinsed the shampoo out of her eyes, climbed out of the shower and dried off, managing to do so only by bracing her hands, elbows and hips against various walls and surfaces as she awkwardly maneuvered the towel. She'd barely finished dressing for the night in a soft, old, floor-length beach shirt when rain began to drum fiercely on the roof.

By the time she left the head to make her way to the captain's quarters, she could barely walk through the wildly tilting rooms, and her heart was hammering. The boat tipped onto one side, slanting the floor steeply, then dropped like a teeter-totter to slant in the opposite direction. Concentrating on remaining reasonably calm, Kate held on to doorknobs, table edges and any surface she could grab.

Remy, she noticed, was pulling shut the windows in the crew's quarters against blustery gusts of rain. In the galley, meanwhile, a coffee mug leaped off the countertop, then a saltshaker jumped from the table, both to roll wildly with ashtrays and cigarettes on the floor. A cabinet door that hadn't been latched now swung on its hinges and banged to the rhythm of the sea, while the canned goods inside slid around and jammed against the inner guardrails. Dishwater sloshed out of the stainless-steel sink. The coffeepot had tipped over on the stove's back burner and now rattled against the metal guards that held it in place.

The chaos added to her sense of impending disaster. Determined to help in the crisis they were surely facing, Kate chased the rolling ashtrays and mugs, latched the cabinet door, drained the dishwater remaining in the sink and struggled to secure every item she could, while her stomach roiled in protest at the motion. By the outside starboard light, she saw Darryl pass by the galley window, his dark, thinning hair matted to his head in a downpour of rain as he strode toward the stern. To "batten down the hatches," Kate would bet.

The sound of rain grew louder, the wind wilder, and her anxiety spiked. She had to see Mitch; had to know how he was reacting, and if she could possibly help. Growing dizzy and disoriented because of the wildly pitching floor and walls, she climbed and slid and treaded through the captain's quarters to the doorway of the wheelhouse, where she stopped and braced herself against the jamb.

Mitch stood at the helm, fighting the wheel, forcing the boat to quarter the waves. He looked intent on his task, but not particularly perturbed. The very sight of him decreased her anxiety, yet somehow promoted a sense of dark excitement within her.

His hair, shirt and jeans were soaking wet. He'd clearly been out in the weather. His hair curled against his neck, and the thin cotton of his dark shirt clung to muscles that bulged and flexed across his back and shoulders with every forceful turn of the wheel. The urge struck her to wrap her arms around his lean waist, press her breasts to his powerful back...and feel those muscles work against her....

Incredulous that she could think of a thing like that in the midst of such drama—and thoroughly dismayed by the impulse itself—she forced her attention away from that well-honed body, and peered through the windshield at the darkness and driving rain. From her vantage point near the helm, she clearly saw the boat sail high over cresting waves, then slide down on a sideways angle to take on the next oncoming wall of water.

She should, by all rights, have been terrified. It seemed that some great, angry beast from the edge of the world had pounced upon them in the murky darkness, howling and bellowing in rage, slashing them with whips of rain, shaking and slinging the boat in vengeful fury. She should, by all rights, be praying.

"You okay, *chèr*?"

She met Mitch's eyes in the navigational mirror, and an odd connection coursed between them. A silent but powerful sharing. Like ancient sea-goers, they were locked in battle with the beast, fighting for their lives, their survival depending on one wooden boat and the skill of their captain. She could well imagine tomorrow's headlines: Shrimp Boat Lost in Storm. Search for Survivors Continues. Yet, exhilaration pumped through her veins, and she swore Mitch felt it, too. The sight of him at the wheel, the sound and fury of the storm, the taste of danger, sent a thrill racing along her spine and brought her alive in a way she'd never felt before.

She didn't answer his question.

He acknowledged her reply anyway. Not with a smile or a nod, but the mere suggestion of both. She felt that she'd been validated. And he, looking vibrantly alive, strong and competent, focused his attention on the gleaming oak wheel and forced the mutinous vessel to do his bidding.

Oh, my! She'd been masquerading as Camryn for too long. What was she doing here, being tossed and taunted by an angry sea—she, Kate Jones, professor of history; the quintessential homebody; the staid, boring, shy one of the Jones twins?

Riding out the storm, that was what…with a fearless captain at the helm who made her heart race. Not a good thing, that. But, for the moment, thrilling.

The storm raged on, and the wet, bedraggled crew gradually made their way to the wheelhouse. Bracing themselves in casual poses on either side of Mitch, they smoked cigarettes, swilled bottles of cola and talked of their confrontations with waterspouts and hurricanes. The three of them laughed, joked and watched the radar screen, while Mitch continued to calmly, ceaselessly, fight the wheel. She sensed an underlying tension beneath their nonchalance—a palpable awareness of danger, a readiness to act—but that only added spice to the moment.

And though Kate's anxiety over the storm hadn't entirely left her, she marveled at their exploits, interjected questions and exclaimed in heartfelt awe. She felt a part of them; as if, in the face of danger, they'd forgotten their differences and embraced her.

All too soon, the adventure drew to a close. They'd "run behind an island," as Mitch put it, to anchor down for the night. She didn't even have time to ask which island they'd run behind. Mitch told Darryl to "drop the hook," and he strode happily out onto the rain-battered bow. Kate wanted to watch him drop the hook, but Mitch ordered her to stay inside.

With a groan, a clang and a slight jerking of the boat, the anchor was, apparently, dropped. Mitch shifted a lever at the control board. The boat surged backward, and the motor cut off.

And the silence was stunning. She'd grown so used to the rumbling and vibration beneath her feet that she had ceased to hear it. She noted its absence immediately. The whine of the wind and drumming of the rain sounded infinitely gentler now, reminding her of cozy nights in a beach cabin rather than a battle with the sea. The motion of the waves had drastically lessened, too. Anchored within the protection of an island, the *Lady Jeanette* bobbed on her tether, slowly rocking like a huge wooden cradle, complete with creaks and groans.

The deckhands didn't return to the wheelhouse. They trekked down the exterior walkways, presumably to the crew's quarters.

Mitch switched off various electronics, leaving the radio on. He faced Kate, looking unquestionably tired after his eventful turn at the wheel. With a brief, casual nod toward the captain's quarters, he murmured, "Let's turn in."

And she realized with a walloping thud of her heart

that she'd forgotten to speak with him about a matter of vital importance. *Bedtime.*

Without another glance at her, he walked past into the captain's quarters, tugging his wet shirt out of the waistband of his jeans. Before Kate had managed to couch her protest in coherent terms, he pulled the shirt over his head and shrugged free of it. The sight of his bare, tanned torso stopped her just inside the doorway. He really was a splendid specimen of masculinity.

But he had no right to undress in front of her. Or to assume that she'd allow him to sleep with her. The thought of falling into bed with him brought a dizzying surge of heat to her face. She hadn't shared a bed with a man for more than a year. And even then, by the time she'd agreed to a physical relationship, he'd seemed more of a dear friend than a lover. The few romances she'd permitted herself had all ended in lukewarm friendships.

Not that these reflections had anything whatsoever to do with her current predicament. She was not romantically involved with Mitch Devereaux, and there was no question of a physical relationship. There was no question of him sharing her bed, either, even in the most platonic way. Yet here he was, hanging his wet shirt on a hook at the far end of the room.

Clearly he'd slept with her last night…and now took his right to do so for granted. She had to disabuse him of that notion!

As he began to unbuckle the belt at his lean waist, she crossed the distance between them in two long strides, grabbed his hands and forced them to a standstill. "Mitch, what in heaven's name do you think you're doing?" She wished she didn't sound quite so breathless.

His gaze narrowed, as if she were speaking an incomprehensible language. "I'm taking off these wet clothes," he explained slowly, "and going to bed."

The warm breath that accompanied his words feathered against her face, and she realized she was standing much too close to him, with her hands trapping his larger, stronger ones against his tautly muscled abdomen. The salty, masculine scent of his skin and hair reminded her of how he'd held her against him, cradled her in his arms, as she'd wept over her sister's death. How he'd stroked her back, her hair. Murmured soothing words. Offered to help her with bills, though she knew he was struggling financially.

He alone, out of everyone who had offered comfort, had managed to loosen the stranglehold of grief from around her heart, if only for a while.

Don't read too much into it. A few gently spoken words in that deep, Cajun-warm voice and a sympathetic squeeze from his big, rugged body didn't mean Camryn had outright *lied* about his abuse, or that he'd be a good, loving father to Arianne. Kate couldn't allow herself to jump to conclusions.

Just as she couldn't allow him to sleep with her.

But he'd clearly stated his intentions of *taking off his clothes and going to bed.*

Abruptly she released his hands and stepped back from his blood-warming nearness. "I don't mind you taking off your wet clothes," she said, striving to rise above her growing sense of panic and strike just the right note between amiability and assertiveness, "as long as it's not in front of me."

He shrugged, and the fluid movement of his broad shoulders sent sensual awareness through her. "I've got no problem with that. I'll change clothes in the other room.'' He opened a drawer beneath the chart table and grabbed fresh underwear.

"Good,'' she replied with an approving nod. "That leaves only one more question.'' She hoped he couldn't hear the slight quaver in her voice. "Which bed are you planning to sleep in?''

He raised his tawny brows in surprise, then nodded toward the only bed in the room. "Mine.''

Nerves tingled all along her spine and down the length of her extremities. "And, um…which bed will *I* sleep in?''

"Same one.''

Her heart kicked wildly in her chest. "I won't sleep in the same bed with you!'' So much for striking the right note. Panic had clearly won out. "For one thing, we're divorced. Maybe not technically, but in every other way. And for another, *I don't know you.* I have only your word for it that we were ever married, or that I've ever even met you before yesterday.''

He shifted his weight onto one cocked hip, ran a hand through his tousled hair and let out a weary breath. "Come on, Cam. I've been up since five-thirty this morning, and I got very little sleep the night before. I'm tired to the bone. I'll wear something to bed, if it'll make you feel better, but—''

"Wear something to bed!'' She gaped at him, taken aback. *Had he worn anything last night?* Flustered by the images flooding her mind, she huffed, "Of *course* you'll wear something to bed. B-but, that's not to say you'll wear it in bed *with me.*'' Heat flared in her face. "I mean…you can't expect me to sleep with a stranger!''

He lifted a shoulder. "Never seemed to bother you before.''

She gasped and glared at him, openmouthed at his audacity, her hands clenching into fists.

Watching her anger rise like mercury on a Delta summer day, Mitch instantly regretted his comment. Though, to be fair, it was true. The "old Camryn" hadn't hesitated to sleep with him the first night they'd met. She wouldn't have hesitated after their separation, either. He'd been the one to keep their relationship nonsexual. It hadn't taken him long to realize she used seduction as leverage to get whatever she wanted. Even before she'd actually moved out of his house, he'd steered clear of sexual involvement with her.

This "new Camryn" obviously didn't remember the times he'd turned her down, though, and now believed *he* was out to seduce *her*. He'd laugh at the irony of it if he wasn't so damn tired. She'd probably scratch his eyes out if he laughed just now, anyway.

"I'm sorry," he offered, impressed that she'd held her anger this long without bursting into rage. "I shouldn't have said what I did. Guess I wasn't giving you credit for how much you've changed." He slanted her an apologetic smile, trying not to notice how her heavy blond hair now glistened from her freshwater shower, and how her curves looked soft, round and too damn touchable beneath a gray, floor-length shift that looked like an oversize T-shirt.

He barely heard her tight-lipped murmur of "Apology accepted" as he perused her choice of nightclothes. Simple. Unassuming. Comfortable, probably. Not in the least bit revealing...unless, of course, you counted the way the thin cotton hugged her bottom, thighs and breasts.

Not that he cared what she wore to bed. He had every intention of keeping his hands to himself, just as he had for the few brief hours he'd lain beside her last night.

She'd been passed out cold, and he'd slept in utter exhaustion.

"Does your apology mean you'll find another place to sleep?" she inquired, drawing his attention to her face as she lofted a golden brow at him. "Or, at least, arrange one for me?"

He lofted a brow right back at her, his attention now caught by the challenge she presented with her suddenly queenlike demeanor. One false move, and she'd have his head. Why did that charm him so? Why did that make him long to rattle her? "As much as I'd love to honor your new sensibilities, Ms. Jones, ma'am," he softly replied, tilting his face to parallel hers, "there's no way I can."

"Oh?"

Just that. *Oh.* But spoken in a tone of authority that would have set many a man to stammering. "Since I sense a disturbing lack of faith in my integrity—" he presented his arm to her "—I'll show you the difficulty we're facing."

With a slight hesitation and clear wariness, she placed her hand on his arm in precisely the right position for a formal stroll with a uniformed captain of a cruise ship. He, in his shirtless state, his belt unbuckled and his face in dire need of a shave, escorted her with stately grace to the crew's quarters.

Banging on the door, he yelled, "Get decent in there, you barbarians. The queen's entourage is coming through."

An annoyed mutter and a curious exclamation in Remy's version of French sounded from within the room before a light switched on.

Mitch pushed open the door and ushered Camryn inside. Darryl frowned at them from his bunk on one side

of the cramped quarters, and Remy grinned from his on
the other side. They'd both been gentlemanly enough to
cover themselves with sheets, but Her Majesty looked
mightily embarrassed, anyway.

Which pleased Mitch to no end. "See anywhere in
here you want to sleep, *chèr'?*"

Rosy color flooded her face. As was true with every
chamber in the cabin, there wasn't even enough floor
space to accommodate a child, let alone an adult. Remy
gallantly offered to make room for her in his twin-size
bed. Darryl snorted. Camryn pivoted and marched out
of the narrow, crowded room without comment.

Mitch smiled, shrugged at his crew, shut their door
and followed her. Slipping a firm hand beneath her elbow, he stopped her in the galley. "If you'll notice, the
benches at this booth and the table itself are a little too
short for an adult to comfortably lie on. And the floor is
made up of two narrow, intersecting walkways that
could use a good scrubbing. See anywhere you want to
sleep yet?"

"Not yet."

"Well, then...I could show you the wheelhouse,
which barely has room to walk through, let alone bunk
in. Then there's the back deck, the bow, the hold, the
engine room and the roof."

"There's got to be some place that either you or I
could spread out a pillow and blanket," she insisted, her
frustration evident.

"You mean, like, brave the rain and sleep outside?
Or ignore the fumes in the engine room, or the ice in
the hold?"

"No, of course not, but—"

"But, nothing." His patience was short. She seriously
objected to sleeping with him, and he found himself se-

riously bothered by that. "I'm captain of this vessel, and I sleep in the captain's quarters—three steps away from the radio and the controls. You're a passenger on this vessel, and you'll sleep where I know you're safe."

Abandoning her elbow in favor of her slender shoulders, he steered her to the captain's quarters and parked her beside the bed. "Right there, on the far side, nearest the wall, is your bunk. Mine is *here*." He indicated the near side of the bed. With a slash of his hand, he then indicated an invisible line down its center. "You stay on your half, I'll stay on mine."

She tossed him a cool glance that spoke eloquently of her disdain. Her silken cloud of hair, meanwhile, brushed across his hands at her shoulders and sent a delicate orange-and-flowers scent wafting his way. Raising her chin to a haughty angle, she kicked off her sandals, tore back the bedcovers and climbed in. Scooting over as close to the wall as humanly possible, she presented him with her back and covered herself with the sheet, leaving only her hair to spill out in a golden wave across the pillow.

He allowed himself a small, rueful smile as he stripped out of his wet clothes, pulled on a dry pair of briefs and settled down onto *his* side of the bed.

His smile didn't last long, though. The bed wasn't big enough for a person his size to share without edging up fairly close to the other occupant. He'd been lucky to find a shrimp boat with a bed larger than a twin. This one wasn't as wide as a regular full bed, though. Keeping strictly to his side would be difficult.

Aggravating the situation was the slow roll of the boat. It made it damn near impossible to stop from nudging up against her. She *had* to be having the same problem, keeping her back stiff and straight in her effort not to touch him.

Neither of them made a sound or moved as much as an eyelid. Rain drummed steadily on the roof. The distant murmur of the surf reached them from the nearby island, and faraway thunder resonated occasionally.

But inside, the silence grew heavier. She lay near enough for him to feel her body heat down the entire length of him. For her personal scent to gradually emerge from beneath the delicate fragrance of her shampoo—the subtle, natural lure of woman. Never before had her scent evoked such hot, breathless tension in him. The effort not to touch her, not to pull her close and fill his senses, only succeeded in reminding him of how she'd looked today, so sweet and soft and pretty. How she'd cried her heart out, and how he'd held her.

What she'd felt like in his arms. *So damn right.*

He swallowed hard. Shut his eyes. Tried like hell to fall asleep. *He didn't want to want her.*

It seemed that he eventually slept. Morning dawned long before he was ready to stir from a deep slumber and lush, hazy dreams. Dreams of silk, and heat, and woman. Of velvet flesh, rounded curves, needful moans. Sweat. Friction. Need.

Her. The One.

He woke with a hoarse groan in his throat. She, with ragged breaths. And in that first instant of awakening, halfway between the dream world and full consciousness, they opened heavy-lidded eyes and met each other in dazed stares of stark, hot longing.

The reason slowly dawned. They were locked in a tight, heart-to-heart embrace...limbs intertwined, hands questing...bodies writhing together in slow, sensual accord.

CHAPTER NINE

SHE COULDN'T FACE HIM. Never, ever again. She'd rather jump overboard and swim a hundred miles than look even one more time into his eyes. His intensely green, intensely sensual eyes, liberally flecked with gold. *Hot* gold. Molten, like lava. Molten, like his body, his touch.

Kate bit her lip to keep from groaning out loud. She should have opted to sleep on the galley table!

Scrambling eggs in a skillet as if her life depended on it—a job Remy hadn't even tried to keep from her this morning—Kate struggled not to think about what had happened with Mitch. And she couldn't even blame him for it. Oh, no…she'd been more than willing. Asleep for the most part, and unduly influenced by lurid dreams, but undeniably willing. He'd been asleep, too. Or at least, not fully awake. She'd seen awareness flood his gaze at the exact time she'd snapped to full consciousness. Good heavens, if they hadn't come to their senses when they had, she probably would have made love to him!

They'd been precious close to it already. She'd been so involved in her sweet, hot dream of strong arms holding her, intimate caresses igniting her blood, feverish moans, both hers and his…dreams more vivid and provocative than any *real* experience she'd ever had. She'd savored his muscular body with slow, bold caresses, locked her legs around his sleek hips, twined her arms around his massive shoulders and given herself over to pleasure.

And to Mitch. As much as she wished she could deny it, her dream lover *had* been Mitch.

By the time she'd awakened and come to her senses, her body was arched and undulating with his. Her nightshirt had ridden high above her thighs, and he'd splayed his hand across her bottom, holding her fast, while his incredible hardness rocked against her. The pleasure had been intense. The very memory shot spears of hot response through her feminine core.

If not for the thin barrier of her panties—those plain cotton briefs he'd mocked just days ago—he would have surged inside her.

Deep, deep, inside.

Heat coursed through her veins, and she drew in a long, cooling breath. How could she have gotten so carried away? He was *her sister's husband*. The fact that her sister was no longer alive did not excuse Kate's wanting him.

And, worse yet, he believed her to be Camryn. Not only was she hiding the fact that his wife had died, but she'd taken her place in bed with him. Perhaps not intentionally, but the result was the same. Her deception had gone to a deeper, more unforgivable level.

What should she do? Confess?

But she hadn't yet achieved the most important goal of her life—securing Arianne's future. She still didn't know if he had abused Camryn or how he would treat his daughter. She hadn't seen his home, his community or the people who would keep the baby while he was out to sea. If she confessed, the best she could hope for was an outsider's glimpse, if they'd allow her even that much. As Camryn, she hoped her tentative truce with Mitch would yield her an inside view.

And if she discovered that he was abusive, or that his care of Arianne would harm her in any way, she'd take the baby and run. She'd work on the legal difficulties later, from a safe distance, where Mitch and his family would never find them.

The thought struck a hollow chord within her. She really didn't relish hurting him. But Arianne had to come first. Kate could not allow sexual desire for a handsome man to influence her judgment, or get in the way of her plans. She couldn't allow herself to fall victim to his charms, perhaps as Camryn had.

The last thing she needed was a broken heart. And something told her that she could easily lose her heart to Mitch Devereaux.

As she lifted the skillet and scooped the steaming scrambled eggs onto a platter, Remy sauntered into the sunny galley with his usual pleasant grin and a hint of caution in his expression. She knew she hadn't been acting herself this morning. She hadn't spoken much to anyone, and was focused too intently on the tasks she'd stubbornly usurped in the galley. With an air of watchfulness that one might accord a quiet but potentially dangerous bear, Remy said, "Mitch wants you."

She nearly dropped the skillet. *Mitch wants you.* How arousing was *that?* Was it equally obvious she wanted him, too?

"In da wheelhouse," Remy added, with a sideways nod in that direction.

Kate set the skillet onto the stove and reached for her mug of coffee with a hand that trembled. When a simple statement infused her with erotic thoughts, it was time to jump ship. Too bad she hadn't done so before they'd pulled anchor this morning. A wistful glance through the open doorway showed miles of choppy blue-gray water between her and the island they'd anchored near last night. Mitch had lost no time in gunning the *Lady Jeanette* into a seaward course again.

So much for swimming to shore.

She supposed she'd have to talk with him.

They hadn't spoken a single word to each other this morning yet. When full consciousness had dawned on them, they'd sprung apart in mutual alarm. Or, more precisely, untangled themselves from each other and leaped into separate courses of action. She'd grabbed an armful of clothes, changed in the bathroom and headed for the back deck, where she'd walked circles around the hatch cover and nearly hyperventilated.

Mitch had closeted himself in the wheelhouse.

And now he wanted her. To *see* her, that was. And talk, probably. Her embarrassment flared. She didn't want to acknowledge her wildly hot response in bed, or to analyze that response too closely. Because even though the incident had mortified her, it had also illuminated a disturbing truth about herself.

Despite her hard-earned success over her twenty-eight years of life and her relatively enjoyable standard of living, she hadn't known passion, real passion, until he'd ignited it in her.

MITCH SET the auto-pilot on a course through the Mississippi barrier islands, about twelve miles south of the coastline, and settled back in his chair. He knew the route without glancing at the markers, the loran or his chart. From a lifetime of shrimping these waters, he recognized the pattern produced by the depth recorder—the hills, valleys and plateaus of the bottom.

Ironic, that he knew the Gulf's bottom better than he'd known what lay beneath his wife's surface. He'd believed she had little interest in anything beyond self-gratification. To learn that he'd been wrong was as shocking as finding a lost continent in his favorite fishing hole.

The surprises just kept on coming. He'd called her in to the wheelhouse to apologize for this morning's misunderstanding. He preferred to think of it by that term rather than an utter breakdown of his self-control. As of yet, though, she hadn't given him a chance to talk about it.

In fact, from the moment she'd nervously perched in the seat beside him, she'd been chitchatting about everything *but* the fact that they'd woken in each other's arms. Instinctively he sensed her desire to avoid the subject. That in itself was a change. The old Camryn would have been smug to think she'd posed such an irresistible temptation that he'd broken his own code of ethics, even if he hadn't been exactly conscious at the time.

The old Camryn was nowhere in sight. *Why not?*

Her conversation baffled him more. After their first few dates, during which they'd concentrated solely on fun and sex, Mitch had found it difficult to talk for any length of time with her. Beyond their common love of a good party, their interests had been too different.

Now, however, she hit on topics that naturally stirred his interest and effortlessly held it. She asked about the electronics in the wheelhouse, and he showed her how to read the radar, loran and depth recorder. She excitedly pointed to a toucan that had landed on the bow with an orange tag on its leg, and spoke of bird-tracking projects she'd read about.

"You won't find more species of birds in one place

than in southern Louisiana," he told her. He couldn't help interjecting a little Cajun humor, and let a casual comment drop. "Yeah, we Cajuns might be known for poaching in the swamps, but we always try to safeguard those protected species. One time my cousin Baptiste accidentally shot a falcon, and he couldn't sleep for weeks."

"A falcon! Oh, my. I don't blame him for feeling terrible."

Mitch nodded in absent agreement. After a strategic pause, he mused, "I'd have thought a falcon would taste like dove, or duck, but it doesn't."

Now, that *really* caught her interest, and she frowned at him in both incredulity and mild disapproval. "You cooked the falcon and ate it?"

He shrugged, as if reluctant to own up to it.

A moment later, she went for the bait. "Well, what did it taste like?"

"Oh, I'd say a cross between a bald eagle and a whooping crane."

Her eyes widened; her jaw dropped. After a horrified stare, though, she twisted her mouth with wry humor. "I almost believed you!" Dramatically she swatted his shoulder.

He laughed. She grumbled. And an odd sense of companionship embraced them. They went on to talk about the wind, the tide and the moon and as he described how each affected the creatures of the sea, she listened, spellbound.

When and why had she developed a fascination for topics that had once bored her silly?

And now, as they passed Ship Island, she turned to him in excitement and talked about its role in the Civil War—a topic that had once glazed her eyes over.

"These barrier islands were used by pirates, too," she was saying, "and all kinds of dangerous smugglers. One of the islands was discovered to have piles of human skeletons. A Frenchman originally named it 'Massacre Island.' I wish I could remember which island it was...."

"Dauphin," he supplied.

She lifted her brows, clearly surprised that he'd known.

"My secret vice," he admitted. "When it comes to the history of the Gulf region, I'm hooked. Spent half my boyhood looking for Jean Lafitte's treasure, or ammunition from the wars."

She stared at him in something akin to awe. At one time, that kind of response from her would require hitting a hefty jackpot. "Did you find any?" she asked in hushed, reverent tones.

"Some. Ammunition, that is."

Her interest was so palpable that the realization struck him harder than it had before: *he didn't know this woman.* The changes in her were too drastic, too profound, to be attributed to memory loss, or the addictions she'd kicked, or guilt over her sister's death.

He began to wonder if she was suffering from some rare split-personality disorder. Perhaps he should try to talk her into seeing a psychiatrist...if she wasn't already seeing one for her memory loss. But then, what if she reverted to the old Camryn? *Sacre Dieu,* he couldn't risk *that!*

Which left him torn over what to do with her. Would it be fair—or wise—to take her to the authorities and charge her with violating the custody order when she didn't remember doing so? But if he didn't put a scare into her, how did he know she wouldn't try to run with

Arianne again? They hadn't discussed their daughter since he'd learned of the accident. How could he talk about custody issues when he no longer knew what was right?

Was she suddenly trustworthy enough to share custody, or would she return to her old, dangerous ways?

Never had he been more confused.

A little while later, after Camryn had left the wheelhouse to watch Remy make oyster po'boy sandwiches for lunch, the marine operator put through a call that brought Mitch out of his chair in surprise. Chuck Arceneaux.

Locking the doors of the wheelhouse to ensure that the call wouldn't be overheard, Mitch greeted the investigator with, "This is a surprise, Chuck. Thought you'd be too busy swilling those rum drinks with little umbrellas to give me another thought."

"Yeah, well, I should be, but that computer report about Camryn's accident had me asking too many questions. I just couldn't leave it alone."

"Your wife'll have my head. Don't worry about the report until you're back from vacation. We'll have plenty of time to gather more facts before—"

"Are you sitting down, Mitch?"

"Sitting down?" He frowned. "Not at the moment. Why?"

"Sit down."

He blinked in puzzlement. Chuck had never been the dramatic type. "Sure you haven't been throwing back those umbrella drinks, Chuck? Maybe you're the one who needs to sit down."

"We've been wrong about a very basic assumption."

"Oh, yeah." The light went on in his head, and he let out a brief laugh. "You mean the mix-up over her so-called alias. I hate to steal your thunder, but she already told me about her sister.''

The silence over the radio was, for a moment, absolute. ''She told you?''

''Yeah. The old man who said that Camryn goes by the name of Kate Jones must have gotten the two sisters confused. Kate owned the house where we found Camryn staying, as well as the car she'd been driving at the time of the accident.'' Mitch paused. ''You know, don't you, that Kate was killed in the wreck?''

Again, a rather ominous silence. Then, ''Sit down, Mitch.''

Foreboding spiraled through his gut. ''Why?''

''There *was* a mix-up about the two sisters. You have that much right. But, uh…'' He hesitated, and went on in an oddly gentle tone that Mitch had never expected to hear from the hard-nosed investigator. ''According to the death records, Camryn was the one who died in that car crash. The gal you have on board your boat can only be Kate. Her identical twin.''

CHAPTER TEN

HER IDENTICAL TWIN. Not "the new Camryn." Not "the old Camryn" playing some kind of game. Literally, *not* figuratively, a stranger.

Her name was Kate.

And Camryn was dead.

Long after he'd disconnected from Chuck, Mitch remained in a stupor, staring blindly into the distance, his thoughts a tangle of disjointed realizations. At least he'd retained the presence of mind to turn the wheel over to Darryl. He'd then wandered out onto the bow, where he leaned against the bulwark, his face to the wind, and struggled to bring the true picture clearly into view.

Camryn had died in the wreck. The news brought surprising pain. Guilt, mostly, for not having found a way to stop her from self-destructing. He felt a sense of loss, too—not for a woman he loved, because he hadn't actually loved her, but for a woman he'd intimately known and cared about. For the mother of his child, despite the fact that she hadn't been a good mother. He had hoped she would eventually find her way to a safer, more fulfilling life and a satisfying sense of self.

Perhaps she finally had.

That reflection tightened his throat, so he pushed on to grapple with other facets of the situation. Apparently, Camryn had left Arianne with her sister. The story Kate had sobbingly told him yesterday probably held aspects of the truth. He believed her grief was real. And her guilt. Thinking back to what she'd said, he guessed she felt the same guilt he did. She hadn't tried hard enough to intervene before her sister had destroyed herself.

Why hadn't Kate contacted him immediately about Camryn's death and turned Arianne over to him? Maybe Camryn hadn't told Kate about him, or their joint-custody agreement. If Camryn had been determined to keep Arianne away from him, he could imagine her hiding that information from a sister who "butted in to her affairs," as Kate had put it. Camryn might have been afraid that Kate would do the right thing and contact him...or simply refuse to get involved with a kidnapping by giving her whatever help she'd wanted at the time. Money, probably. And a baby-sitter.

But he had no way to be certain that Kate hadn't known about him all along.

She clearly wasn't being truthful. Camryn might not have said much about him, but when he'd stormed her house Friday afternoon, he'd been damn clear that he wanted his daughter, Arianne. Why hadn't Kate explained that she was Camryn's identical twin, showed him identification and informed him of his wife's death? "I'm not Camryn," he vaguely remembered her saying. That had been her only attempt to tell him—just that one, unsubstantiated statement. She'd then allowed him to believe what he would.

She'd given him enough rope to hang himself. A disturbing thought. After forcing his way into her house and ignoring her claim that she wasn't Camryn, he'd handcuffed her and carried her off to his boat. Where he'd kept her for days. And forced her to go to bed with him. Nearly seduced her in her sleep.

Sacre Dieu. It was possible, he guessed, that he was

in big trouble. Had that been her intention from the start—to turn the tables on him and charge him with a crime, or *crimes,* as the case may be? His citizen's arrest didn't show in a very good light considering he'd nabbed an innocent party.

But why would Kate want to destroy him? Why had she kept up the impersonation and invented that story about memory loss? No wonder she'd passed all his tests with flying colors. She hadn't remembered anything about their time together because she wasn't Camryn. It was taking him some time to fully digest that incredible truth.

At least the drastic change in personality suddenly made sense.

But now he needed to know who this Kate Jones really was, and why she was pretending to be Camryn. He also couldn't forget the possibility that she'd accuse him of assault, false arrest, kidnapping and whatever other charges her attorney could level at him…then sue for custody of his daughter, her niece.

He had to stay one step ahead of her.

The first thing to do, of course, was call his attorney. He needed to be prepared for any charges Kate might file against him. He also wanted his lawyer to research the legal claims, if any, she might have on Arianne. He'd already asked Chuck to thoroughly investigate her background and her activities with Arianne.

To allow his lawyer and investigator more time, Mitch decided to delay his arrival at port. Now that he knew she wasn't Camryn, he couldn't hold her once they reached shore. She might turn *him* over to the authorities. Or, she might try to find a way to run with Arianne.

Maybe Kate was, in her own way, worse than Camryn. More devious and cunning. More dangerous in her subterfuge. Dangerous because she'd seemed so... perfect. Beautiful, poised, elegant. Intelligent. Sensitive. Honorable. *Desirable*.

Damn her. She'd been playing one hell of a game with him. He wondered what prize she was playing for. He was afraid he knew. *Arianne*. Why did Kate want her? Not that it mattered. No one would take his daughter away from him again.

The thought of Arianne filled him with keen longing to see her. With fair weather, he could make it home as early as tonight. As tempting as that was, he could *not* afford to ignore the threat posed by the woman pretending to be her mother.

Two could play at Kate's game of subterfuge. He was ready to rise to the challenge. Both his attorney and investigator would handle the matter with absolute discretion, he had no doubt. And he himself would tell no one else about her impersonation. He'd wait, watch and listen. When she made her final move—whatever that might be—he'd be prepared to outmaneuver her.

"Mitch?"

The sound of her low, smooth, feminine voice drew his gaze away from the sea. She stood a short distance aft, with one hand braced against the cabin's exterior wall, her hair pulled back at her nape and pretty blond tendrils trailing beside her face. She was wearing pleated denim shorts and a strappy, peach-colored top. She looked fresh, sweet and appealing as hell.

She wasn't Camryn. Her name was Kate. So damn hard to believe that two people could look that much alike. Yet the differences in the way they presented themselves had been plain from the start. She'd made a damn fool of him.

"Yeah?"

"Your po'boy sandwich is still waiting for you in the galley. Remy wants to know if you're going to eat it."

"Later. Ask him to put it up for me."

She nodded, smiled slightly and turned to leave. She then hesitated, and turned back to him. "Remy said that if the weather holds, we should be getting into port sometime late tonight. I was wondering..." She searched his face with clear anxiety. "Will you turn me in to the authorities immediately, or...may I see Arianne first?"

Aha. First clue to her intentions: she wanted to see Arianne. No surprise there. She'd been asking to speak with her all along. She'd cried when he'd taken the baby, and got choked up whenever she talked about her.

"I haven't made up my mind yet."

"I'd love to spend a little time with her. We've been apart for days now, and she's not used to being away from me."

He didn't answer.

Her full bottom lip tightened, and she tilted her chin in that subtly arrogant way that he'd come to think of as her "queen" look. "She's only a baby, with people she doesn't know. She'll be suffering from separation anxiety. At her age, it can be very acute. Traumatic, even."

He stiffened. His daughter didn't know his family because this woman had kept her from them. Had it been deliberate? "Separation anxiety," he repeated. "Meaning, she's missing her mama?"

She reflected for a while on that interpretation, as if afraid to agree; afraid of walking into some trap. With good reason. Her mama was dead. After a short pause, though, this sweet-faced, angel-eyed impostor nodded, her ponytail riffling in the breeze, the shiny blond tendrils dancing around her troubled face. "She's missing her mama, and she doesn't recognize anyone around her."

"By now, she'll be feeling right at home," he assured her, hoping it was true. Joey, his other sisters and his parents would see to it, he was sure. "Which is a good thing, considering we won't be pulling into port for another day or so."

"Another day or so! But Remy said—"

"Remy's not the captain. I am. And I—" he loomed closer, backing her against the cabin wall "—have plans for tonight. And maybe the night after that."

"Plans?" Her voice emerged in more of a whisper, with a throatier quality…or maybe he just imagined so. No doubt about the rising color in her face, though. Was she thinking about this morning—the way they'd hungered for each other; undulated to a slow, hot rhythm; fit together with sleek, utter perfection? "Wh-what kind of plans?"

He couldn't help a slight smile. *She wasn't Camryn.* And she'd gotten herself into this mess by pretending she was…*in his bed.* "You'll see."

There it was in her gaze—clear, bright anxiety. But beneath the anxiety, a smoky intensity grew. And distracted him. Stirred his blood. "About this morning," she whispered, her breath sweet and warm against his face. "It won't happen again. I'll sleep in the galley, if I have to. Or on the roof, or in the engine room."

"What's the matter, *chèr*? Don't trust yourself with me?"

Her lips parted in protest. "If there's anyone I don't trust, it's you. You promised to stay on your side of the bed."

"If I'm remembering right, we *were* on my side of the bed. Which means you were the one trespassing."

"Oh!" Incredulous, she glared at him. "Of all the arrogant, conceited, cockeyed ways of looking at things."

"Are you saying it isn't true? That you…didn't want me?"

The very air around them pulsed with tension while he waited for her answer. "I'm saying," she breathed, "that it won't happen again."

And because he *had* to touch her, he drew the back of one finger slowly down the curve of her face. Her eyes darkened. His body throbbed into hardness. And he knew he was in trouble. Because he wanted it to happen again. He wanted to hold her. Make her smolder in his arms.

Forcing his hand away from her beguiling soft skin, he turned and strode to the wheelhouse. He was glad, damn glad, when she didn't follow him. The last thing he needed was sexual involvement with another beautiful stranger; one with the same entrancing face and body as the last. This one would pose even more of a danger to him, though. She stirred him on too many levels.

He couldn't have her, and that was that.

Darryl glanced at him from his stance at the wheel, and after studying his face, said, "Close da doors, Mitch. We need to talk."

Curious and surprised, Mitch closed all three doors of the wheelhouse, noticing as he shut the starboard side that Kate was headed for the back deck. He'd been a damn fool to touch her.

"You think she's telling da truth, don't you?" Darryl charged.

Mitch faced him with uplifted brows. "Who, Camryn?"

"Of course. Who else? Just because she passed our tests, you're buying her 'lost memory' story."

"Chuck Arceneaux called me with some information. She *was* in an accident. A serious one, just like she told me."

"Yeah, well, dat don't mean she can't remember you. And even if she can't, she's still Camryn. Just because she's acting different don't mean she really changed. You need to get her to da judge. Charge her wit' kidnapping. Put a scare into her."

Mitch didn't answer. He wasn't sure if he'd take her to the authorities or not. That depended on what his attorney advised, and what his investigator learned about her.

Darryl shook his head in patent disgust. "I saw da way you were looking at her, and heard you laughing wit' her dis morning. Don't fall for her schemes, man. She messed up your life once. She'll do it again."

Though Darryl didn't know Kate's true identity, he still had a good point. She couldn't be trusted.

Mitch sauntered across the wheelhouse and clasped him on the shoulder. "Don't worry about me, Darryl. I'll be fine. Pay attention to your own woman problems."

"I don't have any."

"No?" Mitch pursed his lips in reflection, nodded, peered out to sea. "Good for you. By the way, Joey asked how you're making."

Darryl shot an intense glance at him. "She did? When?"

"Yesterday, when I called her."

Darryl pressed his lips into a thin white line and returned his attention to the sea. A while later, he asked in a softer voice, "She's probably passing a real good time wit' dat baby, eh?"

"Yeah, I imagine she is. She'd love another one of her own." Mitch watched his oldest, closest friend struggle to keep his face impassive. "She'll find herself another husband soon enough, I'd think," Mitch predicted. "Henri's been dead for over two years already. I imagine she's tired of being alone."

A slow flush climbed into Darryl's face, but he didn't answer, and Mitch decided to have mercy on him. He'd given him enough hell for one day. "Set the course for Main Pass Hole. I've been hearing talk on the radio. They're marking shrimp."

Darryl frowned in surprise. "Are you saying we're gonna drag tonight?"

"I'd say it's time we made some money, wouldn't you?"

Nodding in puzzled approval, Darryl set the course for Main Pass Hole. And Mitch silently congratulated himself on his foresight. No one would think it strange that they'd delayed their trip a day or two if the shrimp were running. And chances were, he'd find shrimp tonight. The moon, wind and temperature were all perfectly set for a good haul at Main Pass Hole.

As an added plus, they'd be dragging all night long. Which meant Ms. Kate Jones could have that bed all to herself. Both sides of it. And he wouldn't have to sweat it out, trying not to cross that line.

KATE WAS DEEPLY relieved when she learned the nature of Mitch's plans for the night: to shrimp. When he'd mentioned his nighttime "plans" earlier, he'd deliberately given her a very different impression—that he'd been referring to her. *Sleeping* with her.

She hadn't thought of much else since. Other than, perhaps, his hot, intimate stare, and the feel of his long, hard finger trailing down her face. How could one gaze and a simple touch have made her heart race, her insides simmer? But they had.

It wouldn't do. She couldn't get involved with a man who believed her to be someone else. And that was just one of the many complications she faced with Mitch Devereaux. If Camryn had been telling the truth about his mistreatment, Kate would have to betray him by taking his daughter. The farther she could keep from him—both physically and emotionally—the better off she would be.

Then again, how could she learn the truth about his character if she avoided him? And why, in her heart of hearts, did she now believe he wasn't capable of deliberately hurting a woman? Was her perception influenced by her attraction to him?

Never had she been more confused! A night of shrimping would be a very good thing.

"Drop the big ones."

Mitch's command boomed from the intercom, and Kate watched Darryl crank the enormous winch on the back deck. Moments later, the cables ground, the boat quivered and the nets descended from the outriggers to vanish beneath the waves. The engine groaned as if in protest, then the boat sped up to a steady, purposeful hum.

They were "under tow."

Kate couldn't wait to see what they would catch. For the past couple of hours, since late afternoon, they'd been dragging the try-net, a miniature version of the big nets, to see what they'd find. After several drags that turned up a few small shrimp but mostly "trash fish," as Remy called everything they wouldn't keep, Mitch changed his route.

The try-net then yielded ten shiny brownish-white shrimp, almost transparent, along with the trash fish. "Yie, yie! We marking 'em now, *chèr'*," Remy told her. "Nice ones, too. Twenty-six thirties, I'd say."

Even Darryl looked pleased at the count.

Forty-five minutes after they'd dropped the big nets, Mitch called, "Let's pick 'em up." Darryl worked the winch again, and Kate held her breath as huge, bulging nets were hoisted from the water to hang on either side of the boat.

Dressed in faded jeans, a drab T-shirt and heavy gloves, Mitch strode to the stern and tugged at ropes to draw the nets to the deck, the muscles in his neck, shoulders and arms flexing with every forceful pull. Once the heavy, dripping nets had swung over the stern, he gave two mighty tugs and leaped out of the way. An avalanche of wet, squirming creatures cascaded into a pile. A large, glistening seashell rolled across the deck. Angry blue crabs scuttled over a dented license plate, brandishing their pinchers for battle. Eels, squid, shrimp and fish jumped and wriggled in every direction.

Mitch opened the other net, and doubled the size of the pile. Remy dragged baskets, short-handled rakes and low stools into the midst of the catch, while Darryl's gloved hands quickly dove into the pile and snatched out the most valuable fish—flounder, mullet and redfish, mostly, which seemed to please him.

"Go inside," Mitch told Kate. "You'll get hurt out here." He then strode down the port-side walkway to the wheelhouse.

And the deckhands set out the nets again for another drag.

No way would Kate miss the most exciting part of a shrimping trip. Obstinately she remained on the back deck, watching Darryl and Remy rake through the living pile. "Culling," they called it. With nimble fingers, they picked out the shrimp, tossed them into baskets and pushed aside the "trash," which they periodically shoved overboard through scuttle holes in the rail.

In the waning light of evening, Kate watched the trash fish flutter to the sea, and noticed fins following the boat. Big fins. Many of them. And they weren't the curved, graceful ones she'd seen yesterday. These were, undoubtedly, sharks.

"Yeah, dey sharks," Remy replied to her exclamation. "Dey follow da boat, waiting for trash fish. Don't fall overboard, *chèr'*."

She made very certain not to.

She found herself a culling stool, a rake and rubber gloves, and helped the men sort through the pile. She wasn't as quick at picking up shrimp as they were, of course. The spiked heads of the squiggling shrimp tore into her thin latex gloves and hands, the blue crabs pinched her and fish flicked seawater into her eyes.

Kate noticed the puzzled glances Darryl threw her, as if he was surprised at her participation. Camryn obviously hadn't culled very often. Handling squirmy sea creatures wouldn't have been her cup of tea. Kate didn't let that stop her, though. Mitch seemed to have accepted the changes in her personality as a result of the accident and her abstinence from alcohol. She didn't care if Darryl accepted those changes or not.

"Ow!" she cried, smarting from another jab of a shrimp head. "Why don't we wear thicker gloves?"

"Thin is better to pick up da shrimp," Remy replied. "You have to feel what you're doing, or you squish 'em." He went on to warn her of creatures to avoid. Stingrays, saltwater cats, hot jelly and fire fish, to name a few. "Dere's all kind of danger in da sea, Cam. You have to take care."

Action, however, spoke louder than words. The third time they emptied the nets, a huge stingray hit the deck—as big as a kitchen table, and slinging a six-foot-long, razor-sharp barb. As the creature flapped its wings and scuttled, the men laughed and leaped out of its way, like bullfighters in a ring. Eventually they caught it up in ropes and hoisted the monster back into the sea.

Ah, the excitement of it! And the danger.

"How much damage did he do to da net?" Remy asked.

"Not much." Darryl inspected the twine. "At least, not *dis* time." He pulled out his knife and quickly repaired the hole, frowning in Mitch's direction as he headed back to the wheelhouse.

"Mitch don't let us cut off da stingers," Remy explained to Kate. "Says dey need 'em to defend against natural enemies. As if dey aren't *our* natural enemies."

Kate held back a smile; she supposed that anyone in charge of repairing nets would view the situation in a similar light. She felt a surge of approval for Mitch. He respected a stingray's need for defense despite the threat to his nets and loss of his catch. The realization oddly warmed her.

As darkness fell and deck lights illuminated their work area, the men continued dropping nets, dragging, hoisting them in and culling. Kate's back and arms grew tired and her hands throbbed, but she wasn't quite ready to quit. During one of their rare breaks, shortly past midnight, she sat with Remy and Darryl at the galley table, sipping coffee and yawning. Their conversation lulled.

Kate revisited a topic that continued to intrigue her. "Remy refuses to talk about the *A* word, Darryl. He said I'd have to ask you. He mentioned that it's a common item. Something you'd see around the house. Is it *a-s-h-t-r-a-y?*"

"You don't need to know," Darryl grumbled, his frown returning.

"But if I don't, I might say it. How about *a-r-t?*"

Snatching up his coffee mug, he rose from the booth, then stomped out of the galley. Kate bit her lip. She hadn't meant to upset him.

"Don't ask him no spelling questions," Remy advised. "He can't read."

Dismay washed through her. Why hadn't she thought of that? She hadn't meant to put him in an awkward position. And she suspected that an apology would only embarrass him.

"Yeah, dat's why he don't have his captain's license," Remy continued, "and why he don't go after his lady. Just because she's got an office job wit' da Terrebonne Parish Department of Education, he thinks he ain't worthy of her." Remy shook his head in patent disgust and muttered "imbecile" in French, which somehow made it sound more affectionate than insulting.

"Why doesn't he just learn to read?"

"He tried. Can't do it. Don't make no sense, though. I seen him dock an eighty-five-foot boat wit' no rudder and da outriggers down. No one can handle a boat, fix da engine, read da Gulf bottom or make a net like Darryl, except maybe Mitch. So why can't Darryl read?" Again, Remy shook his head, this time in bewilderment.

Kate suspected Darryl suffered from dyslexia, or possibly a visual disability, and her heart went out to him. She longed to talk to him about it—advise him in her professional capacity as an educator—but knew he wouldn't appreciate her concern.

"Pick up the nets" came Mitch's call over the intercom.

Remy downed the rest of his coffee and headed for the back deck. Kate lagged wearily behind him. The night wasn't half over, and she ached in every part of her body. A shrimper's work was far from easy.

Was this how Mitch had spent his childhood—toiling in backbreaking labor? Was shrimping the only line of work he knew? Did he ever long for an escape from it? Had frustration with the job led to violence against his wayward wife?

She found that conjecture too painful to consider, and more impossible than ever to believe. A man who cared about the welfare of stingrays in the deep wouldn't inflict harm upon his wife, would he? But how could she, Kate, know for sure, when she'd only been with him three days and hadn't seen him interact with his family? *Don't lose your objectivity,* she warned herself, hoping she hadn't already done so.

The wind gradually increased the bobbing of the boat, causing her culling stool to shift from side to side and occasionally toppling her off it. She considered giving up and going to bed.

But the men's conversation caught her attention. They were talking about netting crawfish in the swamps.

"You don't actually get into the swamp water, do you?" she asked.

"Sometimes," Remy said.

"But aren't there alligators?"

Both men froze, as if stricken, and shot alarmed glances at her. She frowned in bewilderment. Surely they'd thought about the danger posed by alligators.

"Oh, no, Cam," Remy moaned. "You said da *A* word."

"I knew she'd say it," Darryl muttered. "I knew it!"

"*Alligator* is the *A* word?" Kate cried.

"Don't say it again!" they warned in unison.

"But you told me it was a common word, something you'd have around the house."

"*Mais, oui.* I have 'em around my house all da time," said Remy. "Don't you, Darryl?"

Darryl nodded.

Kate rolled her eyes. "You should have spelled it for me, Remy. Then I wouldn't have said it."

"Too late now. I just hope we make it back to da dock okay."

"Oh, you can't really believe that—"

"Aahrrgg!" Darryl leaped from the stool, dropped his rake, ripped off his glove and clutched his hand. Blood pooled in his palm.

"A catfish?" Remy rose in concern.

Darryl nodded, wincing and cursing, his face ashen as he cradled his hand and staggered toward the cabin.

"Saltwater cats have dem big ol' spikes on der heads," he told Kate as they hurried after him. "A catfish sting'll paralyze you wit' pain. Burn like fire. Make a grown man cry."

Kate swallowed a lump that rose to her throat. Had she caused this by saying the *A* word? At the very least, she'd distracted Darryl from his culling. Mitch had told her to stay in the cabin. She should have listened.

Mitch met them in the galley with a first-aid kit. Darryl refused treatment with an antibiotic, though, insisting that only mashed potatoes and salt would draw out the poison. Remy advised packing the wound with tobacco and spit.

Kate realized that shrimpers—at least these particular ones—would rather argue than breathe. Wincing at the acute pain she saw in Darryl's face, she found a box of instant potato flakes, whipped up a paste, grabbed the antibiotic ointment from Mitch and squirted some into the potatoes. "Here's the mashed potatoes, Darryl. Give me your hand."

"Salt," he croaked. "Dere's gotta be salt in it." Only after a few passes of the saltshaker did Darryl allow her to apply the potato paste to his wound.

But that crisis paled in comparison to the next. She'd barely finished bandaging Darryl's wound when the boat jerked sharply to the left. Remy and Darryl exchanged ominous glances.

Mitch headed for the wheelhouse, looking grim. Moments later, he uttered over the intercom, "Hoist the nets, as far as you can." Darryl worked the winch and Remy tugged on the ropes, lifting the nets above the water. The port-side net, however, remained partially submerged.

The engine cut off. The silence startled Kate. The boat now drifted aimlessly with the waves. Mitch strode past her to the back rail, and the other two men fell in behind him. Kate followed with a growing sense of foreboding.

"Let me do it, Cap'n," Remy said.

"You don't have the lung capacity." Mitch pulled his shirt over his head and discarded it. "Cut back to three packs a day, and maybe I'd let you."

"Let him what?" Kate asked, alarmed by their sober faces—and the fact that Mitch had taken off his shirt. "What's wrong?"

"A net's caught in the wheel." Mitch briskly unbuckled his belt.

"In the wheel?" she repeated blankly. "But how could any part of a net get into the wheelhouse?"

"Not dat wheel," Remy said. "Da propeller."

"Propeller? You mean, the one at the back of the boat?"

"Under da boat," Darryl specified, his face still white and drawn with pain, his bandaged hand held steady in her homemade sling.

Mitch tossed his belt aside, removed his boots, then reached for a coil of rope.

Darryl cursed and grabbed the rope from Mitch. "I'll go. I'm da first mate. I'll go."

"With a puncture wound? Hell, no."

"It stopped bleeding."

"You won't be able to use that hand for another few hours, at least. Forget it, Darryl. I'm going in."

"Going in *where?*" Kate demanded, terribly afraid she knew.

Mitch didn't reply but took the rope from Darryl and wrapped a length of it around his lean, bare waist.

And then she realized what he intended to do. "You're not going in the water, are you?" she cried, horrified.

"It's the only way to get the net out from the wheel." Mitch tied a knot with quick, hard tugs. "Until we do that, we can't go anywhere. We're dead in the water."

Dead in the water. That was exactly what she was afraid of.

"My God, Mitch, what about sharks? There has to be dozens of them. You can't see them now because it's dark, but—"

"I know what I'm doing."

"That's beside the point. The danger is there. It's real. Why don't you call the coast guard for help?"

All three men slanted her scornful looks, as if the idea were ludicrous. "No self-respecting shrimp boat cap'n calls da guard for something like dat, *chèr*,'' Remy told her. "At least, none from Loo-zee-ana. Mississippi, maybe."

They had the temerity to grin at one another. *Grin!*

Stunned that no one was going to stop him, Kate swung a wild-eyed, imploring stare from Remy to Darryl. "Are you two crazy? If you let him jump in that water, he'll be devoured. I saw those sharks gobbling up the trash fish. I saw the movie *Jaws*. And what about those monstrous stingrays? He'll be pierced through the heart. Or tangled in that net and drowned. You can't let him do it!"

Remy evaded her desperate gaze and murmured soothing noises, which only confirmed her worst fears. Mitch continued tying the other end of the rope to the stern ladder, and Darryl narrowed his eyes at Kate, as if she were acting out of character.

She didn't give a flying flip what he thought. The idea of Mitch diving off the boat into the black, treacherous deep filled her with cold, stark horror. She had to stop him!

As Mitch finished securing the rope and turned to speak to his crew, Kate launched herself at him, knocking him against the stern ladder. Coiling her arms around his middle, mashing her face to his chest, she held on to him for dear life. *His* dear life.

"You're not doing it," she shouted, her voice strident with barely checked tears. "I said the *A* word. And we left the dock on a Friday. And…for God's sake…there's a *woman* on board!"

This was, without a doubt, a low point of her life. Remy and Darryl ganged up on her and pried her loose from Mitch. Despite her kicking, fighting and pleading, they restrained her, carried her to the cabin and locked her in the captain's quarters.

And while she banged on the door and shouted herself hoarse, she knew, in the pit of her stomach, in the marrow of her bones, that Mitch was going to die. Anguish clawed at her throat. She'd never see him again. *He would die.* Like her parents and her sister. He would simply be gone.

She curled up on the bed in torment.

She wasn't sure how long she lay there before the door of the captain's quarters opened. Clenching her jaw to stop it from trembling, she braced herself for the unthinkable.

No one spoke, and the door closed again. She glanced up to find Mitch beside the bed, towel-drying his hair. And peering at her cautiously.

Incredulous, she stared at him. *He'd made it.* He'd come back alive. Relief slammed into her with such stunning force that she couldn't breathe.

The sheer power of that relief soon triggered another emotion. Anger. At him, for risking his life. At the sea, for posing such a threat. At shrimpers in general, for shrugging at the danger. At herself, for caring too much.

Cold with fury, she pointed at the door. "Get...out."

He paused in the act of drying one broad shoulder.

"Get out!" In a rage, she leaped from the bed and shoved the heel of her palm into his hard, bare biceps, pushing him toward the door. "I never want to see you again."

He dropped the towel and grabbed her arms, trapping

them at her sides. "I'm sorry for locking you in here. I had no choice. You—"

"You could have been killed!" she cried, struggling to free herself from his grasp.

"I know what I'm doing. I've done it plenty of times before."

"That doesn't make it any better. In fact, it's worse. Barbaric. You didn't even use diving equipment, did you?"

"I wore a mask to help me see. That's all the equipment I ever need. I haven't died yet, have I?"

"Take me to the dock, *right now*."

"Aw, *chèr'*…" He gazed at her in powerful regret, as if trying to find a way to explain the unexplainable. "I had no choice. The boat was too vulnerable. We were all at risk. But everything's fine now."

"Nothing's fine, and don't call me *chèr'*." She choked on the last word and bit her lip to stifle a humiliating sob.

He pulled her close in a warm, strong bear hug. She tried to jerk free, but her struggles only brought her into neater, tighter contact with his body.

And, oh, how she needed that contact. A hard, long, life-affirming hug. She needed to touch him, hold him, squeeze the very breath from him. Punish him, in every way she could. She'd never hated anyone more!

The tension born of fear and anger soon provoked trembling, and she clung to him in desperation, her face pressed against the steady, vibrant beat of his heart. He brought her down with him onto the bed and held her.

After a while, her voice tremulous, she whispered, "I hate you."

He stroked her hair, her shoulders, the small of her

back, gently rubbing away the stiffness and, in the process, molding her body to his. "I'm sorry."

They lapsed into silence, his arms a veritable fortress around her, locking all danger out and all warmth in.

The trembling worsened. Mitch felt it in every part of her slender frame. And in his knees, his elbows and the pit of his stomach. He thought of it as aftershock. The result of an adrenaline surge.

His adrenaline *had* been surging. It didn't matter how many times he'd freed nets from wheels; the possibility always remained that he wouldn't return to the surface alive. He took the necessary precautions and his crew lured most predators away from the stern, but even so, there were no guarantees.

This time had been the worst. He'd seen the fear on Kate's face, heard it in her voice. Fear for him. Passionate fear. And he hadn't wanted to leave her. Too much remained unresolved between them. But the job had to be done or the boat would be disabled. Few things were more vulnerable at sea than a disabled vessel.

So he'd locked her away, dived into the ink-black waves and let his adrenaline rush carry him through. He'd been praying all the while—to return to his family, to raise Arianne. *To hold Kate again. To* know *her.*

Why should she, a virtual stranger, affect him as no one ever had? She was an impostor, with some scheme or another in mind. But she cared deeply for people. Not just him, but her sister. And Darryl, too, despite the fact that he probably hadn't said a civil word to her. Mitch had seen the vital concern in her face as she'd tended Darryl's wound. With potatoes yet. Who else would have made him mashed potatoes?

No one he knew.

And now her body trembled, as did his, and he couldn't seem to gather her closely enough.

"You could have called someone for help," she whispered against the base of his throat, her hand sweeping up his back.

"And have someone else dive for me? I can't see the sense in that." He rubbed his jaw against her temple; savored the privilege, the pleasure, of holding her. Her scent, spiced by the sea, the wind, the night, soon added a different tension to the one that already gripped him. A keen, sensual pull. A familiar heat. The one to which he'd awakened this morning.

"You could've had the boat towed in to dry dock." Her fingers raked and tested the muscles of his shoulders and biceps, inciting a radiance that loosened their tension-wrought stiffness.

Her touch echoed like sonar through his bloodstream, beaming to his very core. "If we had to wait for help, we couldn't have even anchored down," he said in an unnatural rasp. "If a storm hit, we couldn't have quartered the waves."

"But your risk was a thousand times greater by diving into shark-infested waters. I *saw* the sharks, Mitch." She stopped her arousing caresses and tilted her face to his, her eyes wide with emotional turbulence. "Did you enjoy that dive? Are you a thrill seeker, like Ca—" she halted, midword, and her face flushed "—like *I* used to be?"

"No! God, no." Revolted by the idea that she could think he was like her sister, deliberately milking danger for a thrill, he braced his hand along her face and earnestly stressed every word. "I didn't want to do it. I had no choice."

"Don't you care about going home to your family?"

Her voice was rising again, and her tension growing. "Don't you care about seeing Arianne?"

"Yes! Yes, of course I—"

"Then how can you—"

He groaned and silenced her with a kiss. Not a gentle or tender one, but demanding. Maybe a little punishing. She tangled her fingers painfully in his hair, angled her face and drew him in deeper.

And hunger reigned. Here, at last, was the taste, the texture, the sustenance he'd been craving. She met him kiss for kiss, each one wilder, more voluptuous, than the last, until he ached with hardness.

He pressed her beneath him on the bed. He'd never known such need. Breaking from her mouth, he kissed her face, her throat. Filled his hands with her softness. But her clothes prevented full contact. After sweeping the straps from her shoulders, he tugged the thin, chemiselike top from her breasts, unhooked her bra and bent to fill his mouth with her.

"Mitch. Mitch!" Panicked, she caught his face between her hands, her voice again a whisper. "Stop. Please stop. We can't do this."

Through a haze of heat, he peered at her face, which was more beautiful than he could bear. Regret burned golden in her eyes, as golden as her hair fanning across his pillow. As golden as her skin newly darkened by the sun. Skin that beckoned his touch, his kiss, the glide of his tongue...

"This is wrong, Mitch. More than you know."

"Then how can it feel so right?"

Their gazes shifted and sparred in a tense, silent struggle that brought neither of them closer to understanding. Clenching his jaw, he shut his eyes. Dragged in a long, cooling breath. Concentrated fiercely on dousing the fire.

She was right. He couldn't justify going further. She hadn't even admitted her real name. Or, worse yet, her intentions.

Why did all that suddenly seem unimportant?

Alarmed because it did, he drew away from her, rose from the bed, raked an unsteady hand through his hair and paced to a safer distance. He couldn't think clearly around her. Couldn't see past the beauty, the grace. He needed a cold dose of reality, before he did something seriously rash.

Like, fall in love with her.

The time had come to go home…and force their game to a close, whatever that end might bring.

CHAPTER ELEVEN

MORNING HAD DAWNED before Kate fell asleep in the captain's bed—alone, exhausted, emotionally conflicted. She dozed until midafternoon. She'd have slept longer if Remy hadn't banged on the door and startled her awake.

"Better get up, Cam. We almost to da dock."

The dock? She'd expected another day at sea.

"Looks like we beat da odds," Remy said. "We gonna make it ashore okay."

Thankful for that much, at least, she grabbed her terry-cloth robe, hurried to the head and showered, her heart pounding at the thought of what might soon take place. Would Mitch take her directly to the authorities?

If he did, she wouldn't see Arianne or meet his family until after she'd revealed her identity—assuming they'd meet with her at all, or allow her anywhere near Arianne.

Scouring her mind and heart to decide the truth of the matter without allowing her emotions to interfere, Kate asked herself if it was truly necessary to see Mitch with his family, to know how they interacted with Arianne, to meet whomever would care for the baby while he was out at sea.

Yes, it most definitely was!

Her questions demanded answers now more than ever. Why had Camryn violated a custody order and taken Arianne away from Mitch? She'd told Kate that he was abusive and that he hadn't wanted a wife or child. Kate now knew that he *had* wanted his child. Desperately. Why? As a means of controlling Camryn?

She found it impossible to believe that he harbored any dark, disturbing motives, or that he would deliberately harm anyone. Although he *had* forced his way into Kate's home and carried her off in chains, he'd been careful not to hurt her. And he'd allowed her freedom and dignity aboard his boat. Even after she'd screamed at him, shoved him, swore that she hated him, he'd held her in a comforting hug. And he'd kissed her.

As she'd never been kissed before. Heat surged through her at the memory, whipping her emotions into chaos. Guilt, desire, anxiety. Desire.

She leaned against the bathroom cabinet and pressed a hand to her heart. Maybe that was why she saw only the good side of him—because she'd fallen into lust with him.

She couldn't trust her gut instincts where Mitch was concerned. In her gut, she believed he would make a woman deliriously happy. She hated the idea of revealing her impersonation and facing him afterward. And her insides positively twisted at the thought of her bringing charges against him for kidnapping her.

But she had to reveal her identity, of course, and if she didn't bring charges against him, she'd have very little chance of winning legal custody of Arianne.

Then again, should she *try* to win custody of Arianne? Was she morally right in taking her away from her father? Of course not—unless Mitch and his family weren't capable of giving her the love, guidance and support the little girl needed. How could Kate know, though, without a substantial glimpse into the inner workings of their lives?

Another possibility loomed: when she revealed her identity to the authorities, they'd charge her as an accessory to kidnapping. She had, after all, kept the baby for Camryn.

What in heaven's name should she do?

All she really wanted was to see Arianne. Hold her again. Take her home. Carry on with their normal daily lives.

No, that wasn't *all* she wanted. She also wanted Mitch.

Oh, God! Maybe she was suffering from Stockholm syndrome—a captive identifying too closely with her captor. Or maybe she'd spent too much of her life working and striving, as Camryn had accused, without developing a healthy outlet for her sexuality. Why else would she have fallen for the first handsome sea captain who dragged her aboard his shrimp boat and passionately kissed her?

"Remy, tie us off at the bow," came Mitch's voice over the intercom. "Darryl, the stern. Then stand by to unload."

Kate shrugged into her robe, gathered her toiletries from the bathroom and hurried to the captain's quarters. On her way through the galley, she glanced out the open doorways and saw lush, verdant forest on either side of a narrow waterway. The afternoon air lay hot and muggy against her skin—oppressively so—and the smell of diesel fuel, shrimp and mossy woodlands permeated the cabin.

"Camryn, pack your bags," Mitch said over the intercom. "We'll be leaving in about thirty minutes."

Ah, but the question was, *Where would they go?* Needing to know, Kate ventured to the wheelhouse, where she found Mitch at the helm, working controls, shifting a lever, glancing through mirrors and maneuvering the boat into place at a dock.

She held her tongue, afraid of distracting him. She had to admire his ease at docking a boat this size. He seemed to give the maneuverings barely a thought. A friendly shout from Remy on the bow was greeted by an amiable retort from a man on the dock. Darryl called out a gruff greeting, too. With a look outside the wheelhouse doorway, Kate saw that they'd both tied thick ropes to weathered pilings.

The *Lady Jeanette* had landed.

Mitch cut off the engine, and when he turned a questioning gaze to Kate, warmth rose to her face. How could she be so affected by a single glance, especially when her insides were knotted with anxiety? "I need to know where we're going, so I can...dress appropriately." She tugged her robe tighter around her, highly aware of her nudity beneath.

"I'm going home to see my daughter," he replied slowly. "To hold her for the first time in over six months. Do you want to come with me, or would you rather go to the sheriff's office?"

Oddly enough, she sensed tension in him, as if he really wasn't sure which she'd prefer. Why would he think she'd hesitate for even a moment? "I want to see Arianne, of course."

He nodded, appearing to be relieved. A perplexing reaction, to say the least.

She gave the matter little thought, though, because of her gladness over seeing Arianne again. Feeling immeasurably better, she turned toward the captain's quarters to dress.

"Wear something cool," Mitch advised. "We'll go to my parents' house first. Chances are, they'll boil up some shrimp, grill some fish and we'll eat supper outside.''

When she searched her suitcase, she found nothing cool or casual to put on. She'd already worn the shorts and tops she'd packed, which were now in dire need of washing. Her linen pants suit seemed too dressy, as did the tailored dresses she'd brought for court.

''Mitch,'' she called through the door she'd just closed, ''is there somewhere I can do laundry before we go? I'm out of shorts and tops.''

''You can wash clothes at my house later. For now, look in the bottom drawer beneath the chart table. You left some things from your last trip.''

Surprised, Kate pulled open the drawer and found a pair of minuscule denim cutoffs, a red halter top, a black thong bikini and a soft, coral-colored sundress. Hugging the clothing to her chest, she shut her eyes and bowed her head with a pang of grief. She could so easily imagine her twin wearing these clothes, dazzling everyone with her innate sexiness and daredevil smile. She would never dazzle anyone again.

After a long, pain-filled moment, she forced aside her sadness, blinked away a blinding sheen and tried on the sundress. The sleeves were brief and off-the-shoulder; the waist narrow; the skirt light and flowing to below her knees. Though the dress wasn't short, tight or particularly sheer, she understood why Camryn had chosen it. The soft folds molded provocatively to her figure. Definitely Camryn's style.

Not Kate's.

She wasn't playing ''Kate'' today, though. And the dress was comfortable and cool. And she couldn't help but wonder if Mitch would look at her any differently…*if he'd want her more….*

No, no, *that* had nothing to do with it! She didn't want him to want her, just as she didn't want to want him. There was nothing between them. There *could be* nothing between them. She simply had no clean clothes of her own to wear.

Hastily she packed the rest of Camryn's clothing and her own belongings into her suitcase, then turned her attention to her hair, which she rolled into a French twist. She was, after all, meeting his family...and she'd need all the confidence she could muster. Before the day was out, she could be facing a sheriff and judge, too.

Her keen anxiety was lightened only by the fact that she'd also be seeing Arianne again. She ached with the need to hug her, rock her, feed her. Murmur reassurances in her ear. She felt as if they'd been separated for weeks rather than days.

Buoyed by the prospect of reuniting with Arianne, Kate ventured onto the back deck with her purse and suitcase, ready to disembark. Mitch, she noticed, had already climbed off the boat and stood on the wide, modern concrete dock, talking with an older man.

Remy and Darryl milled around on the stern of the *Lady Jeanette,* preparing to unload the shrimp. Their attention alighted on Kate at precisely the same moment, and with a dazed stare, they walked solidly into each other. Darryl flushed, scowled, shoved Remy aside and went about his business.

Remy grinned, his diamond flashing, and whistled at Kate. "You clean up good, Cam."

The wolf whistle and comment halted Mitch in his conversation on the dock. He did a double take.

Perhaps the dress wouldn't keep her as cool as she'd hoped. The intensity of his perusal sent heat spiraling through every part of her. Embarrassed at the attention, she looked away from Mitch, murmured a flustered goodbye to Remy and Darryl and thanked the teenager from the dock who had climbed aboard to carry her luggage.

Mitch himself strode forward and helped her disembark. Her breathing hitched at his nearness, his strong, confident touch. After a few more words to the older man in French, Mitch steered Kate down a flight of stairs and across the graveled parking lot, maintaining a grip on her elbow and a hand at the small of her back.

An odd dizziness overcame her. Surely Mitch's nearness couldn't be affecting her *that* much! Perhaps it was the steady heat and brightness of the blazing Louisiana sun that caused her to reel. Whatever it was, she was glad that he had a firm hold on her.

He opened the door of a gleaming black pickup truck and helped her in. He and the teenage worker from the dock then loaded large coolers of shrimp and an array of boxes into the bed, along with her luggage. Kate rolled down the window to release the ovenlike heat from within the cab, aware that the dizziness hadn't left her.

Mitch's first comment after he'd slid behind the wheel didn't help her condition. "The dress," he murmured, turning the key in the ignition before shifting his gaze to her, "suits you more now than it did before."

The sincerity in his tone and in his look as he met her gaze sent warmth rushing to her head. But how could he possibly believe that? Camryn had had far more panache than she ever would. Kate couldn't help feeling touched that he'd said it, though. Deeply touched.

She struggled to clear her mind—of both the inexplicable dizziness and the feelings crowding her chest for Mitch Devereaux. But soon another odd sensation, sim-

ilar to the dizziness, accosted her as they rode down a
two-lane rural highway. She felt as if they were zipping
along at an outrageous speed, at least a hundred miles
an hour, while the speedometer registered a scant sixty-
five.

Noting her grip on the armrests, Mitch slanted her a
glance. "Does it seem like we're flying?" At her surprised nod, he smiled, deepening the elongated dimples
beside his mouth. "You've gotten used to the cruising
speed of the boat, which is about twelve miles an hour.
If you were driving right now, you'd have a hard time
accelerating past thirty."

"I don't believe I *could* drive right now."

"Dizzy?"

"A little. I thought it might be the heat." *Or your
nearness. Your charm.*

"Could be. But more than likely, your inner ear has
become acclimated to the roll of the sea. Now that
you're not rocking, your sense of balance is off. It'll take
a while for you to adjust to the hill again."

"The hill?"

"Land."

Something about his use of the lingo and the contentment in his sun-bronzed face illuminated a fundamental truth. He enjoyed his life; the challenges he faced
at the sea, the pleasure of returning home.

More surprising still, *she understood why.* She'd only
been on his boat for three days, but she already missed
the salty tang of the breeze, the brisk wind in her hair,
the sun reflecting off jewel-toned waves, the ambience
of adventure, the unearthly communion she'd felt with
nature.

She even felt a tug of sadness at the thought that she
would probably never see Remy or Darryl again. Amaz-

ing, the bond created by a few harrowing days on a shrimp boat. Maybe her camaraderie with Mitch and his deckhands was another symptom of Stockholm syndrome—a twisted sense of empathy with her captors.

She had to banish these nonsensical emotions from her heart and mind. Arianne's future depended on her clear thinking. She had to learn all there was to know about Mitch, his home, his family. Only then could she decide her next move.

She was eternally thankful that Mitch had given her the chance to make any move at all. Regarding him in puzzlement, she wondered why he had. "I'm glad you didn't handcuff me again."

A shadow of discomfort crossed his face, but he didn't reply.

"Do you no longer feel it's necessary?"

A smile edged a corner of his mouth. "Take a look around."

She did, and gradually realized they were now surrounded by thick, junglelike greenery and black-water marshes, interspersed with oil wells, canals and sugarcane fields. No houses, stores or even other vehicles on the road.

"We're in my neck of the woods now, *chèr',*" he murmured. "Even a native-born son would think twice before setting out on foot around here. I damn sure wouldn't try it if I were you."

Uneasiness trickled through her like the beads of sweat beneath her dress. If she decided to run with Arianne, she'd need to do some serious planning. The very thought that she might have to go to that extreme upset her, for more reasons than she cared to analyze.

"Where exactly are we?" she asked.

"Terrebonne Parish."

"Near any big towns?"

"Big?" His eyes lit with mild humor and creased at the corners. "Let's see…there's Gibson. Dulac. Chauvin. Cocodrie."

She could just imagine how "big" those towns were. "How far are we from New Orleans?"

"Seventy some miles to the south."

"And how far are we from your home?"

"Ten."

Kate had a sinking feeling that every one of those miles would carry her deeper into swampland.

Her intuition proved correct. They crossed several bridges over wild, grassy marshes and lazy-moving waterways that Mitch identified as bayous. Occasionally she'd see a roadside sign with a picture of an alligator, indicating an "alligator crossing." And when they turned off the paved highway onto a maze of narrow gravel roads, Kate peered around her in awe.

Huge cypress trees stood with their craggy bases under water and their limbs draped with ghostly gray Spanish moss above swampy terrain. Palmettos, black willows, tupelo gums, muscadine vines and tawny bulrushes surrounded her. Dappled sunlight streamed in slanted beams through a surrealistic twilight. Birds screeched; frogs croaked; insects hummed. Brownish-black water gleamed in stretches on both sides of the road, covered with wide-leafed water plants, white amaryllis, clusters of purple hyacinths and something that looked like thick, dry, green sawdust.

The air felt damp, close and heavy, but not as oppressively hot as it had at the dock. The breeze wafting in through the windows of their slow-cruising truck smelled of brackish water, foliage, muscadine and flowers.

She saw an alligator sunning on a log. A long, fat alligator. And she could almost hear the snakes slithering beneath the brush.

Her dress, she discovered, was sticking to her damp skin.

For the umpteenth time in three days, Kate marveled that she, the quintessential homebody, a career-minded suburbanite, had landed in such an alien dimension. In her world, she worried about parking tickets at the university, tardy thesis papers, homeowners' association causes and swim lessons for Arianne. Not killer sharks, storms at sea, alligators in swamps, voodoo curses…and long, hot kisses from a Cajun sea captain!

She wasn't sure why she'd thought of his kisses just then. Maybe because the heat they'd provoked hadn't really left her. Maybe because he was gazing at her with intense, green eyes; eyes that suddenly reminded her of subtropical foliage—hot, deep, mysterious. Dangerously alluring.

Suddenly he pulled over and stopped the truck. He settled his arm along the back of the seat, casually against her bare shoulders, and studied her. "I know you've changed in a lot of ways, Cam," he murmured in a deep, gruff voice subtly spiced with a Cajun cadence. "I'd go so far as to say you're not the same person you were when you ran away with Arianne."

Her heart did a slow, uncomfortable roll. He didn't know how right he was. Or…did he? No, surely not.

He leaned his broad shoulders closer, slid two long, bronzed fingers beneath her chin and held her face in steady alignment with his. "But let me make something very clear, *chèr'*. If you try to run with her again, I'll come after you. And you'll wish you hadn't."

She stared at him in stark dismay. Not because she

feared him. She didn't. Even here, in the heart of this alien and dangerous swampland, with an ominous threat hanging between them, she didn't believe he'd intentionally hurt her. But she wanted to promise him that she'd never run with Arianne, that she'd never intentionally hurt *him*...and she couldn't make that promise.

"Did you bring me here to scare me, Mitch?"

His gaze intensified, then followed his fingers as they skimmed from beneath her chin, along her jawline, to linger in her hair. "No, not to scare you. Warn you, yes. Tie up loose ends. Settle things between us." He met her eyes with a probing stare and retracted his hand slowly, as if the withdrawal took some effort. "But not to scare you. And if anyone does, let me know. I won't allow it."

Visions of clannish, backwoods strangers with hateful intentions sent another pang of unease through her. "Does your family know I'm coming with you?"

"Yeah, I called ahead. Told them about your accident and memory loss. Your sister's death." He frowned. "I doubt if you'll get much sympathy. They're goodhearted people, but they rally around their own. You made enemies when you took Arianne."

"I realize that." She wished she could apologize, at least, but she couldn't. Not until she knew if Camryn had been justified in taking Arianne away. Hating her need for deception, Kate sat perfectly still, her eyes locked with his, the eerie sounds of the swamp buzzing, humming and screeching around them. "Are you one of those enemies, Mitch?"

He searched her face, then chose his words carefully. "At one time I thought I was. Now I'm not so sure. Guess that remains to be seen. I'm willing to keep an open mind about you if you're willing to do the same about me.''

She chewed her lip and nodded, inexplicably choked up by a welling of emotion. She was just so very glad that he wasn't going to continue holding Camryn's sins against her. Of course, he hadn't learned of her own yet.

''Maybe we won't have to bring any criminal charges into our personal affairs,'' he mused.

''That would be…nice.''

His gaze meandered to her mouth. And hunger flashed in his eyes; the hunger they'd felt for each other last night. Hunger that stole her breath and warmed her blood. *He was going to kiss her.*

And she longed for it.

He didn't, though. He shifted away from her, settled behind the wheel, threw the truck into gear and drove down the narrow, twisting road, through denser, more surrealistic foliage.

It took Kate a while to breathe again.

She soon heard sounds through the thicket that seemed out of place in such raw wilderness: the murmur of voices, the peal of a child's yell, a cackle of laughter. The rousing beat of swamp-rock guitar by Creedence Clearwater Revival, with John Fogerty singing, ''Better run through the jungle.''

Maybe those sounds weren't out of place, after all.

Mitch drove past a hodgepodge of pickup trucks, Camaros and SUV's parked along one side of the narrow road, some new and gleaming, some old and rusted. By the time the road widened into a clearing, Kate realized a fairly large crowd of people had gathered.

''Why are all these people here? They can't all be family.''

"At least half of them are. The rest are neighbors and friends. I'd say they're here to celebrate the reunion."

"Reunion?"

He tipped her a speaking glance. "Mine and Arianne's."

Unsettling emotion rose in her throat again, and she swallowed to dislodge it. She didn't like playing the villainness against him. It seemed unfair that she had to. Yet she'd taken on the role willingly. For Arianne's sake. The child of her heart. The sweet, loving, brown-eyed girl she'd nurtured as her own from an infant.

Kate had to learn all there was to know about the people who would take her place in Arianne's life.

CHAPTER TWELVE

MITCH PARKED the truck between a scenic view of a wide, moss-draped bayou and a huge, pink-flowering mimosa tree, opened Kate's door, took her arm and leisurely ushered her toward the activity. She was fervently grateful for his calm, solid presence at her side—more for moral support than anything else.

She knew she wouldn't be welcomed.

Music played and laughter rang as people of all ages milled about the front yard of a stone-and-cedar house. A surprisingly spacious, expensively built house, from what Kate could see. For some reason, she'd been expecting much less.

Children romped about with squirt guns, some the size of cannons, happily saturating one another and any adults who crossed their paths. An old man in striped swimming trunks and a straw hat fought back with a garden hose. Other kids fished from a weathered wooden pier. Some swam and frolicked in another section of the bayou. Dogs barked and romped with the children.

Men drank bottles of beer and smoked cigars while grilling fish and stirring the contents of simmering kettles. Women chatted and arranged covered dishes on a long picnic table. A few of the younger women sunbathed on picnic blankets, their bikinis skimpy, their skin oiled and deeply tanned.

Older folks lounged in rockers on a wide front porch,

some with babies on their laps. None of those babies was Arianne, though. Kate searched in vain for sight of her.

As they ventured closer to the house, more attention swung to Mitch, and Kate felt hostility aimed her way. Smiles for him turned to frosty glares for her. Bystanders muttered to one another from the sides of their mouths, and a harsh-faced old woman spat very near to where Kate walked.

Mitch's prediction proved true. Despite the fact that he'd told them of her supposed memory loss and the story of her sister's death, she would get no sympathy here.

Holding a firm hand at her elbow, Mitch strode with easy confidence, his air naturally commanding as he guided Kate into the midst of the crowd. Though he wore his usual dark T-shirt and faded jeans, his tanned, muscular body and ruggedly striking face glowed with an innate masculine splendor. More than one stunning, skimpily clad Cajun lady smiled at him with pointed warmth behind casual greetings.

A disturbing jolt of possessiveness shook Kate. The reaction bothered her all the more. He was nothing to her. At least, not in that way.

"Where's my daughter?" Mitch asked no one in particular, his gaze seeking her. Kate set aside her musings and tuned in to the strong anticipation she sensed in him. Her own need to see Arianne was simply too strong to focus on. Perhaps that was why she was diverting herself with inappropriate feelings for Mitch. Otherwise, she might very well shove through this maddening throng and snatch her baby away from these strangers.

"Oh, Mitch, she's just the cutest little sweet potato!" A slender, barefoot woman with long, dark, Gypsy-like tresses and laugh lines etched pleasingly around her green eyes stepped forward. She had to be his sister; the family resemblance was strong. Kate knew from the sound of her voice that she wasn't Joey. "*Mémère* brought out baby pictures of you, and I swear, Arianne's your living image."

"She is not, Lisette," countered a cute, petite woman setting napkins on the nearby picnic table, her short, shaggy hair the same light brown as Mitch's. "She looks exactly like her aunt Joey."

Kate recognized her voice, of course, as Joey's.

Joey shifted her regard to Kate, and the teasing light faded from her vivacious dark eyes. Her lips twisted and she said something to Mitch in French.

He uttered a quiet but dismissive reply. Kate wished she knew what he'd said about her. Clearly it wasn't to Joey's liking, because she frowned and looked away.

"Take me to Arianne," Mitch said to the woman Joey had called Lisette.

"You know who's got her, eh? *Mémère.* Won't turn her loose. Felicia played with her all morning, since Joey brought her. I've been waiting my turn all day."

Mitch put his free arm around her. "Hate to break it to you, *mon coeur,* but you'll have to wait awhile longer. It's her papa's turn."

Lisette smiled and led him and Kate toward a cluster of mostly women and children beneath a huge cypress tree. As they neared, Kate saw a robust woman with the Devereaux green eyes, graying brown hair and a Madonna-like gentleness about her face, seated on a blanket with Arianne between her thighs. The woman's head was bent close to the baby's, her voice soft and lilting, as she walked her fingers across the blanket. "You see dat little ol' mud bug? Ooh, he's coming to kiss your toes!"

Arianne laughed and reached her chubby little hands for the woman's fingers fluttering toward her feet.

Kate's heart stood still. In a sweet pink-and-white sunsuit and tiny white sandals that someone must have recently bought, her blond ringlets caught back with matching bows, her brown eyes bright and smiling, she looked so…happy. Well cared for. Loved.

Mitch sank down onto one knee beside her, his expression one of awed reverence. Kate's heart lodged in her throat, her attention divided between his dark, emotion-filled face and the child she'd missed so badly. He said nothing, but his mother halted in her game, smiled lovingly at him and said to Arianne, "Look, *ma petite chér'*, who is dis man?" Directing her attention to Mitch, *Mémère* exclaimed, "Why, it's your papa!"

He didn't reach for his daughter. Not without her permission. He merely spread his hands in a silent invitation for her to come to him. Arianne's gaze focused on him— his radiantly tender face, his hopeful eyes. She then gifted him with a sunny, dimpled smile.

And leaned toward him.

His throat muscles worked; his eyes filled. And then he was lifting her, holding her; bracing the fair-skinned baby in his large brown hands, cradling her next to his heart.

It was the most painfully poignant moment Kate had ever experienced. He murmured hoarse endearments, some in French, some in English. The language didn't matter. Even a newborn would have known what he meant.

Arianne patted his clean-shaven jaw with her fat little hands, her brow puckering in concentration as she explored new territory. He turned his face and kissed her palm, surprising her into a grin. He then blew a loud, vibrating raspberry against her hand. She squealed with laughter. And her dimpled smile so resembled Mitch's that Kate's throat physically ached.

He was her father. And he loved her. He would give his life, his freedom, his everything, to protect her. He would give her the very best he possibly could. Only a fool would doubt it.

Kate forced her blurry gaze away from them in a desperate attempt to collect herself. All around her, she saw overly shiny eyes focused on the reunion of father and daughter, and unmistakable looks of tenderness for them both. She didn't know these people, but she knew what they were feeling. Many glanced at one another and shared embarrassed little laughs at being caught with teary eyes and constricted throats.

"Uncle Mitch, Uncle Mitch!" The jubilant cry cut through the moment as a pint-size boy with eyes like Joey's dashed to a skidding halt beside Kate. "Did you bwing me a seashell, Uncle Mitch?"

Mitch reached out and tousled the boy's hair, his one-handed grip on Arianne so easy and natural that Kate knew he'd held many babies in his time. "Of course I did, Claude. From the bottom of the Gulf. I told you I would, didn't I?"

The boy hopped and skipped, his dark curls bouncing, his eyes sparkling in clear adoration of his uncle. "You like *ma petite cousine?*" he asked with a distinctly French flair.

"I love her."

"*Mais, oui…*but she likes me best." His mischievous grin told Kate that these Cajun men learned how to tease at a very early age. He couldn't be more than four, she guessed.

From her comfy perch on her papa's hip, Arianne

pointed at Claude, kicked her feet in excitement and babbled a bonny sound that, in Kate's opinion, could be construed as his name.

But then her gaze alighted on Kate. And after a stunned stare, her smile crumpled. "Mama! Mama-Mama!" Huge tears welled up, and she stretched her dimpled arms to Kate, pitching herself forward in clear anguish. "Mama, Mama!"

Kate took her. No one could have stopped her. She hugged her fiercely, buried her face in baby-scented ringlets and choked back sobs of her own. Arianne cried and wailed and clung with all her might. Kate knew what she was saying. *Where were you? I wanted you! Why did you leave me?*

"No, no," Kate whispered, "I didn't leave you. I didn't want to. Shh. It's okay, sweetheart. It's okay." She rocked her and murmured in her ear, stroked her back, patted her diapered bottom and, without a thought, paced toward a more private corner of the yard.

A woman briskly cleared her throat, and Kate glanced up to find Joey, Lisette and a buxom redhead who had to be Mitch's eldest sister blocking her way. Their narrowed eyes spoke succinctly. *Where you going wit' dat baby?*

It hit Kate then as it hadn't before. She could go nowhere with her. Arianne was Mitch's daughter. She belonged with him.

And she, Kate, would be lucky to play the part of an aunt who might visit her now and then. Chances were, when Mitch learned of her deception, he wouldn't trust her even in that minor role. She couldn't blame him. She had lied to him repeatedly. The rest of his family would despise her, too, of course, and believe the very worst about her.

"Take your daughter back, Mitch," Lisette demanded. "Camryn's had her long enough. Six months too long." The others nodded in stony-jawed agreement.

Kate tightened her hold on the baby. *Arianne needed her.* At least, for now.

"Why don't you three lovely hostesses round up some boys to carry the shrimp from my truck," Mitch said to his sisters, his low, pleasant rumble of a voice sounding from directly behind Kate, "and leave my business to me."

Their chins came up. Their mouths thinned.

Joey strutted forward, pulled him aside and whispered furiously, "Why did you bring her here, Mitch? You don't believe her story about an accident, do you?"

Kate couldn't hear Mitch's reply, but his sisters soon trudged away, and a strong arm came around Kate's waist.

"Come, sit," Mitch said, and shepherded her to an unoccupied blanket at the far edge of the shade. She settled down onto the blanket as Arianne clung to her and continued to cry—no longer an aggressive wail, but a quiet, droning complaint.

Shutting her eyes, Kate huddled with the baby, her emotions too sharp and ragged to easily control. *She would have to give her up.* The matter didn't require any in-depth research or screening of backgrounds or even further insight into Mitch's life. Love, loyalty, pride and devotion didn't shine with such totality in the eyes of so many for a man who didn't do right by them.

Even as a despised outsider, Kate couldn't miss the warmth this family shared, and though her heart was breaking, she wanted that for Arianne. Nothing would do her more good throughout life. Nothing.

But Kate wouldn't leave her just yet. An abrupt severing of their mother-daughter bond would hurt Arianne profoundly. Kate knew from personal experience. She'd lost her parents at an early age, then continually lost beloved teachers at the children's home and treasured friends there whom she'd come to regard as siblings. The pain of those abrupt departures had left Kate feeling that no one cared as deeply for her as she did for them, or they couldn't have abandoned her.

Maybe that was why she'd shied away from emotional relationships—because all the ones that had mattered the most had ended in heartbreak.

She wouldn't leave Arianne until she had to. Until then, she'd prepare her the best she could. Help her strengthen new bonds and get used to her new surroundings.

But she knew she couldn't hope for much time with her. Perhaps no longer than today.

RECLINING BESIDE THEM on the blanket, Mitch propped himself up on an elbow and watched Kate hug and rock Arianne, whose crying had gradually declined into an occasional full-body hiccup. Kate's eyes were closed, her face against the baby's hair, her arms snugly around her.

She was crooning a lullaby. Her voice had the same pitch and quality of Camryn's, but was untrained. Not a polished work of art, but slightly flawed. And natural, warm and sincere. He'd never heard anything more beautiful.

And he'd never seen anything more beautiful than the two of them together, Kate and his daughter. Kate's hair, much of which had escaped her smooth French twist in loosely curling tendrils, was only a shade darker than Arianne's mop of blond ringlets. The baby's face, now resting on Kate's shoulder in sweet repose, had to be the closest he would ever see to an angel's. What had struck him the most forcibly when he'd gotten his first full view of her—after six months of longing for that view—was her resemblance to Kate. And to Camryn, of course. Same golden-brown eyes, heart-shaped face, adorably cleft chin. Same angelic beauty. No one would take Kate and Arianne for anything but mother and daughter. Especially now, when their bond was so damn obvious.

Questions pulsed through him with every beat of his heart. What did Kate intend to do? Why was she carrying on this impersonation of Camryn? He could simply ask her, but then he'd have no way of knowing whether her answer was true.

And he badly wanted to know the truth. All he could think to do was wait and see what she did. Actions spoke louder than words.

He expected to hear from his attorney with legal advice soon. Would Kate charge him with crimes against her? Would she fight to gain custody of Arianne? Would she try to run with her? He was having a hard time believing she'd do any of those things.

At least he knew a little more about her now. This morning while she'd been asleep, he'd taken a peek in her wallet. Not a thing he would normally do, but she'd waived her right to privacy by staging her impersonation. Identification cards became fair game, in his opinion.

Kate Jones, Ph.D., Florida State University.

He still couldn't get over it. She was as different from Camryn as night from day. A professor of history, by God. No wonder she'd been fascinated by his mention of Jean Lafitte and civil war relics. He wondered what she'd think of nearby places he could take her where history lingered so palpably that one could feel the ghosts. She'd be enthralled. He wanted to take her.

Fat chance of that. She probably couldn't wait to resolve the situation with Arianne, shake the Louisiana dust from her sandals and get back to her highbrow life in the city. She'd probably been appalled to learn that Arianne's daddy was a lowly shrimper from the swamplands.

But when he thought back to the time they'd spent together on his boat, he remembered only her vital interest in everything, and her enjoyment of the sea. He also remembered every kiss they'd shared, every heated gaze. Had she just been slumming, since she had little else to do?

He didn't want to believe that.

Why the hell wouldn't she just be honest with him? When did she intend to admit the truth? What did she have up her sleeve?

Needing to reestablish communication with her, Mitch glanced up at the moss-draped cypress tree. "You know, Civil War soldiers used Spanish moss to bind their wounds."

Kate opened her eyes at that. Arianne even peeked at him from beneath her lashes, surprised, no doubt, by the proximity of his voice.

"Yes," Kate finally responded with a slight smile. "I know."

"Did you know we Cajuns sometimes stuff it in our shoes to make 'em fit better?"

She lifted a golden brow. "You do?"

"Well, maybe not me personally, but I've heard it's a common practice." As he spoke, he held his hands out to Arianne. She hid her face against Kate. That would have bothered him a lot more if she hadn't come so willingly before. With patience and time, he'd win her over again.

He wished he could be as sure of Kate. Rising higher on his forearm, he searched her gaze, which hadn't left him. She looked deeply troubled. "The world isn't ending, *chèr*," he said softly, brushing a blond tendril from her face. "I believe we can work things out, you and I."

Hope sparked in her eyes like a tiny silver fish in a murky sea, but vanished just as quickly. She forced a smile through her sadness. A breathtakingly tender smile. "I know you'll be a good father to her, Mitch."

It occurred to him then that she hadn't known that. How could she have, when she hadn't known *him?* And when she'd finally met him, he'd forced his way into her house and dragged her off in handcuffs. He'd been an angry stranger, and she'd been afraid...not only for herself, but for Arianne.

Was that why she was impersonating Camryn—to see just how badly he'd treat her, and what she could expect for Arianne? If so, he couldn't blame her for going to any lengths for answers to those vital questions. Had he been in her shoes, he'd have done the same.

"I'd like to meet your parents," she said.

Ah. So the appraisal was still going on. It seemed that she'd reached a favorable opinion of him but hadn't decided about his family yet. What would she do if she concluded they weren't good for Arianne?

Whatever it took to get her away from them. He knew that much about her already.

The heaviness that had settled in his chest now swelled to a new fullness. How could he feel so damn proud of her, so grateful for facing hostile strangers to protect his daughter...yet also want to shake some sense into her? *Tell me who you are, damn it. Prove to me that I'm right about you. That you're honorable to the very core.*

"Let's go talk to my parents." He stood up, held out a hand and helped her rise with Arianne. "Keep in mind that they...well, might not entirely believe you lost your memory, or that you've, uh, changed."

"Don't worry, Mitch. I'm not expecting an outpouring of warmth."

Which was probably a good thing.

The usually lively gathering of neighbors and friends had grown subdued since he'd escorted Kate into their midst. Clusters of adults stood around chatting, idly watching the children play, and sneaking concerned glances in his direction.

His mother looked at the picnic table, spreading out newspapers on which to set the boiled shellfish. His sisters hovered nearby. Their eyes were all fixed on him and Kate. They watched her like a dog tending sheep, as if she might try to make a run for it with Arianne. At one time, he might have worried about that, too.

But no longer. *I know you'll be a good father to her, Mitch.*

Keeping her hand firmly in his, which drew worried frowns from his sisters, he led Kate first to his father, who had propped his tall, burly body against the base of a tree—again, strategically placed for an unimpeded view of his prodigal daughter-in-law. He now sat whittling a chunk of pecan wood into the shape of a dog.

Considering that his father had snorted at the idea that Camryn had lost her memory, Mitch decided to forgo a formal introduction. Settling in the grass beside him, he struck up a casual conversation. Kate sat beside Mitch with a sweetly contented Arianne in her lap.

Before long, Kate got around to asking his father about his whittling. His father replied in monosyllables.

Mitch brought up the subject of his ducks. He saw his father's mouth flatten. Though he was a world-class carver of decorative wildfowl and had won prestigious awards for his work, Camryn had found it funny that a grown man would spend his time making wooden ducks. She hadn't been openly contemptuous. Just mildly amused.

"Duck carvings?" Kate said. And from the tone of her voice, Mitch knew what was coming next. She had to learn more. "You mean, like the ones the Ward brothers display?"

His father lifted a stunned gaze to her. The Ward brothers were pioneers in the art of wildfowl carving, and sponsors of the championship competition. Kate went on to talk about their museum, which she'd visited in Maryland, and soon had his father expounding on topics such as primary flight feathers, the speculum colors of certain ducks and his vermiculation techniques. Before long, he allowed Mitch to bring out a sample of his carvings.

Kate reverently examined every finely detailed feather. "It's exquisite. Truly a masterpiece." She then showed the duck to Arianne. "Ooh, look. A duck. See his head, his eyes, his bill? And all these *beautiful* feathers." She guided her tiny fingers lightly over the handiwork. "Your grandpa made this. He's making something else now. See?"

Arianne was too young to understand that information, Mitch knew, but she seemed to take interest in most everything Kate brought to her attention. She was now bringing his father to her attention.

His father, the strong, quiet type, wasn't a man who

actively sought interaction with babies. Despite this fact, his grandchildren always ended up gravitating to him eventually.

Kate somehow sped up the process. His father couldn't resist Arianne's wide-eyed perusal of him. He spoke to her in soft, gruff tones. Showed her the carved dog. Made the dog bark, which delighted her. Before they walked away, Kate held Arianne to his cheek to give him a kiss.

His father's stunned, bemused stare followed Kate as Mitch led her away.

Mitch took keen pleasure in watching her flabbergast the rest of his family, too—mostly by her interaction with the children, whom she drew into lively conversations with questions about the bayou, Cajun festivals and their fishing-hunting prowess.

She surprised everyone, as well with her fastidious care of Arianne, who refused to be parted from her. He knew his mother and sisters were having a hard time reconciling this woman with the one who had focused strictly on the adults' entertainment at social gatherings, leaving others to care for her baby.

Only once did Kate ask for help with that task. Procuring a blender from his perplexed mother, she showed Mitch how to puree fresh fruits and vegetables, then asked him if he'd like to feed Arianne.

Grateful for the unexpected lesson and the chance to interact with Arianne, he bungled through the task—one he'd rarely performed with his nieces and nephews—but won sloppy smiles and gurgles from his daughter.

Kate and *Mémère* sat at the kitchen table and watched. Kate's teasing comments and soft smiles soon relaxed his mother's spine. Before long, she'd unwound enough to show Kate the family photos.

Kate paid particular interest to the ones of Arianne during her first three months, and pictures taken of Camryn and him at their impromptu wedding. She also spent a good deal of time leafing through pictures of him, from infancy to manhood.

Mémère, of course, beamed with motherly pride.

"I'll send you pictures I have of Arianne," Kate promised her. "Videos, too. Expect three or four crates, at least," she said with a small laugh. She then bit the corner of her lip, blinked back tears and looked away. "I...I think it's important for children to know they were loved from the very start of their lives."

Visibly moved and conflicted by Kate's obvious emotional distress, Mitch's mother wholeheartedly agreed with her theory, and showed her the "trophy corner" of her bedroom, where she displayed her children's achievements.

By the time they returned to the party outside, his mother was regarding her with the same dazed expression his father had. And when Kate exclaimed in incredulity over the spread of food on the supper table—a subject close to his Cajun mother's heart—she urged Kate to try some of every dish. Mitch had to stifle a grin. That would be a Herculean task for all but the very hungriest.

Boiled crawfish, shrimp and blue crabs were piled on spread-out newspaper, accompanied by platters of steaming corn on the cob, tiny new potatoes and sweet onions. Fish, both fried and grilled, widened the selection, as did spicy white beans and crusty French bread. Which had to be followed by pie—pumpkin, pecan or sweet potato.

By God, she put a little of each on her plate. A *very* little, but the effort *was* made.

All the guests sat down at two long picnic tables, or on surrounding chairs and blankets, to partake of the feast. His sisters and parents joined him and Kate at one end of a table. Arianne relaxed enough to go to Mitch, but granted him the honor of holding her only as long as he sat beside Kate. He wasn't averse to that. He couldn't think of anywhere else he'd rather be.

Besides, her conversation with his sisters was simply too interesting to miss. She asked who would be watching Arianne while Mitch worked. Suspicious of her motives, they declined to answer. So she addressed them all as she described the things Arianne liked best. Back rubs when she was upset. Cuddling on the rocking chair when she couldn't sleep. Lively music during play time. The company of other children whenever possible. Vanilla wafers, bubble baths, dogs and kittens. Long walks in the stroller. Happy cartoons on TV. Picture books. The blanket she called her "bankie."

Kate's voice grew choked; her eyes filled. Unable to blink the tears away this time, she excused herself from the table and practically ran to the house, the skirt of her pretty, coral-colored sundress wafting behind her.

His family sat staring at one another in confoundment.

Mitch himself, however, was no longer confounded. He now realized what she was doing. *She was letting go.* She was turning Arianne over to them and trying to make sure that all went well.

She was going to leave him. He'd understood this all along, of course, but suddenly, her departure seemed too real. Too close. She hadn't even confessed her deception yet! When did she plan to do that—on her way out the door? Or...*sacre Dieu*...never?

Anger took root inside him. She wasn't being fair, wasn't giving him a chance. What did she think he'd do if she confessed the impersonation—feed her to the gators?

Arianne, who'd been contentedly chewing on a thick crust of French bread, looked at Kate's empty chair and let out an agonized cry. ''Mama! Mama-Mama!''

And as Mitch rose from the table to distract his squirming, bucking daughter from her distress, he suddenly knew what Kate was afraid of. *Being locked out of Arianne's life.* He had the power to do just that. Kate clearly believed that once she admitted to the impersonation, he'd wash his hands of her. Forbid all contact with his daughter.

He could set her mind at ease on that score…as soon as she confessed. But not until then. Because if she didn't come clean…and soon…he would know he'd read her all wrong. That she was, in every sense, a stranger. And he *would* be afraid to trust her with his daughter.

Unable to tolerate the thought, he distracted Arianne from her anguish by whistling for Molly-goo, his mother's Catahoula pup, with a patchwork coat, one blue eye and one brown. So enraptured was Arianne with the lively scamp that she barely noticed Mitch shift her to Joey's arms.

He then strode to the house to talk to Kate. Maybe she just needed the right opening to explain her impersonation. He'd give her one. He'd say that he'd decided to honor their joint-custody agreement, with a few minor modifications that would require her signature on legal forms. Her response would tell him what he wanted to know.

But as he entered his parents' house, he heard Kate's voice murmuring from the guest bedroom. With a covert glance around the corner, Mitch saw she was talking on the phone. He hadn't caught her words, and now she seemed to be on hold.

He ducked back around the corner, into the hallway, and waited for her to speak again. Who was she calling, and why? Her lawyer, maybe? The sheriff? Someone to come and get her?

Another possibility hit Mitch like a fist to the gut. Could she be calling a man, a lover, someone who shared in her *real* life? She could be engaged. Or married. No, she hadn't been wearing a ring, and she hadn't *acted* as if she were committed elsewhere. And when he'd asked if she had a man, she'd told him ''no.'' But had she been talking as Camryn then, or as herself?

Mitch shut his eyes and waited in silent torment to hear her speak.

''Yes,'' she finally said, her voice a near whisper, ''I'd like to make a reservation for tomorrow, from New Orleans to Tallahassee. One adult. One way. Coach fare. The name's Kate Jones....''

Mitch released a long breath and quietly headed outside. At least she hadn't been calling a lover. But she *was* planning to leave. Tomorrow. Alone.

Incredible, the feeling of abandonment that gripped him. She was willing to walk out of his life before they'd even had a chance to really know each other.

He loitered tensely on the front porch, exchanging quips with his musically inclined neighbors and his irrepressible Uncle Mazoo, who were setting up a microphone and tuning their instruments for the dancing portion of the party—the *fais do do*.

Mitch's mind wasn't on the casual chatter, though. He'd decided to wait there, right there, near the front door, until Kate stepped foot outside. Then he'd whisk her to some private place and test her with that joint-custody proposal. Would she admit to the impersonation?

The door opened, and Kate stepped out. Before he said a word, she took hold of his arm and drew him to a far corner of the porch. "Mitch, I need to talk to you. There's something I've got to tell you." And he saw it there, in her golden-brown eyes—the decision to bare her soul. To come clean. To put a definite end to the game.

A heavy feeling of foreboding pressed down on him. What then?

He hooked his arm around her waist and swept her down the porch steps, around the corner of the house and into the small, deserted backyard. Without releasing his hold on her, he guided her to the garden swing, where they sat side by side.

Anguish, guilt and anxiety showed in her face. "I haven't been entirely honest with you, Mitch. All I can hope is that you'll understand the reason I wasn't. Arianne..." She paused, pressed her lips together, blinked against a tears. "I wanted to make sure she'd be okay. I thought she'd need me. But now I see—" She paused again, swallowing hard this time. "I'm only making the transition harder. As long as I'm around, she won't accept anyone else as her primary caregiver. The longer I stay, the more difficult it will be for both of us. I think it's best that I make a clean break and let her start fresh. With you. Now. Tonight."

He couldn't utter a word. She really was going to leave them, him and Arianne.

Dragging in a breath, she forged on, "But first, I have to tell you something that will come as a shock, I'm sure. Please keep in mind that I had the best of intentions when I...deceived you."

From the finality in her tone, he knew what would happen once the words had left her lips. She'd apologize, kiss Arianne goodbye and fly off to her own life. Nothing he could say would stop her, because she was leaving for Arianne's sake. And once she left, Mitch Devereaux would be nothing more than a reminder to her of the loss she'd suffered. The cause of her heartbreak.

He couldn't bear that.

"Mitch." Her gaze grew soft and misty with compassion as she took his hands in hers. "Do you remember when I told you that my sister died in that accident?"

He nodded slowly, fighting against a rising sense of desperation. What reason could he give her to stay? He hadn't had the chance to show her his good side. In fact, he was amazed that she'd decided he'd make a good father. She'd seen him angry, hostile, cynical and preoccupied. She believed he'd dived off the boat for kicks, and had intended to jail her sister. What cause had he given her to prolong their relationship? He hadn't once shown her a good time, or danced with her, teased her. Made her laugh.

He hadn't made love to her. How could he let her leave when she didn't yet understand how damn good they'd be together?

"My sister was my identical twin," she pronounced in a tone of weighty revelation. "And I—"

"Don't talk about your sister now," Mitch cut in, running his hands up her bare arms to her silky shoulders. "This isn't a time for sadness, or grieving, or even confessing whatever's on your mind. Tomorrow's soon enough for that. Tonight, let's celebrate the good things. After months of worrying about Arianne, wondering if I'd ever see her again, she's back home and doing fine. That's cause to celebrate."

"But, Mitch, you don't understand. What I have to say is very important, very—"

"Tomorrow." He cupped her face in his hands, looked insistently into her eyes. "Tonight will be for us. For me and the woman who took such good care of my daughter."

She stared wordlessly at him, clearly stunned. Clearly touched. Clearly…tempted. Which sparked a fire of hope within him.

As the early-evening sun slanted golden rays to gild the shadows of the mossy garden, lively strains of accordion and fiddle music beckoned from a distance.

"Dance with me, *chèr',*" he implored. "Come dance with me."

CHAPTER THIRTEEN

HE WASN'T ASKING for much, really. Just a single night of celebration with his family and friends, and for the best of reasons—his daughter's safe return. Kate hated to ruin the party for him with shocking news. She remembered what Darryl had told her about Mitch. That Camryn had stolen his *joie de vivre,* his zest for living. She hoped this need to celebrate signaled its return. In light of her deception, she felt she owed him at least this one night of carefree revelry.

She also had to admit to herself that she felt relieved at not having to confess just yet. In fact, she dreaded having to tell him. He might understand that she'd acted in the best interests of his daughter, and allow her to visit as Arianne's aunt. Or, he might be furious that she'd withheld the news of his wife's death and impersonated her, planning all the while to take his daughter away if she judged him an unfit parent. Who could blame him if he was outraged? *He might banish her from his home, from his life, forever.*

The very possibility broke her heart.

Maybe waiting until morning wasn't such a bad idea. She'd already come *this* far in her deception. He'd either forgive or despise her. How could one more night make much of a difference? He needed an evening of carefree partying, and she would give it to him.

But she wasn't able to ignore her anxiety, guilt and

heaviness of heart enough to actively join in. "*You*
dance, Mitch. I'll enjoy holding Arianne and watching."

That seemed to satisfy him...at least, until they
reached the front yard, where four musicians stood on
the porch playing an accordion, two fiddles and a triangle, while a lanky Cajun cowboy sang a fast, lighthearted ballad. Everyone was dancing, even the children,
with adults and one another. Lisette held a laughing Arianne in her arms, dipping and swaying to the lively,
jumpy sound of Cajun music.

With devilry glinting in his eyes, Mitch caught hold
of Kate's arms and pulled her toward the action. "You
know da two-step, *chèr'?*" he asked with a deliberately
exaggerated Cajun accent.

"No! Well, a little, but—"

He wouldn't take no for an answer. And before she
knew it, he was guiding her with sure hands, irresistible
rhythm and a wide, white smile that she couldn't help
returning.

It had been a long time since she'd danced, and never
in quite this way. The steps themselves weren't intricate.
At least, *hers* weren't. But the turns, twirls, pivots and
fancy arm work required true mastery. Mitch maneuvered her around the yard with such flowing ease that
she suspected he'd been dancing this way since he was
a small boy. A glance around showed her that the tiniest
of tots were learning the basics, and having a grand time
at it, too. A fast waltz followed the two-step, without a
moment's break, and Kate found herself laughing breath-
lessly as Mitch whirled her around in another pattern of
movement.

Couples sped merrily past them, their feet moving in
synchronicity. To her surprise, she spotted Remy among
the dancers, the diamond stud in his teeth flashing in the

summer evening sunshine when he grinned, his grungy old sports cap missing and his grizzled ponytail swaying as he partnered a spry, grandmotherly type in red tasseled boots. Kate also noticed Darryl whirling Joey about, their movements so perfectly choreographed that they seemed to be gliding on air. They smiled into each other's eyes with such warm, adoring expressions Kate barely recognized either of them.

The singer's lyrics took a personal turn, grabbing Kate's attention. "Arianne, oh Arianne," the cowboy crooned, "we're glad to have you home. Now dat we all on da bayou again, *we gonna let da good times roll!*"

Joyous cries of "Ahh-*eee!*" rose from the dancers, including Mitch, who caught Kate up in a fast, hard spin that made her shriek with laughter. The old man playing fiddle echoed in French, *"Laissez les bons temps rouler!"*

Never had Kate felt such a strong, cohesive spirit of celebration...of community, of family. Of life. And poignant gladness filled her knowing that Arianne would always have this. Envy gripped her, too...that she herself wouldn't be here, and wouldn't see her niece blossom in the rare, wonderful warmth.

She wouldn't let the sadness in, though. Not yet. Not tonight. She needed this laughter more than she ever had. Needed Mitch's arms around her, and his smile energizing hers.

How could she have been so wrong about him and his family? She'd presumed the worst. Because of what Remy had told her, she'd expected them to be relatively uneducated, but *Mémère* had shown her Mitch's degrees from a private college in Dallas. He'd won academic scholarships and earned an MBA. His years away from the bayous accounted for the subtlety of his dialect, Kate guessed, although now that he was home, the Cajun cadence had grown more noticeable—in an inexplicably *sexy* way. And she'd seen pictures of his boats. Four of them, all seventy-five-foot trawlers. He may have had to sell a boat to free up funds, but Mitch Devereaux was clearly successful in his chosen field.

Joey, Lisette and Felicia had achieved admirable goals, too. Joey was rapidly moving up in rank at the Terrebonne Department of Education, and her sisters owned a flourishing day-care business.

"I home-schooled my children," *Mémère* had told her. "Back den, da public education wasn't good. Now, we win national awards for our schools. Took a lot of work, but it's worth it, eh?"

Kate felt ashamed of herself for her assumptions.

And now that she saw Darryl with Joey, and knew she worked for the DOE, Kate realized she was the woman Darryl loved. The woman he felt unworthy of. Remy had been right when he'd called him an *imbecile*. The girl plainly adored him.

Why did it seem so hard nowadays to find couples who were happily, mutually, in love? And why, as she asked herself that question, did her eyes return to Mitch and her heart contract with painful longing?

She couldn't fall in love with him! She had no legitimate place in his world, and he certainly had no place in hers. More important still, when she confessed her deception, he might very well despise her.

She tried to keep that in mind as the music slowed, children left the dancing and couples merged into each other's arms. Mitch pulled her close, his embrace warm, strong and utterly compelling, his gaze remaining locked with hers and glimmering with new intensity.

He felt it, too. The longing, the sensual heat that had

only intensified since the first time he'd held her. The realization made it harder for her to resist her feelings for him, but all the more crucial that she did. *Because he believed her to be someone else. The mother of his child. The woman he'd married.*

Was he still in love with Camryn? The thought tolled through Kate like a death knell. Why hadn't the possibility occurred to her more clearly before? She'd taken every glance, every touch, every kiss, in a deeply personal way, meant only for *her,* Kate.

But he didn't know Kate existed.

What an empty-headed fool she'd been! If he still loved Camryn, she was doing him a terrible wrong. She might be giving him hope of reconciliation, when the woman of his heart was actually dead.

"No, *chèr'*. No sadness now," he murmured, sliding his thumb lightly across her bottom lip, as if to guide it into a smile. "Tomorrow will be for problems. Tonight will be for us."

"But that's just it, Mitch. We're not 'us.' There *is* no 'us.'"

"I used to think that, too." He searched her eyes, as if trying to summon a truth buried deep within her soul. "But then I got to know the new you." His hand glided up her back, molding her body to his, and his voice grew hoarse. "Now I want there to be 'us.'"

Her heart surged and thudded. Did he mean he hadn't loved Camryn, or that he hadn't held out hope for their future because of her refusal to change? Either way, she had no business thrilling to anything he said, especially while he believed her to be Camryn.

"Time to change partners, *mes amis,*" a cheery, gruff, familiar voice broke in. She turned to find Remy standing beside them.

"Go away." Mitch kept his arms around Kate.

"Hooo, dey ain't gonna like dis," Remy muttered as he moved on.

And Kate knew without looking that his family watched in growing alarm. They wouldn't want Mitch involved again with the woman who had seriously disrupted his life.

Kate couldn't force herself to break away from him, though. His family would have their peace of mind tomorrow. And she'd walk away with nothing. Not Arianne, not Mitch. In her heart, she knew she'd never get over losing her baby—even if she were permitted visiting rights—and she'd never feel this blood-stirring desire, this sense of absolute rightness, in any other man's arms. Ironic, that, since her staying was absolutely wrong.

"It's time to leave," he said. "Time to get our daughter and go home."

Our daughter. Home. How she loved the sound of that! But the emotion provoked by those words was just one more reason for her to leave Mitch now, before she did something disastrous. Which was too, too easy to imagine.

Because she'd fallen in love with him, she realized with a pang. Thoroughly, hopelessly in love. He was everything she'd ever wanted in a man, and then some. *Oh, Kate, talk to him! Tell him who you are.* Yes, she had to do that. In a truly private place, where they could discuss the matter openly, and he could rail at her, or even cry over Camryn's passing, if need be. Where could be more private than his home? *No, no, tell him here and now.*

At her hesitation, he frowned and swept her away from the dancers to the shadows of a nearby willow, and tipping her face to his, he kissed her. A grazing. A mere tasting. Then a deep, possessive thrusting, silky and hot.

The heat grew too quickly, and she gasped at the fierceness of her response. She wanted him desperately. But she couldn't have him. She couldn't! Certainly not *here*…

He broke from the kiss with a needful groan, and they both fought to normalize their breathing. "Don't think," he pleaded hoarsely. "Just come with me."

Come with me. Such simple words. Oh, but his meaning was far from simple. There was no mistaking his intent, and by accepting the invitation, she would be declaring hers.

"To talk," she breathed, needing to strike a compromise; hoping to be saved from herself by some last-minute, cavalry charge of fortitude.

His gaze burned into hers and his mouth flexed at one corner, as if he strenuously objected to her stipulation. Instead of arguing, though, he concluded the discussion by weaving her fingers tightly through his. She *would* be coming with him.

He then led her around the dancing crowd to where they found *Mémère* in a rocking chair. Arianne slept soundly in her arms, cuddled against her cushiony bosom. With a smile of gratitude and affection for his mother, Mitch reached for his daughter. *Mémère* shook her head and cast him a speaking frown.

Lisette took him by the arm and turned him away from their mother and his sleeping baby. "I need to talk to you, Mitch. Alone."

"I'm about to head home with Arianne. We'll talk tomorrow."

"Camryn's going with you, too, isn't she?" It sounded more like an accusation than a question.

A tense pause stretched between them. "I know you don't mean to stick your nose in my business, *chèr'*," he finally murmured, with only a hint of steel beneath the amiability.

His sister huffed in frustration and tugged him into the long shadows of nearby trees. Even from a fair distance, Kate could hear her furious words. "If you want to risk your own happiness by trusting her again, so be it. But don't put your daughter at risk, too. You'll wake up in da morning and dey'll be gone."

"Don't worry about Arianne or me. We'll be fine."

"Don't worry? Do you realize how you've been looking at Camryn? Like she's da only woman in the world, and you can't wait to get her alone. I never saw you act dat way wit' her before...or wit' anyone else, either."

Kate's heart did another flip. Could that be true?

He made a dismissive sound and turned to leave.

"Please, Mitch, let us keep Arianne here tonight," Lisette urged. "Just until things are more...settled."

After a long, brooding silence, Mitch lifted a palm and let it drop in a distinctly Cajun gesture of surrender. "Tell *Mémère* I'll be back in the morning for Arianne."

With that, he strode away from his sister, slid an arm around Kate and hurried her toward his truck. She felt a multitude of worried eyes follow them. When they reached the pickup, they found that other vehicles had blocked it in. Not to be deterred, Mitch grabbed her suitcase from the bed. "We'll go by boat."

"Boat?"

He smiled at her surprise and led her toward the swampy shore of the bayou. "I live just around the bend."

"We can't walk?"

"I wouldn't recommend it."

She fought a feeling of mild trepidation as he pulled a pirogue out from the high reeds at the water's edge and set it afloat amid an emerald carpet of duckweed. He then placed her suitcase into the boat's center and helped her into the high-sided, flat-bottomed pirogue. She supposed there was nothing really dangerous about boating in the bayou or families wouldn't have been swimming in it.

Shortly after he pushed away from the shore, though, she revised that opinion. They were headed in the opposite direction from the swimming area, down a narrow, twisting offshoot of the bayou, where three-hundred-year-old cypresses stood knee-deep in dark water, and the soupy air smelled of dense, damp greenery. Strains of Cajun music grew faint, like a timeworn memory. Fog hovered in places on the slick black-green water in ghostly apparitions, and wispy trails of Spanish moss hanging from the trees diffused the sunlight, giving the place a murky, mystical feel.

They glided dreamlike through the eerie stillness, into a cacophony of croaking, squawking, trilling and buzzing. All around her, Kate sensed subtle movement—a flutter, a hop, a slither, a splash. Startling, really, in contrast to the utter stillness of the dense air, the black, mirrorlike water and the thick green vegetation carpeting its surface.

Forcing aside her unease, she peered closer and glimpsed a furry brown nutria scampering through the underbrush. Herons roosted among the tall reeds. A red-shouldered hawk dived into the water. A plethora of other unusual birds preened and flitted between the cypresses, bay-leaf trees and willows. An egret, white and long necked, glided over the treetops.

So much to see, to learn! She wished she'd brought binoculars.

Mitch guided the boat with strong digs of a long pole, steering them away from densely overhanging moss and huge, knobby roots of cypress trees protruding from the water, which the children had pointed out earlier as "knees."

The boat glided near a leafy, low-hanging limb, and Kate leaned nervously away from it. "I suppose there are quite a few snakes in the water *and* the trees."

"A few." The quintessential understatement.

She glanced around at the water. "And gators, too."

"Not in the trees, *chèr'*."

She slanted her mouth in wry rebuke. A teasing light glinted in his forest-green eyes, and the dappled sunlight illuminated his bronzed skin and tawny hair with an exotically golden hue. He seemed a creature vitally in tune with the wilds; a natural-born ruler here, with the strength, cunning and grace to easily protect his mate.

His mate. Oh, my. Heat suffused her at the thought.

"The gators won't get you," he said, "as long as you keep your hands in the boat." He then cupped his fine, strong hands to his mouth and emitted a sound like a wild bird call, except deeper, more commanding. "Haah, haah, haah."

After a few repetitions, Kate saw bubbles gurgling about a dozen feet from the boat. An elongated form then rose slightly from the surface of the water. As the form moved closer, she made out eyes...and a long, reptile snout...and a gray-green scaly body. An alligator. A smaller one followed, their eyes seeming to float on the water.

Mitch watched with a pleased air, which helped ease Kate's growing tension. "The big one's Alice," he said, ''and her baby is Cat. Short for Cheshire Cat. My nieces and nephews have named just about every blessed creature in the swamp.''

She smiled, charmed by that thought, and watched the mighty lizards glide peacefully alongside the boat. A silly spurt of contentment breezed through her. She felt as if she belonged here, at this man's side, wherever he happened to lead her, be it bayou, jungle or the great blue sea.

But that feeling was an illusion. Wishful thinking at its worst. *She didn't belong with him.* And the longer she kept up this pretense, the harder it would be to remember that.

She had to confess her identity. Tonight. And since they'd already left the party, she didn't have to worry about ruining his celebration. She wouldn't begin her confession, though, until they reached his house. She didn't want to distract him from his navigation. So she rode with him in silence through twisting, mossy waterways, through fragrant stretches of floating purple flowers, across slow-moving eddies of black-brown water that glinted with the last golden glare of a long midsummer's day.

When they rounded a particularly sharp turn, the water opened up into a wide cove. And the breath literally caught in her throat at the dazzling beauty.

A huge, fiery sun was sinking just beyond the moss-laden cypresses, igniting the sky and water in a blaze of crimson, vermilion and gold. The brilliance shimmered in rays all around the boat, bathing their faces in its glorious heat.

And as they coasted through the colorful radiance, the beauty filled Kate's soul to the very brim, until she ached with the need for someone else to catch and savor the overflow. She glanced at Mitch, and he shifted his stare from the incandescent sky. Keen appreciation coursed between them.

In a devout whisper she marveled, "It's…it's like a divine manifestation."

"That's exactly what it is." And from his gruff, solemn tone of discovery as he stared at her, she knew he wasn't referring to the sunset but to their profound sharing of it.

And she loved him with every fiber of her being.

Which wasn't good. No, not good at all.

Before she could collect herself, the sun sank beyond the horizon, the brilliance cooled to a purplish pink, and Mitch guided the boat to the shore of the cove. The evening shadows thickened as he tied the line to a small wooden pier, hooked the strap of her suitcase over his broad shoulder and helped her disembark. She saw no house or yard—only trees, dense foliage and growing darkness.

Mitch mentioned something about mud and snakes, and Kate didn't protest when he swept her off her feet. She slid her arms around his taut shoulders, immediately aware of the tension in his body; the heat of his arms around her back and thighs; the musky, male scent of his skin and hair; the accelerated thrumming of his heart.

He was bringing her here to make love to her. She hadn't forgotten that.

He moved with silent purpose through a subtropical thicket that smelled of peat moss, muscadine and honeysuckle. Tension tightened between them with every brisk stride. Her pulse drummed; her blood roared in her ears.

She wanted him! She wanted to taste his kiss again,

feel his strength, his heat. Wanted to provoke him to wildness; to ride the power of his storm.

But the storm she was about to provoke was not the kind she wanted. She wasn't the woman he believed her to be, and almost everything she'd told him had been a lie. Would he despise her?

A small cypress cabin with a pillared front porch appeared within a copse of huge, ancient trees. Lights glowed golden from a window. Mitch took the porch steps in one impatient bound, shoved open the unlocked door and carried her inside. In three thudding heartbeats, he crossed a cozy, lamp-lit room and set her on the edge of a low counter that divided the living room from the kitchen.

She released her arms from his neck, expecting him to move away.

He didn't. He dropped the suitcase from his shoulder and commandeered her gaze, while his hands coursed down the length of her thighs, his touch simmering through the thin, damp fabric of her dress. Parting her legs, he pressed his hips between them and pulled her closer, tighter, against him. "We're home," he said in a drawn-out whisper, searching her face with blood-stirring intensity. "I didn't think I'd ever get you here."

Powerful desire rose in her, and kept her silent when she knew she should speak; kept her aching for more of his hardness and heat when she knew she should back away.

With a harsh breath, he slid his hand around her nape and took her mouth in a long, lush, intricate kiss. She closed her eyes and courted the heat, wishing the kiss would never end.

Eventually it did, though. And before he led her into another, her moral sense reared up in protest. She had to put an end to this! To her deceit. To his passion. To *them*.

With an anguished groan, she pushed her hands against his muscled chest and staved him off. "I'm sorry, Mitch." Her heart tied itself into knots. "I'm so, so sorry. I don't know the best way to explain what I've done, and why I did it, but—" She paused to gather her words. To get her explanation exactly right, so he wouldn't immediately close his mind and heart to her.

But as he waited for her to continue, his jaw squared, his brows knitted, his masculine beauty so blazingly potent that she could barely think straight, she couldn't summon the first coherent word.

"Don't make this so hard, *chèr*,'' he murmured in a gruff voice, his expression heated and tender as he brushed a stray blond tendril back from her face. "Just tell me, Kate. Tell me who you are."

CHAPTER FOURTEEN

IT TOOK A MOMENT for the meaning of his words to fully register. *Just tell me, Kate.* He'd called her Kate! *Tell me who you are.* She stared at him in stunned silence, unable to think beyond one incomprehensible fact. He knew.

He raised a tawny brow, silently prodding her for a reply.

"You...*know?*" she managed to utter. A ridiculously inane thing to ask, but those were the only two words running through her head.

"A loaded question," he said, studying her. "Let's start with the fact that I know who you're *not.*"

Mortification weighted her down. He knew she wasn't Camryn, and that she was a liar. Those two facts couldn't have been more damning. How could he ever forgive her?

Other questions rushed at her. How long had he known? How had he found out? Why hadn't he confronted her and put an end to the deception? *Why had he kissed her?* The most pressing question rose above the others, though, and wedged painfully in her chest. She had no choice but to ask it, and she braced herself for his response. "Do you know, then, about... Camryn?"

Somberness shaded his face, and he nodded.

She shut her eyes, overcome by regret over what she'd

done, as well as grief. "I'm sorry," she whispered, unable to say more.

"I'm sorry, too, Kate. I know you loved her. And though you might not believe it after all my ranting and raging, *I* cared about her, too. I was hoping she'd find her way to real happiness eventually."

She swallowed convulsively at that and struggled to tamp down her grief. She'd hoped the same for her. Slowly, then, she opened her eyes to see what she'd find in his face. She saw compassion—*for her*—and unmistakable warmth. Her heart slowly thudded back to life. He didn't despise her. And he wasn't devastated by Camryn's death. Amazing, how those facts allowed her to breathe again.

Her relief was too acute, his nearness too overwhelming. Sliding down from the counter, she sidestepped him and paced across the hardwood floor, past handmade throw rugs and a wide oak-and-leather chair near a stone fireplace. Her emotions were too chaotic to face him just yet. "How did you find out?"

"I started believing your amnesia story," he said, causing warm color to suffuse her face. Another lie she'd told. How could he ever trust her? "I wanted to know more about the accident, so I had the private investigator who found you do a little more digging." Through the mirror above the mantel, she saw that he was leaning casually against the countertop and watching her. "By the time he got back to me, I wasn't really all that surprised to learn you weren't Camryn. Your personalities are too different to be explained by amnesia, or anything else, for that matter."

Kate wrapped her arms around herself and kept her back to him. Remembering the time they'd spent together only made her emotions more volatile. *How long had he known the truth?* She struggled to keep her voice reasonably nonchalant. "When did you, um, get the news from your investigator about my...identity?"

He didn't answer, but through the mirror, she saw him stroll toward her, his hands in his pockets, his face dark and serious. "Kate." He stopped directly behind her. "Come sit down and we'll talk."

She didn't budge from where she stood. In fact, she turned her face from the mirror so she couldn't see him. She didn't want to look in his eyes. Her control was too fragile. Who knew which of her emotions might break free?

"I'll get us some wine," he said, "or whatever you'd like. Coffee, cola, water..."

"Nothing, thank you." It seemed that an emotion was indeed emerging as dominant. Anger. He'd let her carry on with the impersonation and anguish needlessly over the prospect of confessing. "Does your family know who I am?" She tried to keep the sharpness out of her tone. "Are they all in on the...game?"

"Game?" His hands closed on her shoulders and he turned her to face him. "Is that what we're doing... playing a game?"

She couldn't help glaring at him. "Do they know?"

"No. I'm the only one who knows who you are. But that's about *all* the information I've been given—your name. Oh, and I also learned your occupation, professor...courtesy of the ID card in your purse."

"You looked in my purse?"

"Yes, ma'am, I did. That doesn't upset you, does it? But I have a feeling you're upset, anyway. Why? Because I wasn't open and up front? Because *I* kept something from *you?*"

His point struck home, of course. She really had no

room to complain. Guilt diluted her anger, but not enough to entirely douse it. She raised her chin and leveled him cool with a glance. "Why didn't you tell me you knew?"

"I wanted to see what you intended to do."

"And have you?"

"I think so, but I'd like to hear it from you."

She compressed her lips. She didn't want to be put on the defensive quite yet. "You didn't answer my question. When did your investigator tell you about me?" When he merely gazed at her in stubborn silence, she asked, "Did you know who I was while we were sitting on the roof of your boat and I told you about my sister's death?"

"No. I believed every lie you told me." She flinched at that, and he pressed for the advantage. "Now answer a question for me, Kate. Why did you spend the past four days pretending to be *my wife?*"

Oh, he was good. He'd finessed his way right out of answering her real question. She wanted to know, *needed* to know, when he'd discovered her identity. Realizing her chances were slim of getting a reply unless she answered him first, she rested her fists on her hips and glowered. "You were *barbaric* when you broke into my home, and I didn't know who you were, where you lived, or where you'd sent Arianne. All my sister ever told me about Arianne's father was that he was mean."

"Mean!"

"That's right. Abusive. And I was afraid that if you knew I wasn't Camryn, you'd just disappear and I'd never find Arianne."

"You were planning to run with her if you had to, weren't you?"

"Yes."

They stared at each other with flushed, angry faces. "And what do you think now, Kate? Do you think I was abusive to your sister, or to my daughter?"

How, oh *how*, had he gotten her so far off the subject? She wanted *her* question answered, damn it. "No. I think you tried to save Camryn from herself. And I think you'd rather die than hurt Arianne. I think you'll give her the very best life you can, and that you're kind, and f-fair, and—" Her throat closed; her eyes moistened. Now *she* was getting off the subject. "When did you know I wasn't Camryn?" she asked in an uneven whisper.

He loomed closer, his expression losing all anger but gaining a new intensity. "That's a hard question to answer, Kate. I guess on some level, I knew you weren't Camryn when you smiled about taking that damn saltwater shower. And again when you thanked me for helping you through your seasickness. And when you refused to share my bed…and most of all, when I couldn't keep my hands off you, even in my sleep."

Heat welled up in her, and she bit her lip.

He wasn't finished, though. "I'd rather that you ask the question the way you really mean it. *When did I know who you were.* That's a hell of a lot more important than when I knew you weren't Camryn." He moved nearer, until his heat and his scent enveloped her. "I knew who you were, Kate, when you made mashed potatoes in the middle of the night to bandage Darryl's hand. I knew who you were when you fought to keep me from diving off the boat, and when we held each other afterward. I knew who you were when you hugged my daughter like there was nothing in the world more vital. And in case that doesn't answer your question…I knew who you were when I kissed you. Every time."

The quiet fervor of that statement trapped the breath in her lungs. "Or I wouldn't have done it, Kate."

And she was right back to where she'd been when he'd first carried her in here—*thoroughly, helplessly, in love with him.*

He caressed her face with both hands, swept his thumbs alongside her mouth. "I want you," he said in a husky tone. "Now, Kate. Tonight. All night."

Yes. Oh, yes. She wanted him, too. And if a little voice in her head warned her not to mistake his passion for love, she ignored it. If reason begged from some distant part of her soul to take things slower, to protect her heart, she shifted her attention elsewhere. She, the girl who had spent an eternity in a children's home watching prospective parents pass her by; she, the woman who had invested her heart in a child who would never be hers; she, the one who had lost every blessed person who had ever loved her, refused to think beyond this one night.

She answered him by weaving her hands into his thick, silky hair and kissing him, not on the mouth, but just beside it...then in a tender, lingering brush of her lips across his jaw and face; a sensual exploration of the strong, masculine planes, angles and clefts that so beguiled her. With each new sweep of her mouth, his breathing deepened, and her need for him grew.

Exhaling in a hard rush, Mitch shut his eyes and caught her body to his. *She was going to make love to him.* The realization awed him to his very core. And the feel of her soft, lush mouth skimming his face, her fingers sifting through his hair, her breasts pressing against his chest, sent desire shooting to his loins.

Her lips neared his, and hunger broke through his control. He splayed his hands across her back and hip and brought her down with him onto the leather sofa, where he captured her mouth in a deep, hot, sexual kiss. If life was a banquet, she was his bread, his wine, his spice… and he couldn't get enough.

Heat flared between them with awesome intensity, and their hands quested beneath clothing in needful caresses—hers, beneath his shirt, along the muscles of his back and chest; his, beneath her dress, along the silky length of her thigh, around the curve of her hip and up to the warm fullness of her cresting breasts.

His need swelled into an ache. Breaking from their kiss, he released her from his arms, rose from the sofa and briskly worked at doffing his clothes while his gaze traveled over her. Most of her hair had escaped from the French twist, looking tousled and sexy around her flushed face. Her honey-brown eyes were on him as he undressed, her lips rosy and kiss swollen, her breathing labored, her coral sundress riding low beneath her tanned shoulders. He wanted her with a desperation that shocked him.

She reached behind her to unzip the dress.

"No." His voice emerged as a rasp. "Let me."

He cast the last of his clothing aside and reached for her. His hands nearly shook as he stripped the clothes off her—the close-fitting, gauzy dress he'd been trying his damnedest to peer through all day, and the prim little cotton panties he'd probably never see again without thinking how they'd looked being tugged down her long, wicked legs.

His heart thundered; his blood rushed. His appreciation bordered on painful. She was simply too beautiful in her nakedness to casually behold. Her physical perfection came as no surprise. He'd been married to her identical twin. Yet Kate's beauty transcended any he'd ever seen. Just as the sunset had somehow glowed with unparalleled radiance, so did Kate. And her golden eyes were heated with desire and calling to him.

She would be his, he swore. Not just for now, but forever.

He set about making it so. With need throbbing through his veins, he blazed a meandering path down her body with his mouth, kissing, suckling and swirling his way into a swelter, until she lay gasping and trembling, her hips undulating between his hands. Only then did he thrust his fingers into her heat.

She would be *his*.

He brought her to a wild, shuddering completion. And by the time she wrapped her legs around his waist and he drove into her, hard and deep, they were both slick with sweat, feverish with passion and lost to everything but the need to possess.

His climax nearly blinded him.

And Kate finally understood what she'd been missing from her life—not only love and family and adventure, but *this*. The most exhilarating fire in her blood, in her loins, in every fiber of her being, and pleasure so intense her body quaked with it. She'd had orgasms before, but they'd been only pale foreshadowings of what she'd felt with him…not once, but twice, in rapid succession. She felt as if her soul had left her body to somersault through the heavens.

The intensity left them both gasping for breath, collapsed on the sofa, entwined in a tight embrace that anchored them while the world slowly drifted back into place.

She expected nothing more from the night, sexually speaking. She already felt enriched beyond her wildest dreams, and would have been content to merely hold him.

He had other things in mind. He brought her home-made elderberry wine, fragrant and full-bodied, which they shared along with a blanket to cuddle under, dreamy candlelight and spontaneous, wine-flavored kisses. And when they finally forced themselves up from the sofa, he set their glasses aside, tugged her into the shower with him and teased her into laughter.

She'd never before associated laughter with lovemaking. Yet somehow the two blended naturally. One moment they were playing in the driving water and billowing steam, smiling into each other's eyes, lathering fragrant shampoo into each other's hair. But then he nudged her out of the direct flow of water and reached for the soap. The sight of his wet, muscled body, and the sensations coursing through her from his strong, virile, workman's hands as he sudsed her shoulders, back and hips, turned her playfulness into keen sensuality.

That sensuality soon possessed her. Transformed her. She turned into a purely sexual being, one of movement, heat and desire. While his sudsy hands rounded her breasts, cupping and kneading, tweaking her nipples into highly reactive points, her back arched, her eyes closed. Her hands flexed in compulsive rhythm through her lathery hair as her body writhed in sinuous, voluptuous gyrations.

His playfulness left him. His hands surged with new urgency, everywhere. *Every*where. His breathing turned harsh, interspersed with deep-throated groans, and he dropped to his knees before her. Running one hand around her undulating bottom, he worked the other to lather suds between her legs.

Pleasure coursed through her like lava, and a glance

at his dark, rugged face filled her with an intoxicating sense of power. Through hooded eyes, he watched her hips roll and his hand glide. His jaw was tight; a pulse beat at his temple; his chest rose and fell in hard contractions.

The rhythm of her gyrations quickened. Sensation flashed through her with each slide of his hand, each delve of his fingers, building her need to a fierce intensity. With a breathless cry, she forced her movement to a halt and closed his hand between her thighs. She wouldn't relinquish the power to him just yet.

"Stand up," she urged in a tremulous whisper.

"Kate," he groaned on a hot breath, ignoring her command, shifting her until the water sluiced down her torso and rinsed away the suds. He then ran his tongue across her glistening skin, back and forth, just above the blond, water-slick triangle. And then downward.

Her breath came in gasps, and her legs shook. She couldn't let him get away with this! She'd lose all control. Digging her fingers into the water-beaded brawn of his shoulders, she pried him away. Forced him to rise.

On his way up, he scoured her face with a desperate stare.

"Hands against the wall," she murmured, her voice unrecognizable in its huskiness.

A muscle flexed in his jaw. His eyes flashed. But he did as he was told, flattening his palms against the wall on either side of her, bringing his face close to hers. He angled in for a kiss. She evaded him. And soaped her hands. And applied them with a vengeance to his sinewy body—across wide shoulders and a heaving chest, her fingers working the suds through fine whorls of hair and around peaking nipples. She raked her hands downward, then, to his washboard abdomen and strong, lean hips…and around to his tautly muscled backside. The feel of him streamed from her fingertips to sizzle through her blood.

He watched her with barely contained savagery. Animal-like hunger.

She wasn't done with her tormenting, though. She stroked between his legs in rich, soapy lather—first the velvety heaviness underneath, then up along the hard, pulsing strength of his erection. With a hissing intake of breath, he shut his eyes, pressed harder against the wall and moved in a sinuous dance of his own. A glorious male beast, roused and ready, undulating in subtle yet powerful thrusts.

Her hand gripped and slid through the suds, harnessing the pulsating power. Heat fluxed through her, simmering, radiating, deep within her core.

A helpless moan vibrated in her throat.

He opened his eyes. Met her gaze. Pulled back from the wall, curved his hands around her bottom and lifted her. Her legs slid around his hips, her arms about his neck.

And he surged into her.

Ah, the power and fury of that storm! Lightning, thunder, hurricane force…she experienced all, with pleasure rising in her like a tidal wave, until the crest broke over them with a stunning potency.

It took a long, long while of huddling together against the shower wall before either of them could move. Kate felt as if she'd been profoundly transformed. A new persona had emerged from within the staid, prudent Kate. A freer, stronger woman…yet somehow utterly bound to *him*. Her wild, green-eyed lover. Her oh-*so*-willing sex slave. She reveled in her newfound sexual prowess.

The utter freedom she felt with him. The poignant satisfaction.

Afterward, when the water ran cold and they stirred back to life with dazed expressions, prunelike fingers and chilled flesh, they dried each other off with fluffy towels and probed each other's gazes, as if searching for yet a deeper connection. *Feeling* a deeper connection. Drifting then on a warm euphoria, she curled up with him in bed and slept in exhausted slumber, her naked body curving with sleek perfection to his.

Mitch stirred first at dawn, his dreams saturated with the flavors and textures of their lovemaking; his consciousness dawning with awed awareness of her in his arms. Life could get no finer. He brought her awake with slow, hot caresses, and this time, they made love without the sound and the fury; without the hurricane force. They moved, instead, in subtle synchronicity and savored the most sumptuous tenderness he'd ever known.

And in the jaw-clenching, hip-grinding heat of it, he marveled at how much he loved her. She was, without a doubt, the One.

The power of the sea, the beauty of the sunset, the physical high of making love—all these had taken on a whole new dimension because of her. Though each had filled him with the old soul-deep yearning, it hadn't been an empty yearning. He hadn't longed for a woman he might never meet, but for *her,* the woman at his side.

And now, in the clear light of morning, after a full night of incredible lovemaking, the longing for her hadn't lessened. It had grown into something powerful and relentless. He had to find a way to keep her here, in his world, or make a place for himself in hers. She was the woman meant for him. His mate.

Should he tell her how he felt, or would he scare her

away? After all, she'd only known him for four days. *Four days.* Yet he'd known *her,* searched for her, longed for her, his entire life.

Lying with their bodies entwined, her face tucked against his neck, her silky, fragrant hair pooling across his chest, he didn't want to let her leave his bed. Didn't want to end the bliss. But bright sunlight streamed through slim openings in the curtains, and he knew the day would begin whether he wanted it to or not.

As if reading his thoughts, she lifted her head and rested it on the pillow beside his. With a small but heart-stirring smile, she murmured, "You're very good at what you do, Mitch Devereaux."

Humor momentarily lightened his intensity. "Shrimping?"

"Well, that, too. But I meant, making love."

Fervently glad for that, he reached out and touched a golden tangle of hair beside her face, savoring its luxuriant softness. Again he wondered, should he tell her that he loved her? Or would that be rushing things too much?

Before he could decide, she said in a warm, drawn-out whisper, "I've never made love like that before."

His heart expanded. "I haven't, either."

Her delicate golden brows knitted. "I find that hard to believe."

"Why?"

"I just assumed that you…well, made love many times, and with women who—" She broke off and blushed. "I'm sorry. I didn't mean to lead you into a discussion about what you've done, or haven't done."

He smoothed the back of his fingers across the creamy softness of her face, wanting so badly to keep her with him for the rest of their lives. "I've made love *with* women before last night, but never *to* them."

She frowned in clear puzzlement. "The difference being…?"

"I'd say it's the difference between singing a song *with* someone—" he paused, choosing his words to get his meaning exactly right "—or *to* someone. The first is a shared activity. Fun, rousing. Companionable." He searched her eyes for understanding. "The other is a form of communication. A way of expressing what's in your heart. I was singing my song *to* you, Kate. Not just with you."

Kate felt her chest expand with the warmest of hope. Was he saying that he loved her? But she couldn't allow herself to jump to that conclusion. She was probably reading too much into a beautiful, poetic sentiment uttered after a night of passionate lovemaking.

"My song's all about you, Kate," he said, slanting his face across hers, his arousal once again stirring to life between them. "About you and me, together."

And, oh, how she thrilled to that song, wanting to hear it again, and listen more closely this time to the lyrics. But before they'd even properly kissed, a noise intruded from beyond their closed bedroom door. The sound of the front door opening.

"Mitch, you home?" came a man's shout.

Mitch pulled away from their kiss and cursed beneath his breath. "Kip Landry, my lawyer. An old friend. One with lousy timing." Swinging his legs over the side of the bed, he raised his voice to answer. "I'll be right out, Kip."

He drew a change of clothing from his dresser and hurriedly donned fresh jeans and a light chambray shirt. It was the first time she'd seen him in anything but

T-shirts. He looked so vitally strong, tanned and hand-some, even with his hair all mussed and a morning shadow darkening his jaw. "Don't you dare go any-where," he told her. "I'll be back as soon as I can." He then strode out to meet his guest, closing the bed-room door firmly behind him.

She heard the lawyer's greeting, only slightly muffled through the closed bedroom door. "Stopped by to talk about the Kate Jones situation."

Kate sat up straight from the pillows, her heart gearing into a slower, heavier beat. *The Kate Jones situation?*

"Outside, Kip," Mitch said.

"Why, you got somebody here?"

"Outside."

Kate fought free of the tangled bedcovers and nearly tripped over her own bare feet as she hurried to the open bedroom window. Pushing aside one corner of the cur-tain and virtually pressing her ear to the screen, she heard the lawyer's hearty voice, although Mitch had ap-parently led him a good distance away from the house.

"Yessir, you were right to worry. It'd cost you a pretty penny to defend yourself if she brings you up on assault or kidnapping charges. As far as a claim to cus-tody for Arianne, she doesn't have many grounds, unless she has you locked up in prison."

Dismay shot through Kate with such sickening force she could barely hold back a cry. Mitch's reply was too low to hear, but as she peered through the curtains, she saw that he was practically pushing Kip into a black luxury sedan.

"What do you mean, later?" the lawyer boomed. "I just spent half my holiday weekend doing research to keep you out of jail."

Again, she couldn't make out Mitch's answer.

The car door slammed, the motor started and Kip called through the open car window, "Like I told you before, get on her good side. Cozy up all you can. Knowing your way with the ladies, that shouldn't be too hard." He then drove away.

With her heart slamming painfully against her rib cage, Kate grabbed her toiletries from her suitcase, slipped to the bathroom and locked the door. She then reached into the shower stall and turned on the water, full blast. Ignoring the provocative memories they'd made in this stall last night, she leaned against the bathroom wall and wrapped her arms tightly around herself.

Please, don't jump to conclusions! You can't judge Mitch by a few overheard remarks. She'd always believed in giving people a fair chance to prove themselves before drawing unfavorable conclusions. To do less now would be highly unfair to Mitch *and* herself.

Yet, those few overheard remarks couldn't be ignored, either. Like a dowsing of cold water, they'd shocked her out of a dreamlike euphoria unlike any she'd ever experienced. She couldn't judge him on the basis of *that,* either. She'd been so carried away by his charm and his lovemaking that she'd actually believed he was falling in love with her. After only four days!

"Kate," Mitch called through the locked bathroom door, trying the knob. "How about opening up? We could pick up where we left off."

She didn't answer. Let him think she was already in the shower and couldn't hear him. She needed time to gather her scattered thoughts. To deal with the mind-numbing blow.

Oh, come on. *It's not that bad,* she told herself. *He didn't do anything wrong.* She couldn't blame him for contacting his lawyer. If she had discovered he was abusive, she *would* have pressed charges against him and sued for custody of Arianne. At least now she understood why he'd waited to confront her about the impersonation. He'd been buying time for his lawyer to prepare.

To find a good defense against charges she might level against him.

Oh, God. Why hadn't she realized Mitch might have that concern in mind?

Get on her good side. Cozy up. She cringed at the remembered words. She also thought back to all the nice things Mitch had said and done, and how she'd taken every one of them to heart.

He might have been sincere, she reminded herself, wanting to believe it. Just because he'd consulted a lawyer about her didn't mean he hadn't really wanted her. But the practical, world-weary voice in her head cut in, *You've only known him for four days, and you've lost your objectivity.*

That much was undeniably true. And if she discovered that he *had* sweet-talked her, made love to her, led her into loving him, all for the purpose of "cozying up," she'd never get over the heartbreak. But how would she ever know what his motivation had been? He would never admit to a hidden agenda. Even if she swore she had no intention of filing charges, she could change her mind, right up until the statute of limitations ran out, which might be years from now. The fact that he hadn't talked to her about his concern, hadn't cleared the air, left her doubting his sincerity.

Humiliation scalded her at the possibility that he'd courted her passion with an ulterior motive. She wouldn't jump to that conclusion, though. That wouldn't be fair to him. But she couldn't close her mind to it, either. And she certainly didn't intend to let him know what she'd overheard, or he'd bend over backward to assure her that the legal issues had nothing to do with their personal relationship. What other response could he give without utterly alienating her?

No, she wouldn't let him know she'd overheard. She'd employ the acting skill that helped keep her pride intact all those years ago, when potential parents had looked the orphans over and passed by her and Camryn in favor of an infant.

Kate hadn't blamed them back then for preferring a baby, and she didn't blame Mitch now for doing everything he could to protect himself and his daughter. At least, that was what her rational mind was telling her. But a strident inner voice cried out, *Don't you know that love is for other people, never for you? You'll always be on the outside, looking in. Haven't you learned that by now?*

The pain that pierced her was not new but very old, an integral part of her spiritual makeup, and far too strong to fight. She realized then that even if she hadn't overheard Kip Landry's remarks, the euphoria couldn't have lasted. Her entire life experience proved as much.

She had to get away to think straight. Away from Mitch, his intoxicating touch, his mind-drugging words. She had to get back to *her* world, to the levelheaded, clear-sighted Kate Jones she knew and understood.

Maybe then she could sort through the chaos that was her soul.

CHAPTER FIFTEEN

MITCH WAS DISAPPOINTED to find the bathroom door locked. He would have loved to join Kate in her shower. Thoughts of their last one still sent rushes of heat through him.

Damn Kip for interrupting them this morning! He'd sent him away as fast as he could. He no longer needed his advice regarding Kate. He knew she wouldn't bring charges against him. She would do all she could to make Arianne feel at home with him. He hoped that would include staying with them.

She hadn't mentioned the flight to Tallahassee he'd overheard her booking for today. That was a good sign. He would ask her at breakfast to stay an extra week or two. Didn't want to spook her by pressing for more. By the end of that time, though, he would convince her to stay permanently.

He looked forward with keen relish to the persuasion tactics he intended to employ.

Forcing his thoughts away from Kate in order to function as a rational being, he sauntered into the kitchen to scrounge up breakfast. As soon as they'd eaten, they'd go to his parents' house and pick up Arianne. What could be more perfect than having them, Kate and Arianne, together forever in his life?

A goal well worth pursuing.

He would take the next week off from work to do just

that. To become an integral part of their lives. He'd already installed captains on all his boats. When his week of vacation had ended, he'd finalize the deal on a purchase of a dock, perfectly situated on a deep-water canal. With the help of a few savvy investors, he'd shape it into a commercial enterprise to cater to boats other than his own.

Highly pleased with the turn his life had taken, he whistled an old Cajun tune as he reached for the coffeepot. Through the open kitchen window, he caught sight of two familiar pickup trucks pulling into his yard. His parents and Joey were in the first, and Darryl and Remy in the next. He assumed they were bringing Arianne to him, and he smiled with anticipation.

He soon realized, though, that Arianne wasn't with them.

"Mitch isn't thinking wit' his brain anymore," Joey was saying to his parents as they climbed out of his father's truck. "If he won't have Camryn arrested, I will. Da sheriff's a good friend. If I call him, he'll charge her wit' violating dat custody order."

"Just talk to Mitch about it, Joey," his mother implored as she and his father trudged along with her toward the house.

From a few paces behind them, Darryl growled, "Don't go messing in Mitch's business, Jo."

"It's my business, too. I won't let that siren steal my niece again."

"I'm telling you, she ain't da same woman she used to be," Darryl said, surprising Mitch. He'd never heard Darryl take such a fervent stand against anything Joey wanted. Amazing that he'd do so over Camryn—or the woman he thought was Camryn. "She won't run wit' Arianne."

"Tu m'dis pas! And when did you get to know her so well, hmm?"* Joey's tone spoke volumes about her feelings for the man who'd grown up next door to her, although she'd never admitted those feelings, as far as Mitch knew. "Did she work her siren magic on you, too?"

Darryl's face reddened. "Don't be crazy."

Deciding to put an end to Joey's ranting before Kate finished with her shower, Mitch ambled out onto the porch. "Where's Arianne?"

No one answered, but Joey barged forward with that determined expression that usually made Mitch groan. "Lisette has her. We didn't want da baby upset by anything dat goes on here dis morning." Glancing at the house, she lowered her voice. "Is Camryn still here?"

"Jo, you're making a big mistake getting involved in something you don't know about," Darryl warned, lumbering to her side with a scowl.

"You be quiet and mind your own—"

"Darryl's right, Joey," Mitch cut in, his brusque tone effectively drawing her attention. "You don't know anything about the situation. None of you do. If you'll have a seat on the porch—" he nodded toward the rockers and swing "—I'll explain some things that'll make it clear."

"On da porch?" Joey said. "You mean, we're not welcome inside?"

"That depends on how open-minded you are to what I'm about to tell you."

She gaped at him in affront and alarm. His parents exchanged worried glances. He knew what they feared— that he was about to announce his reconciliation with Camryn. He wasn't sure his real news would make them feel much better. How to explain that Kate had deceived them only for Arianne's sake…and that he'd forgiven her and intended to keep her around for as long as she'd stay?

He wouldn't explain anything, of course, until Kate was standing beside him. "My houseguest and I will be out in a few moments to talk."

With that, he strode to the bedroom to see what was taking Kate so long. As he pushed open the door, the sight of her brought him to a surprised halt. She was slipping into the tailored jacket of a cream-colored linen pantsuit, which she wore with an apricot silk shell and high-heeled pumps. Her hair was coiled in a shining braid on top her head, with tiny wisps framing her face and small pearls glinted at her ears and throat.

She looked elegant, beautiful and, somehow, beyond his reach. He wasn't sure what gave him that last impression, but it made his insides clench with foreboding. "My, don't you look nice."

She tossed him a smile, then turned to the mirror to smooth her hair. Not a single strand was out of place.

He shut the door behind him. "But…why are you so dressed up?"

"Well, I told you yesterday that I was out of clean shorts and tops. All I have left are suits and dresses. This was the most casual." She met his gaze in the mirror. Reluctantly, it seemed. "Which is fine, really, because I'm going to be…traveling today."

He stared at her in disbelief. *She hadn't changed her mind about leaving.* Their kisses, their lovemaking, their intimacy…none of it had changed her mind. Her suitcase stood beside the bed, ready to go.

But maybe she'd come back. Maybe she'd handle business in Tallahassee, then catch a return flight. "What exactly are your plans?"

"I'm going home," she answered with devastating simplicity. "My flight's this afternoon, out of New Orleans. I probably should have told you earlier, but I guess I was too...distracted." She offered him a weak smile.

He felt as if he'd been kicked in the head. The world suddenly seemed off-kilter. "Kate." He approached her in a daze. "You can't leave yet. We have things to talk about. Loose ends to tie up. Besides—" he slid his arms around her and pulled her near "—I'm not ready to let you go."

Her expression warmed, thank God, and her hands skimmed up his chest, but then regret clouded her face. "I had a wonderful time with you last night," she said softly. "And what I said was true. I've never before felt the way you made me feel. I'll always treasure the memory."

Always treasure the memory. Oh, God.

"Now it's time for me to go," she said, "and get back to my own life."

"Your own life?" His voice had gone dry and gruff.

"I *do* have a life, you know." She meant to sound rueful, he knew. Droll. The attempt at humor fell flat. "Classes will be starting next month, and I have to prepare my lesson plans."

"You have a whole month to do that. Stay longer, Kate. A week or so. Here, with me and Arianne." He ran his hands up her back, pressed her tighter against him...willed her to lift her face to his for a kiss.

She didn't. Emotion darkened her eyes, and she drew back from his embrace. "I'm sorry, but I can't stay. And I think it's better that I don't see Arianne before I go." Her bottom lip quivered, and her eyes gleamed too brightly. "There's no sense in upsetting her. Maybe after some time has passed...a year, I'd say...I can see her again, and it won't disrupt her transition.'' Tears welled up, and she dashed them away with her hand.

Anger reared in him. "You're ready to just walk away from her—" *and from me* "—and not see her for a whole year?''

"It won't be easy, believe me. But she needs time to adjust to her new home without being reminded of... of..." She finished on a whisper, "Me.''

"She needs all the love she can get, and as far as she knows, you're her main source. You're running away, Kate. Why?''

"I'm going *home,* not running away. Please don't make this any harder. If you or your mother would drop me a line now and then, just to tell me how Arianne is doing, I'd be very grateful.''

Drop her a line. He or his mother. He couldn't have been more stunned if she'd slapped him. "Are you saying you don't want me to call you, or...visit?''

When the moment dragged on and she hadn't answered, he tipped her chin up to better read her face. "It's not that hard of a question. You either want me, Kate...or you don't.''

She regarded him in clear dismay. And an ache grew inside him. Averting her face, she paced away. "Things happened so quickly between us, and I...I was in a place and frame of mind that made me feel—" she spread her hands "—unlike myself. I need to get back to reality. *My* reality.'' She paused, gathered her thoughts and delivered her answer. "I would prefer you didn't call, unless it has to do with Arianne.''

He couldn't breathe for quite a long moment. He wasn't part of her reality...except as Arianne's father. He found that impossible to accept.

"I want to stay in Arianne's life, as her aunt,'' she

said. "A sexual relationship between you and me will only make things…awkward."

Pain and anger mounted in his chest. She saw their relationship as only sexual. And *awkward.* "You didn't mention that concern last night."

"Last night wasn't for problems," she whispered, her eyes shining with an intensity that twisted the knife in his gut. "We saved those for today. Remember?"

He hadn't expected his own words to come back and ambush him. And after last night, he hadn't expected her to shrug aside their relationship as if it were a minor faux pas. Just this morning, they'd made the sweetest love. He couldn't believe she'd consider that casual entertainment. Camryn would have. Kate would not. He knew that in his heart, his bones.

Something had changed drastically between them since earlier this morning. Since…*Kip's visit.*

The realization flashed like light in a thickening fog. When Kip had walked in the house, he'd said, *"I've come to talk about the Kate Jones situation."* He'd said it quietly enough, though, that Mitch hadn't thought Kate heard. Maybe he'd been wrong.

He searched her face. "Did you, by any chance, overhear Kip say that he'd stopped by to talk about…you?"

"About me? Your lawyer came by to talk about *me?*"

He scrutinized her. Had she really not overheard what Kip had said before he'd hurried him outside? Things would be much easier to fix if that was the problem. A simple matter of explaining. "When I first learned you weren't Camryn, I called him to ask for advice. Dragging women from their homes and across the Gulf of Mexico isn't something I do every day. Could get a man into trouble."

She gave a soft, understanding smile. "Don't worry,

Mitch. I understand why you did it, and I admire your determination to bring your daughter home. Don't give it another thought. I'd never do anything to hurt you or Arianne.''

Oh, but she was. She was tearing their hearts out.

''I should get on the road,'' she murmured, looking pale and distraught, despite the cavalier attitude she'd assumed. She looped the strap of her slim, beige handbag over her shoulder. ''I know New Orleans is quite a distance from here. Will you be able to drive me, or should I…find other transportation?''

Her courteous detachment washed through him in cold, stunning currents, dousing the last of his doubt. *She really intended to leave him.* Just like that, without a backward glance. Which meant she didn't give a damn about him, or the love they'd made, and hadn't given a thought to a future with him. What had all those tender kisses been about? All those mesmerizing, heart-in-her-eyes gazes?

Why hadn't he known she'd only been playing?

Fighting to keep the pain and anger from his voice, he asked in a flat, cool tone, ''What time's your flight?''

''One-thirty.''

He pursed his lips and nodded. ''I'm sure we'll find plenty of volunteers who'll be more than happy to drive you.'' Turning his back on her, he walked to the door, then paused. ''I'd take you myself, but I have a daughter who's going to need me more now than ever.'' And the truth of that statement tore him in two. Happy though he was that Arianne was home, it pained him to know she was losing Kate.

And that *he* was losing Kate.

''I hear people talking outside,'' she remarked, drawing his attention to the murmur of conversation coming from outside. "Is it your family?"

"Yeah." He suddenly wasn't sure he could explain much about her without losing his hard-won control. He didn't have a choice, though. "I'd say it's time we tell them who you are."

"Yes, of course. I'd been hoping for the chance to do that." Straightening her spine, she firmed her lips and lifted her suitcase. "I'm ready."

Swallowing a curse, he took the suitcase from her and gestured for her to proceed him out the door. As much as he wanted her to struggle with her decision to leave him, courtesy was too deeply ingrained in him. He would carry her luggage, damn it, and find her a ride to the airport. Then he'd do his best to forget her.

Bleakness loomed just beneath the surface of his anger like a black hole. Clenching his jaw, he followed her out of the bedroom.

And as she strode across his living room in her classic leather pumps, her pearls glistening, her posture straight and authoritative, he saw her in a new light. She was every inch Kate Jones, Ph.D.

With a sickening squeeze of his heart, he realized what a fool he'd been, believing she felt anything for him. She, a professor at a university. And a city girl, to boot. She probably dated her esteemed colleagues, or tycoons with luxury cars and mansions in the suburbs. Why the hell would she want a bayou-bred shrimper with a pickup truck and a cabin in the woods?

He had to give her credit for not scoffing at him when he suggested they carry on with their relationship. She'd just been slumming. Oh, she'd miss Arianne, all right…but she probably couldn't wait to put the swamp-lands behind her, along with his highly opinionated, openly antagonistic family. For all he knew, she'd run back to her safe little academic community and write a paper on the hostile, backwoods clans who live on the bayous.

He stifled a painful laugh. And he'd thought she was his mate. The woman meant for him.

No, worse. Much worse. He *knew*.

She pushed through the door and stepped out onto the porch, where his sister and mother halted in their whispered conversation. The men were out in the yard, but they'd directed their attention to the porch. Mitch sauntered out directly behind Kate.

All eyes were fixed on the slim, elegant, stylishly coiffed blonde. Surprise shone on everyone's faces. Yesterday she'd worn Camryn's sultry sundress—a sexy little number they'd come to expect from her. Camryn had never worn a prim, tailored pantsuit, or carried herself with this graceful sophistication.

Mitch drew the attention away from Kate by setting her suitcase down. He could practically hear the questions racing through their minds. Who was leaving—Camryn, or both of them? When, where, why?

The answers were locked too tightly in his chest to pry loose. But he did manage to summon his voice. Or, at least, a rusty, dry facsimile. "You may think you know this woman, but you don't. Her name's Kate Jones. Professor of history at Florida State University." The bewilderment around him thickened. "Camryn's twin sister."

Their astonishment was absolute. His mother gaped from a rocking chair, Joey from the swing, Remy and Darryl from their stances near his pickup truck and Mitch's father from a lounge chair beneath an oak tree, his wood and whittling knife forgotten in his hands.

Kate's fingers tightened nervously on her purse strap as she offered a wan, tentative smile to each thunder-struck face.

If things were different, Mitch mused, he'd have his arm around her, and he'd say something silly to tease her. By the time his family gathered their wits, she'd be smiling at him with rueful humor. Regarding him with tender warmth. Making them all understand, before another word was spoken, that she belonged to him. That they were meant to be together.

But of course, things weren't that way. She would never belong to him. He wasn't even part of her "reality."

Sliding his fists into his pockets, he leaned against the pillar and kept his pain and anger strictly to himself.

"I'm, um, sorry," she said to the group at large, her summer-soft voice breaking the silence and sharpening the ache in his gut, "for misleading you. But when Mitch found me with Arianne, he assumed I was Camryn. And I...well, I decided it would be better to let him go on believing that. You see, Camryn was killed in a car crash in January."

Their stares grew all the more incredulous. No one said a word.

Kate bowed her head, then hurried on with her explanation, clearly not wanting to dwell on her sister's death. "I didn't know who Mitch was when he came and took Arianne. Camryn hadn't told me anything about Arianne's father. Except that he'd been...abusive."

"Abusive," Joey scoffed. "Dat's a low-down, dirty lie. Mitch has never, in his entire life, lifted a finger against anyone, let alone—"

"Hush, Joey." His mother's face was pale and her lips tight. "I want to hear what this young woman has to say for herself, letting my son believe she was his wife...when all along, his wife was dead.''

Hearing it spelled out in those terms made all of them glance at Kate. Mitch squared his jaw, crossed his arms and let her take the heat. She'd done exactly as his mother had described, hadn't she? She'd also made him fall in love with her—kissing him as though she'd found her one-and-only—then walked away without a care.

''I had to pose as Camryn until I found Arianne,'' Kate said, her color rising, her tone a plea for understanding. ''I had to learn more about Mitch.''

''Hooo, I'll bet you learned plenty about him, from what we saw of you two last night,'' Joey retorted angrily.

Mitch felt his throat go dry. He supposed he hadn't been too subtle—the way he hadn't been able to keep his eyes off her. The way he'd refused to leave her side. The way he'd held her hand. Danced with her. Kissed her. Taken her home.

''Don't go there, Joey,'' he warned, his voice hoarse and harsher than he could help.

And Kate looked nothing less than mortified.

As she should be.

''Answer me one thing, Dr. Jones, please, ma'am,'' his mother bit out in her soft, steel-edged way. ''Were you planning to run wit' Arianne?''

''Yes,'' Kate whispered. ''Yes, I was. If I...had to.''

Mitch shifted his eyes to the rafters of the porch. Now she'd done it. They'd be ready to feed her to the gators before she had a chance to explain.

''But I'm not going to run with her,'' she continued, her voice tight, ''because I can't give her the things you can. Like, family. A *real family.*'' There was no mistaking the awed reverence in her tone. ''She'll have you,

Mrs. Devereaux. Her *grandmère.* You'll hold her in your
rocking chair whenever she needs it. Put her trophies on
display…and keep photos of her from every special
event in her life. She'll have her *grandpère,* too. And
just by watching him work, she'll learn to appreciate art
and all the little details other people might not notice.
Her uncles will play fiddles for her, and start water
fights. And her cousins…well, she'll be tearing around
the yard with *them* in no time. Claude's already the apple
of her eye.''

Mémère inclined her head in agreement, and Joey responded with a glint of acknowledgment in her gaze.

"And she'll have her aunts," Kate said with a soft,
almost rueful smile as she paced across the porch. "Oh,
my…yes, her aunts. They'll fuss over the cute little
things she does and argue over who's going to get to
spend time with her. Do you have any idea how rare and
wonderful that is?" She stopped her pacing and stared
at the bunch of them. *"Do you?"*

No one answered. Her intensity held them all mes-
merized.

"Maybe I see it so clearly because I didn't have that.
From the time I was five, I lived in a children's home.
Camryn might not have told you. She didn't like to think
about it. But she and I…well, we…" Her words dwindled; her lips wavered and slanted. She looked away.
After a moment, she returned her gaze to them and went
on in a huskier, quieter voice. "We would have given
anything…*anything*…for a grandma and grandpa.''

Silence bore down on them with throat-aching heaviness.

"And if family isn't enough reason for Arianne to
grow up here, there are plenty of others. The community,
for one. She'll have so many friends! And you can't

underestimate the value of her heritage. The Cajun language, the food, the music, the dancing. She'll know she's part of a proud, grand tradition. And then there's all *this*." Descending the steps into the yard, she held her arms wide. "The bayou, the forest, the birds, the animals. And the...sunsets." Tears welled up in her eyes—Mitch swore they did—and she looked his way. Just the slightest, briefest meeting before she pivoted away.

But his heart kicked into a harder rhythm. Sunsets. Why would the mention of sunsets bring tears to her eyes? Sure, she was talking about leaving Arianne, but she'd looked at *him* when she'd said "sunsets."

She wouldn't be thinking about that sunset unless it had meant something special to her...would she?

"The bayou will be a wonderful place for Arianne to grow up," she whispered in a choked voice. She blinked away unshed tears and visibly gathered her composure.

Mitch fought against the compulsion to go to her, to pull her into his arms. Her fine, warm emotions were for Arianne, not him...and he wouldn't put himself through the pain of holding her when he'd only have to let her go again. If she'd wanted his embraces, she wouldn't be leaving.

And heading back to *her life*.

He gritted his teeth, and the pain spiking through his jaw made him realize he'd already been gritting them.

Kate, meanwhile, glanced around at the others with determined self-control. "So, you don't have to worry about me trying to take Arianne away from you. I'm so very, very *glad* for her." No one could doubt her sincerity. With a quirky twist of her mouth and tilt of her head, she added, "I might worry a little about the snakes and the alligators, though."

His mother and sister nodded in maternal understanding and uttered reassurances.

Kate felt her chest constrict. She really would be leaving her baby, her sweet Arianne, to start a life without her. But she couldn't let herself grieve over that now or she'd fall apart. She had to keep a stout heart, a stiff upper lip…at least until she boarded that plane.

Needing to distract herself from the grief, she angled a look toward Darryl and Remy, who leaned against a pickup truck. "When Arianne is old enough, I hope you'll warn her about the *A* word. Tell her to shorten it to 'gator' when she's riding in a pirogue."

Remy squinted at her, confused.

Darryl cast a self-conscious glance at the others, clearly embarrassed to admit he paid any attention to the old sea myths. "Da *A* word's only bad when you're on a shrimpboat," he quietly informed her.

"Oh. I didn't realize that."

"But I'll tell her, Kate."

Maybe it was his use of her name, or the simple sincerity of his assurance. Whatever the reason, a surge of sentiment crowded Kate's chest. "I'm glad she'll have *you*, too, Darryl. She'll learn about loyalty and hard work. And courage." She smiled, took a breath, then forged ahead, determined to do him a good turn, whether he appreciated it or not. "Of course, if you don't use that courage to tell Joey how you feel about her, you might not have the place in Arianne's life that you should have."

Surprise and dismay sprang into his eyes, and Joey rose from the porch swing with her mouth slightly ajar.

Kate knew she shouldn't say any more, but she was leaving, and had no time to see to these important matters. Turning to Joey, who was slowly approaching, Kate told her, "He thinks he's not worthy of you because he has difficulty reading."

With a gasp, Joey cried, "Not worthy of me? Do you really believe dat, Darryl? You think I care so much about how well you read?"

"I don't have 'difficulty' reading, Jo." Shame whitened his face. "I flat out can't do it."

"I know you can't, but you never told me it mattered to you. I work wit' specialists who can diagnose reading disabilities and teachers who can overcome them."

He shook his head, his scowl deep.

Kate recognized the doubting, frustrated look in Joey's eyes. She clearly wasn't sure how the man felt about her.

And it really irked Kate. What was it with these men, always keeping their feelings to themselves? Here stood Darryl, deliberately withholding the fact that he loved Joey, just as Mitch had withheld the fact that he didn't give a flip about Kate.

That last fact was becoming more obvious every moment. Mitch had set her suitcase on the porch, then strolled away to lounge against the pillar, looking nothing more than bored. His eyes no longer held a special warmth for her, or even a glimmer of interest. Now that she'd assured him she wasn't going to press charges, it seemed his need to "cozy up" wasn't quite as pressing.

The pain of that realization was bearable only because of her anger. Her anger would carry her through…at least until she boarded that plane.

Shoving her misery aside, Kate focused her intensity on Darryl. "If you love Joey, it's wrong not to tell her. And if you don't love her, you need to tell her that, too. It's clear she loves you, and nothing's worse than being led on, and given false hopes that can only break your heart.''

She couldn't help shooting Mitch a pointed glance.

That glance, it seemed, caught his attention, and he pushed away from the porch pillar. ''That's right, Darryl,'' he murmured, his stare fixed on Kate as he descended the steps and strolled their way. ''It's wrong to lead someone on, to make them believe you want them and care about them, when you really don't.'' He stopped near Kate, the boredom gone from his expression. His jaw was taut, his mouth tight and his gaze confrontational. Or was that…repentant? Was this his way of admitting what he'd done and telling her that he regretted it? ''Anyone who does that deserves to be horsewhipped.''

''Horsewhipped!'' Darryl spluttered. ''Damn it, Mitch, I never meant to lead Joey on!'' He turned away from Mitch, whose attention remained on Kate. ''You have to know I love you, Jo.''

''Do you, Darryl? Do you really?''

''I don't think Mitch was talking about you, Darryl.'' Kate was seething. If this was Mitch's idea of an apology, it was a lousy one. But what did that matter? An apology wouldn't change the fact that he'd used her for ulterior motives. In fact, an apology only made the humiliation worse. ''I think he was talking about himself. And yes, I agree…anyone who 'cozies up' for no good reason ought to be *horsewhipped*.''

Mitch blinked and frowned.

Kate whirled away and stalked toward the house, past his mother standing on the porch and his father sitting beneath the shade tree. ''I have to go now,'' she announced, retrieving her purse from beside her suitcase. ''I have a flight to catch.''

"A flight?" his mother said. "Why you going so soon, *chèr'*?"

"I have to get back to work."

"No time to tell me more about my granddaughter, eh?"

Mitch stood where she'd left him and watched Kate stumble over explanations about why she had to catch that one-thirty flight. He didn't hear much of what she said, though. He couldn't think beyond the mystifying confrontation they'd just had.

He was the one who had been wronged. *She* was the one who had led *him* on, who had given *him* false hopes, with her supercharged kisses and passionate lovemaking. Yet, she'd implied that *he* should be horsewhipped. And she'd used a term that he'd heard fairly recently. *Cozy up*.

No sooner had he repeated the phrase to himself than the memory surfaced. Kip Landry. This morning. "Cozy up to her all you can."

Sacre Dieu. She must have overheard! But she couldn't believe that he'd been acting on that advice, could she? She couldn't possibly think that he was the kind of low-down, unprincipled, heartless bastard who would take her to bed for a reason like that.

One word resonated through his mind. *Horsewhipped.*

Hell, yes, she believed it. She'd deduced the very worst about him, and about every word they'd spoken, every kiss they'd shared, every intimate moment they'd spent together. She was ready to leave, shut him out of her life, without even explaining why.

Of course, what the hell could he say, even if she'd confront him with it? He could hear the conversation now: *"Have you been 'cozying up' to me to stay out of jail?"* "No, *chèr'*..."

Fury filled him. Shook him, like thunder. Never had anyone incited an anger so deep and cutting. And that included Camryn.

Through a reddish haze, he saw the others had gravitated around her near the porch steps. Only his father remained aloof, casting a casual eye in that direction as he sat whittling.

"So, you see, even though classes don't start until next month," Kate was saying, "I'll need time to prepare."

"Speaking of time, Kate…" His mother crossed her arms and peered at her, then turned her scrutinizing stare at Mitch. "Just how long has Mitch known you're not Camryn?"

Color rushed into Kate's face, and Mitch sensed she was doing her best not to look at him. "You'd have to ask *him* that, Mrs. Devereaux, but I believe his investigator told him a couple of days ago."

"Days?" That one-word inquiry was indeed directed at Mitch.

If anyone else had butted into his business, he'd have turned a deaf ear. As it was, he shrugged.

And though he hadn't actually admitted to anything, he saw perception seep into her gaze. A glance around showed him the same perception dawning in everyone's faces. They knew now how he felt about her. They knew that at the party last night, he'd been hungering for *her,* Kate. No one else. And if they had any sense at all, they could look at her face and know he didn't stand a chance of keeping her. That he wasn't part of *her life.*

His anger burned.

"As much as I'd love to stay and talk, Mrs. Devereaux," Kate said, "we'll have to do that by phone. I have to leave now or I'll miss my flight. Would any of you be willing to drive me?''

No one volunteered.

Mitch was surprised. He knew they'd all been charmed by her, and would probably drive to Mississippi if it would please her. Yet no one said a word to break the awkward silence. And one by one, they stole sidelong glances at him, as if looking for guidance.

He gave them none.

''I'll pay for gas, of course,'' she added hopefully. Everyone evaded her gaze. ''Remy, would *you* drive me?''

The look of dismay on his craggy face might have been comical under other conditions. ''Aw, no, *chèr'*. I mean, I would, but—'' he rubbed the back of his neck, beneath his grizzled ponytail ''—I don't have my own vehicle. Darryl's gonna need his, and I—''

''Take mine, Remy,'' Mitch said. ''The cargo van. It's in the backyard.'' Digging in his jeans pocket, he found his keys, slipped one off the ring and threw it to him.

Remy caught it, looking painfully reluctant to carry out the task. ''If you say so, Cap'n.'' With a grim set to his mouth, he grabbed Kate's suitcase off the porch and trudged around the corner of the house.

Kate didn't acknowledge Mitch's loan of the vehicle by as much as a glance, let alone a thank-you. She pointedly ignored him, busying herself with goodbyes.

Just as well. He was too furious with her to carry on a polite charade. But he couldn't help wondering what she felt for him, if anything. What would have happened if Kip Landry hadn't shot off his big mouth? Would Kate still have insisted on taking this flight and bowing out of his life? Or would she and he have spent the day with

Arianne…and another night in his bed, making love as if they really meant it?

It hurt like hell to think about.

"Kate," his mother said with outstretched arms. "You're my granddaughter's aunt. Dat means you're part of dis family now, too. You come visit, eh? I better see you at Christmas, for sure. Hooo, you never passed a good time like you will at a Cajun Christmas."

Tears rose in Kate's eyes. "Thank you."

And Mitch took another jab to the gut. He could just picture what Christmas would be like. If she accepted the invitation, it would be hell…seeing her, wanting her. Not having her. And if she didn't accept, it would be worse.

"Keep in touch, *chèr*," *Mémère* urged, hugging her.

They were both teary-eyed when Kate pulled away. She then turned briskly, bowed her head and hurried in the direction Remy had taken.

The silence following her departure was deafening. When it dragged on and grew too oppressive, Mitch tore his attention away from the path she'd taken. They were all watching him—his mother, Joey and Darryl. Not his father, though. His father kept on whittling.

"You gonna go after her, son?" his mother asked, maternal anxiety puckering her brow.

"After her?" Mitch kept his face impassive. "What for?"

She returned his cool stare with a searching one. "I was worried at da party last night. Didn't make sense, you acting dat way wit' Camryn. But wit' Kate—" she paused, then finished with devastating gentleness "—it makes sense."

His pain worsened, and his anger seeped deeper into his bones.

At his continued silence, his mother's lips bowed up in disapproval. "If you don't want her, dat's your business. But we don't let our guests leave wit'out even saying goodbye. I didn't hear you say goodbye to her."

A very intentional thing.

"I don't know what you did to get her so upset, but you need to go straighten things out."

"What *I* did to *her?*" he said, finally riled into a response.

"Don't think I didn't hear her say you ought to be horsewhipped."

"I can't believe," Joey said in a fervent undertone, "dat you're gonna let her leave. You're tearing her baby from her arms."

Good God Almighty! Arianne was suddenly *her* baby. But he couldn't argue with the truth of that. "No one's forcing Kate to go."

"I'm not too sure," *Mémère* muttered.

Mitch squared his jaw, crossed his arms and settled more solidly against the side of his pickup truck. The women of his family glared.

"Leave da boy alone" came his father's low but imperative rumble from beneath the oak tree. "He'll handle things his own way."

It didn't take more than a minute longer for Remy to appear at the corner of the house, striding purposefully toward Mitch. "Dere's a problem, Cap'n. Can't get dis key to fit. Won't even open da doors. Must be da wrong one."

Mitch took the key without glancing at it and slid it back onto his ring. "Guess I'll have to find one that fits." He opened the door of his pickup, reached into the glove compartment and located what he was looking for. "The locks on that old cargo van can be tricky," he murmured to Remy. "Might take me a while to get it open. Why don't you just wait here?"

Remy shrugged and nodded.

"Better yet—" Mitch glanced around at their watchful faces "—why don't you all go home."

Eyebrows lifted. Gazes shifted and connected. His father lumbered to his feet from the lounge chair, leisurely pocketed his pecan wood and whittling knife and led the silent retreat toward the trucks.

"How 'bout me, Cap'n?" Remy asked, the only one remaining at Mitch's side. "You still want me to drive Kate to da airport?"

"Nah. Take my pickup. Go enjoy your time off."

"Feels funny calling her 'Kate' instead of 'Cam,' eh?"

"No, Remy, it doesn't."

He accepted that with a philosophical shrug, glanced cordially at him, then peered closer. "You *sure* you don't want me to drive her?" His hesitation suddenly seemed to border on discomfort. "I mean, she did ask *me*. Wouldn't want you two arguing, or something, and her being stranded wit'out a ride. I already told her I'd take her."

"Oh, don't you worry, *mon ami*." Mitch headed for the backyard. "I'll take her."

CHAPTER SIXTEEN

IN THE DENSE, flower-fragrant heat of midmorning, Kate shrugged out of her linen jacket and leaned against the passenger door of the cargo van, grateful for the shade of the mossy cypresses. She'd been expecting more of a minivan, but instead had discovered a full-size truck. She wouldn't have cared if it had been a combat tank, as long as it would get her to the airport.

A glance at her watch upped her anxiety. She hoped Remy would return with that key soon.

And not only because of her flight schedule. She felt as if her chest would explode from the pressure of the emotions she was holding in check. The most overpowering was far too familiar—the grief of parting with people she loved. Although she refused to focus on Arianne, her heart bled for her, anyway. The emotional departure from Mitch's family hadn't helped. How had she come to care for them in such a short span of time?

You're a part of this family now, too, Mémère had told her. She couldn't be, of course. Not in any meaningful way. Because then she'd have to see Mitch again, and she couldn't bear it. No, she wouldn't be having any Cajun Christmases, Thanksgivings or Fourth of Julys.

She knew Mitch would be relieved by her absence. She'd seen the look on his face when his mother invited her—stark, utter dismay. Nothing had convinced her of his desire to be finished with her as that reaction had.

Oh, Mitch. How could I have been so wrong about you?

It didn't help to know that his impatience to have her out of his life probably stemmed from guilt. He'd clearly gone too far in his determination to prevent her from filing charges. He could have "cozied up" to her without all that seductive passion.

But then, how many men would have thrown away the opportunity for a night of wild sex with a more-than-willing partner? And if truth be told, no woman in her right mind would complain after a night like that with Mitch Devereaux.

Unless she fell in love with him. A stupid, useless, self-destructive thing to do.

What was keeping Remy? She needed to put distance between Mitch and her as quickly as she could or her chest might very well burst.

With a rush of relief, she heard footsteps crackling through the underbrush just beyond the grove of trees. But then a tall, broad-chested figure came into view, and Kate's heart virtually stopped.

Mitch.

He moved with long, purposeful strides, his dark face aloof and unsmiling. He'd clearly come to open the truck, nothing more. He barely spared her a glance as he approached.

Tense and shaken by the sudden force of her heartbeat, Kate straightened from her reclining position against the door, which seemed to be his destination. Stepping aside to allow him access to the lock, she asked in an impressively steady voice, "Where's Remy?"

"Last time I saw him, I believe he was heading for the phone," Mitch murmured, digging in his jeans pocket and drawing out a ring of keys.

Highly aware of his potent masculinity and mind-clouding nearness, she watched his large, sun-bronzed hand as he slid the key into the lock, jockeyed it about and finally turned it. Odd, how just the sight of his hands could bring a surge of sensual memories to warm her blood.

He swung open the door and a blast of Louisiana summer heat poured from the cab. Rolling down the window to let in the gentle Delta breeze, he said without inflection, "Don't get in until I open the other door and the truck's had time to air out, unless you're in the mood to bake."

She waited while he stalked around to the other side of the truck, opened the door and left it ajar. Glancing at her watch, Kate said, "Remy didn't intend to be very long, did he?"

"Didn't say."

He rounded the back of the van and ambled to a halt beside her. "Should be cool enough now." Curtly he took her jacket and purse from her and tossed them up onto the truck's bench seat. He then turned to her and, in a distinctly impersonal manner, held out a hand to help her in—an awkward step up, she realized, for someone in heels.

Embarrassed at her initial hesitation, she forced her foolishness aside and set her hand in his. With easy strength, then, he boosted her up, turned her around and guided her onto the seat, which brought her to eye level with him. His hands were gripping her bare arms, and his dark, rugged face loomed very near.

"Thank you," she murmured, flushed with awareness of his heat, his scent, his nearness.

When she gathered the nerve to meet his gaze, a pang of dismay went through her. The vivid green eyes that had so captivated her, so enchanted her, just hours ago, now regarded her with unmitigated coolness.

The sense of loss she felt startled her.

Oddly enough, he didn't entirely release her. He let go of her right arm, but his hand slid down the length of her left arm, the friction leaving a tingling path. She'd barely had time to catch a breath, to get past the feel of his hand running along her skin, or to reconcile the action with the aloofness on his face, before a jangle sounded, then a startlingly familiar *click-click.*

And metallic coolness encircled her wrist. A tug at her hand made the situation shockingly clear. He'd handcuffed her! To the handgrip on the dash!

She blinked in disbelief at the cuff, then shot him a stunned, uncomprehending gaze. His expression hadn't changed...except, perhaps, for an added tightness to his jaw and intensity in his stare.

"Wh-what are you doing?"

He braced an arm along the back of her seat. "Ooh, *chèr',*" he murmured, the softness of his tone at direct odds with the hardness of his gaze. "I'm *'cozying up.'*"

The words brought a welling of pain to her chest, even while she struggled to make sense of them.

"What's wrong, darlin'? Is this latest maneuver of mine not up to par with all my others?" The fury in his face was suddenly unmistakable.

The shock of this unexpected confrontation sent her own fury flaring. "No, I'd have to say your maneuvers in the shower last night were of a much higher caliber, *and* the ones in bed this morning."

His scowl deepened; his eyes flashed. "Your low opinion of me is bad enough...but what's worse is that you took something beautiful and made it ugly."

The words struck her like a blow—especially since he

was calling their time together beautiful. It made her want to cry and deepened her confusion. "No, *you* took something ugly and tried to pass it off as beautiful." But she was no longer sure he had. How could she think clearly, when his very presence shook her from the inside out? That was exactly why she had to get away—to regain her presence of mind. "Let me out of these handcuffs."

"No. Scream, if you want. Might draw a few nosy gators from the swamp, but that's about all. The folks went home. The nearest neighbor lives miles away. It's just you and me, *chèr'*."

"Where's Remy?"

"I told him to get lost."

Her anger glowed. "That's enough of this nonsense, Mitch. You're going to make me miss my flight."

"That's right. You're going to spend the day—and the night, too—shackled to this truck." A startled gasp escaped her, and he drew a cell phone from his shirt pocket. "Your only way out, Kate, is to call the sheriff. Have him send his deputies. The number is programmed in the phone. Hit the star key, and the one. A direct line."

Stunned, she stared at him. He couldn't mean it! But beneath the force of his stare, her surprise deepened into dismay. He did indeed mean it.

"Call, Kate. Tell them I took you from your home in Florida, held you prisoner on my boat, and now I've got you handcuffed to my truck. They'll see that part for themselves when they get here." He hit two buttons on the phone, then pressed it into her hand.

She took the phone with an angry jerk and disconnected the call.

"What, you don't want to face the drama of a big

arrest scene?'' he taunted. ''Then call a friend from your *real life*. Have him come to your rescue. He can report me to the cops for you, if you can't stomach making the call yourself.''

''I'm not calling *anyone*.'' She flung the phone onto the truck floor. ''I get your point.'' And she did. She could so easily have him thrown in jail right now—for a long, long time—and she believed he would keep her chained until the deputies arrived. So much for cozying up! Yet her anger wasn't appeased. ''Why weren't you honest with me, Mitch? You could have told me you were worried that I might bring charges against you.''

''Do I look worried that you might bring charges against me?''

''You must have been. You called your lawyer about it.''

''That was before I knew you. It didn't take me long, Kate, to realize that you wouldn't do anything to hurt me. And that has nothing to do with our cozying up. It has to do with Arianne, and your love for her. You want her world to be a happy one. You're not about to throw her papa in jail.''

Kate's throat tightened and her vision blurred. He was, of course, right. And she'd been so wrong.

''What kills me, Kate, is that after all of our 'cozying up,' you jumped to such an unfair, unfounded, degrading conclusion about me.''

''I didn't jump to any conclusion. I doubted you, yes, but I didn't entirely believe you'd done anything wrong…until you *showed* me how little I meant to you.''

''Showed you? What the hell are you talking about?''

''The moment I assured you I wouldn't press charges, you were ready for me to leave. You practically pushed me out the door.''

"I didn't push you. I didn't touch you. I didn't even look at you, more than I could help."

"Exactly." Her voice wavered with an overload of emotion. Swallowing against a painful lump in her throat, she finished in a whisper, "I hadn't known you could be so cold."

Regret and something deeper flashed in his eyes. "I've never *felt* that cold, Kate. Or that hurt."

Her breath stalled. *She'd hurt him?* His pride, maybe. But to actually hurt him, he'd have to really care. A painfully twisted sense of hope, regret and confusion added to her emotional upheaval. Fighting off the onset of tears, she choked out, "Then why don't you want me here for Christmas?"

"Christmas?" He said it as if he'd never heard the word.

"I saw you when your mother invited me. You almost groaned out loud."

He muttered a curse, glared at her, leaned in close and lodged his fingers around her jaw. "Hell, no, I don't want you here...not if I can't have you. I can't take the torment, Kate. If you're near me, I'm going to want to hold you, and kiss you, and take you home." Intensity blazed in his stare; his voice grew gruff. "And if you're not near me—" he clenched his jaw "—I'm still going to want you."

Her heart surged into a thudding beat, and she searched his taut face, her feelings so poignant they made her chest ache.

"And if you'd show up with another man," he rasped, "I might have to do something drastic. Like feed him to the gators."

She bit her bottom lip. She loved him so much! And it frightened her. Terrified her. He couldn't possibly feel the same for her. Desire, maybe. The chemistry between them was, without a doubt, explosive. Needing to subdue the fear, to distract herself from it, she forced a half smile and asked half jokingly, "Have you *ever* fed anyone to the gators?"

"Not yet…but you better not test me."

Their gazes melded, shifted and probed. Her longing for him intensified. "Don't be feeding anyone to the gators, Mitch Devereaux, because if the sheriff came and took you away, I believe it would kill me."

He expelled a long, violent breath, hooked his hand around her head and kissed her—a needful, demanding kiss that kindled a fierce yet tender heat. When the kiss drew to a reluctant close, he whispered, "Don't be afraid to trust me."

She ran her free hand up the strong, commanding contours of his face, worshipping every angle. "I'm so sorry, Mitch. I don't know why I doubted you. One minute I was happy and thinking about postponing my flight. The next, I heard what Kip said and started worrying that…that…"

"That what we have together is too good to be true."

She stared at him, wide-eyed, amazed that he understood how she'd felt…and that he thought their relationship was "too good to be true." Tumultuous emotions rose with such force she couldn't speak. She'd fallen too deeply in love with him, and it scared her witless. He brought too much precious bounty to her life—everything she'd ever wanted—which meant he *had* to be out of her reach, ultimately. Triumphs of that magnitude never happened to her. When the inevitable day came that her illusions were shattered, her heart and soul would shatter right along with them.

"Don't *do* that, Kate," he said with quiet desperation.

"You're running from me again. I've got you hand-cuffed to my truck, *and you're still running*."

She couldn't deny it.

With a tightened mouth and brisk moves, he drew his keys from his pocket, unlocked the handcuffs and tossed them onto the floor. His expression of anguished intensity mirrored what she was feeling. "I'm not going to try to hold you, Kate. Tell me that you don't see *any* kind of future for us, and that I'll never be an important part of your life, and I'll drive you to the airport right now, and call you only about Arianne...."

She groaned, frowned and hushed him with a kiss. She didn't want him to let her go! He opened his mouth wider on hers and deepened the give and take. When they parted, she whispered unevenly, "I never meant I didn't want you. I'm just so afraid of jumping to conclusions again...but in the opposite direction. Of taking our relationship too seriously."

"Too seriously?"

Better to scare him off now and spare herself the heartbreak. Struggling with contracting throat muscles, she nodded.

"I can't believe you don't know," he said fervently, "that I'm so crazy in love with you I can't see straight."

And her heart rolled like a drum to a pause. *So crazy in love with her.*

"Did you hear me, Kate?" He tilted her face. "I love you. You might think it's too soon, but I *do know*. I grew up around lots of love. I understand how it works...and I recognize it when I feel it."

Oh, how she longed to believe that love *could* last. But she'd had to let go of love so many times. If he decided some day that he had, after all, made a mistake, the devastation would destroy her.

And it wasn't as if he'd never made a mistake in matters of the heart. Gripped by a sudden, urgent need to know, she asked with her heart pounding in every vein, "When you married Camryn, did you think you loved her?"

He drew back, considered the question, then swung her down from the truck. Grabbing a blanket from behind the seat, he took her hand and led her to a soft, grassy spot beneath a tree, where he lay beside her, propped up on an elbow.

He regarded her in wary silence as he searched for a place to begin.

He couldn't blame her for needing to understand about his failed marriage with her sister. How could she trust in his promise of love if he'd been so wrong before?

And he *had* to make her trust. The future of his heart, his home, his everything, depended on it.

"I married Camryn," he began slowly, "because she was having my baby. I believed that was only right. But, there *was* a moment, Kate…one blinding moment, when I first saw her, that I swore she was the woman for me. Something about her face, her eyes, her voice, called out to me on such a primal level, I felt that I'd come face-to-face with my destiny. And I acted on that belief. But as I got to know her, I realized there was nothing for me there."

He shook his head in remembered confusion. "How could I have been so wrong? I asked myself that a thousand times." He paused, then stroked her cheek. "But I see now, Kate, that I wasn't wrong. I just misinterpreted what fate had in store for me. Camryn *did* lead me to my destiny. And the woman meant for me does have that same face, same eyes, same voice…but a whole different heart and soul.''

Her eyes shone with sweet poignancy, but his need for her was too great for him to clearly judge its significance.

''I don't want to rush you, Kate, but I can't seem to help it. I don't want to live without you, even for a little while. I've got captains running my boats. I can manage them from anywhere. I can live in Tallahassee, if you want, and build a dock near Carabelle. Or…you can live here and teach at Nicholls State University, which isn't far, or even LSU. We'll make it work, Kate. I swear we will…if you love me.''

Tension held him hostage.

''I can't believe,'' she finally said, weaving her fingers through his hair and drawing near, ''that you don't know I'm so crazy in love with you I can't see straight.''

Joy rose in him like an incoming tide. Pulling her into his arms, he pledged his life to her in a kiss. She joined him in the celebration, and the fire of their love leaped and blazed.

A while later—a good while later—he pinned her down, not only on the blanket, but on the details. ''You *do* understand that I'm asking you to marry me, don't you? I want you for my bride. My wife. My partner.'' He smoothed a thumb across her mouth, and added in a gruff, lingering whisper, ''My lover.''

Her chest rose on a swelling intake of breath, and she nodded, her eyes answering a resounding ''yes.''

''Then let's go bring our daughter home.''

''Our daughter,'' she repeated, her happiness shining.

''And tomorrow, we'll get married.''

''Tomorrow?'' She knitted her brows and slanted her

mouth at him in protest. "I believe in careful, detailed planning...and long engagements."

Long engagements. He felt his heart grow still. He didn't like the sound of that. It seemed he'd waited forever for her already.

She brushed a kiss across his lips. "Let's make it next week."

His mouth slowly spread in a consenting smile, and his spirits once again soared. He knew when to compromise.

Heady with her success, she pressed on. "And I'd like to live here, on the bayou, and teach nearby. Life just wouldn't be the same without that Cajun spice."

"I promise you plenty of that, *chèr'*."

As always, he delivered on his promises.

And oh, *chèr'!* Dey passed a good time.

A brand-new story of
emotional soul-searching and family turmoil
by *New York Times* bestselling author

Featuring her famous
Crighton family!

STARTING OVER

Focusing on the elusive Nick Crighton and his
unexpected exploration of love, this richly woven story
revisits Penny Jordan's most mesmerizing family ever!

"Women everywhere will find pieces
of themselves in Jordan's characters."
—*Publishers Weekly*

Coming to stores in October 2001.

HARLEQUIN®
Makes any time special ®

Harlequin Romance®
Love affairs that last a lifetime.

HARLEQUIN *Presents*®
Seduction and passion guaranteed.

Harlequin® **Historical**
Historical Romantic Adventure.

HARLEQUIN® *Temptation.*
Sassy, sexy, seductive!

HARLEQUIN® *Super*ROMANCE®
Emotional, exciting, unexpected.

HARLEQUIN® AMERICAN *Romance*
Heart, home & happiness.

HARLEQUIN® *Duets*™
Romantic comedy.

HARLEQUIN® INTRIGUE®
Breathtaking romantic suspense.

HARLEQUIN® *Blaze*™
Red-Hot Reads.

HARLEQUIN®
Makes any time special ®

If you enjoyed what you just read,
then we've got an offer you can't resist!

Take 2 bestselling love stories FREE!

Plus get a FREE surprise gift!

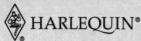

CALL THE ONES YOU LOVE OVER THE HOLIDAYS!

Save $25 off future book purchases when you buy any four Harlequin® or Silhouette® books in October, November and December 2001,

PLUS

receive a phone card good for 15 minutes of long-distance calls to anyone you want in North America!

WHAT AN INCREDIBLE DEAL!

Just fill out this form and attach 4 proofs of purchase (cash register receipts) from October, November and December 2001 books, and Harlequin Books will send you a coupon booklet worth a total savings of $25 off future purchases of Harlequin® and Silhouette® books, AND a 15-minute phone card to call the ones you love, anywhere in North America.

Please send this form, along with your cash register receipts
as proofs of purchase, to:
In the USA: Harlequin Books, P.O. Box 9057, Buffalo, NY 14269-9057
In Canada: Harlequin Books, P.O. Box 622, Fort Erie, Ontario L2A 5X3
Cash register receipts must be dated no later than December 31, 2001.
Limit of 1 coupon booklet and phone card per household.
Please allow 4-6 weeks for delivery.

**I accept your offer! Enclosed are 4 proofs of purchase.
Please send me my coupon booklet
and a 15-minute phone card:**

Name: _____

Address: _____ City: _____

State/Prov.: _____ Zip/Postal Code: _____

Account Number (if available): _____

---

097 KJB DAGL
PHQ4013